A PENGUIN MYSTERY

Murder in the Rue Dumas

M. L. LONGWORTH has lived in Aix-en-Provence since 1997. She has written about the region for the *Washington Post*, the *Times* (UK), the *Independent*, and *Bon Appétit* magazine. In addition to the Verlaque and Bonnet mystery series, she is the author of a bilingual collection of essays, *Une Américaine en Provence*, published by Éditions de La Martinière in 2004. She divides her time between Aix, where she writes, and Paris, where she teaches writing at New York University.

ALSO BY M. L. LONGWORTH

Death at the Château Bremont

Death in the Vines

Murder on the Île Sordou

The Mystery of the Lost Cézanne

Murder in the Rue Dumas

A VERLAQUE AND BONNET
MYSTERY

· M. L. LONGWORTH ·

PENGUIN BOOKS

PENGUIN BOOKS
Published by the Penguin Group
Penguin Group (USA) Inc., 375 Hudson Street, New York, New York 10014, USA ·
Penguin Group (Canada), 90 Eglinton Avenue East, Suite 700, Toronto, Ontario M4P
2Y3, Canada (a division of Pearson Penguin Canada Inc.) · Penguin Books Ltd,
80 Strand, London WC2R 0RL, England · Penguin Ireland, 25 St Stephen's Green,
Dublin 2, Ireland (a division of Penguin Books Ltd) · Penguin Group (Australia), 250
Camberwell Road, Camberwell, Victoria 3124, Australia (a division of Pearson Australia
Group Pty Ltd) · Penguin Books India Pvt Ltd, 11 Community Centre, Panchsheel Park,
New Delhi – 110 017, India · Penguin Group (NZ), 67 Apollo Drive, Rosedale, Auckland
0632, New Zealand (a division of Pearson New Zealand Ltd) · Penguin Books (South
Africa) (Pty) Ltd, 24 Sturdee Avenue, Rosebank, Johannesburg 2196, South Africa

Penguin Books Ltd, Registered Offices:
80 Strand, London WC2R 0RL, England

First published in Penguin Books 2012

1   3   5   7   9   10   8   6   4   2

Publisher's Note
This is a work of fiction. Names, characters, places, and incidents either are the product
of the author's imagination or are used fictitiously, and any resemblance to actual persons,
living or dead, business establishments, events, or locales is entirely coincidental.

LIBRARY OF CONGRESS CATALOGING IN PUBLICATION DATA

Longworth, M. L. (Mary Lou), 1963–
Murder in the Rue Dumas : a Verlaque and Bonnet provençal mystery / M.L.
Longworth.
p. cm.—(A Penguin mystery)
ISBN 978-0-14-312154-1
1. Murder—Investigation—Fiction.   2. College students—Fiction.   3. College
teachers—Fiction.   4. Aix-en-Provence (France)—Fiction.   5. France, Southern—
Fiction.   I. Title.
PR9199.4.L596M87 2012
813'.6—dc23   2012023725

Printed in the United States of America
Set in Adobe Caslon Pro · Designed by Elke Sigal

For Ken and Eva

Murder in the Rue Dumas

Chapter One

❧

Hoping to Impress

*T*he friendship between Yann Falquerho and Thierry Marchive had surprised everyone at the university. Not only were they competing for the same doctoral fellowship, they were also physically and socially different in every way. Yann was tall and blond, the son of a television producer from Paris now divorced from Yann's mother, an interior designer. Thierry was dark, short, and stocky, and came from more humble origins: his father was a French teacher in a Marseille high school, and his mother—still married to his father—an underpaid dietitian at the Hôpital du Nord.

The two students walked quickly, speaking loudly and with few pauses, for they were both the youngest of three children—here was something they shared—and were well versed in the effort required to be heard at the dinner table. "Hurry up," Yann said over his shoulder to his friend. "All of the choice food will be gone by the time we get there."

"I can't help it if I don't have your giraffe legs," his friend replied, skipping in order to keep up. "We would have left on time if you hadn't answered the telephone and had that long conversation with what's-her-name."

"Suzanne," Yann said slowly. "Suzanne, she was named after the song."

"Right . . . your childhood sweetheart . . . her father the town doctor in Carnac, where your bourgeois family spent their idyllic summers." Thierry stopped to mimic playing a guitar and did a very acceptable imitation of Leonard Cohen.

> *"And she feeds you tea and oranges*
> *That come all the way from China . . ."*

he sang, until he slipped off of the narrow sidewalk and onto the street.

"Shut up, you imbecile," Yann laughed. "Yeah, idyllic summers, all right. So idyllic that my parents divorced. Maybe it was all that rain in August . . . they were stuck together inside our impeccably designed beach house." That was one of the things that Yann liked about Thierry: the fact that he wouldn't recognize, nor care about, an impeccably designed interior even if it hit him in the face. Yann walked on ahead, frowning, as he thought of his mother and father with their respective new partners, neither of whom he cared for.

The two young men reached an elaborately carved wooden door on the place des Quatre Dauphins and rang the buzzer that was set into a polished brass plaque, marked "Professeur Moutte." The door buzzed back and clicked open with a thud, Thierry holding it open for his friend and saying, "After you!" Thierry saw that Yann had suddenly become quiet, as he often did when the subject of his parents came up—they had divorced two years previously—

and Thierry thought he should try changing the subject. He pictured the Falquerho family sitting in a living room with furnishings that were impractical for a vacation house—white, for example— watching in silence the gray waves crash onto the shore. He spoke, trying to remind Yann of other, happier things. "All you think of is food. And Suzanne, naturally." Yann laughed and walked into the apartment building's cold, damp foyer, looking forward to this evening's free dinner, and Suzanne, whom he would see at Christmas break.

Weight gain had been a problem for Thierry ever since junior high, and he had never had a girlfriend in high school. His first romance with a female had been in his second year of university. But what an encounter it was. Ulla had been a Swedish exchange student—a cliché that even Thierry, who had never left France, could recognize. He smiled to himself as they mounted the wide stone stairs to Professor Moutte's third-floor apartment, but the image of Ulla naked in his bed faded as he looked around the seventeenth-century mansion. Thierry marveled at the building's entrance hall—so different from the apartment where he was raised and the one he now shared with Yann, whose steep red-tiled steps were so narrow that getting an armchair or even a bicycle up to their apartment was next to impossible. He purposely set his foot into the dip in each step, worn away by centuries of wealthy Aixois—and their servants—coming and going out of this aristo- cratic mansion, now divided into three elegant apartments.

"I can smell the hors d'oeuvres," Yann commented, taking two steps at a time. "Puff pastries, little bits of pizza, perhaps a tray of cold cuts and a wheel of brie or two—supermarket cheese, I bet. Why do the well-off often serve such cheap food?" He stopped on a step and looked down at his friend, who had been awakened out of his daydream. "Are you listening? I'll bet the wine will be bag-in-box." He watched his friend place his small, wide foot in a groove in one of the stone steps.

"Beggars can't be choosers," Thierry replied. "Besides, I am a connoisseur . . . of bulk wines."

Yann laughed and knocked on the door. He turned to his Marseillais friend, who was now panting, and quickly said, "I promise, when I am fully employed, hopefully in the near future, never to buy supermarket cheese or cheap wine."

Thierry nodded in mock sincerity and replied, "Noted." With his father's teacher's salary, Thierry had been raised on industrially produced cheese, but thanks to his Parisian friend he now knew what artisanal cheese tasted like and secretly hoped that he too would be able to buy quality food—quality everything—someday. The Easter week he had spent at M. Falquerho's penthouse overlooking Les Invalides had been one of the highlights of his twenty-four years. He had never eaten in so many fine restaurants, and in each one the Falquerho father and son were given the best table and chatted happily with the owners, staff, and chefs. Thierry admired M. Falquerho, for despite the hoards of money and famous friends, Yann was given the same meager student budget as his peers.

The apartment door was opened by a tall, handsome woman in her midforties with thick black hair and large brown eyes. Thierry was happy to see that she was wearing the scoop-neck black wool dress that he particularly liked on her—it showed off not only her perfect olive skin but also her ample chest. "The gruesome twosome," she said, laughing. "Come in! You're just in time!" she whispered, winking. "The table has just been laid!"

"Thanks, Professor Leonetti!" they replied in unison. While both Thierry and Yann appreciated the scholarship of their host,

Dr. Georges Moutte, they preferred the dynamic, often humorous lectures of the younger Dr. Annie Leonetti. But it was Dr. Moutte who had the last say on the Dumas Fellowship, and so here they were, giving up their traditional Friday night of trying to charm the American girls who hung out in Aix-en-Provence's pubs, to hobnob with their professors. Thierry's stomach tightened as he saw the sea of heads—many of them gray—and was relieved that Dr. Leonetti was there. Yann was more comfortable in large groups, and although he usually watched Yann in order to follow his cues, tonight Thierry vowed to be more independent.

Dr. Leonetti led the students to their host and then disappeared. "Try not to gawk around at the apartment," Yann warned his friend under his breath.

Thierry didn't miss a beat. "As long as you don't say 'indeed' in that phony tone of voice you always use when speaking with the doyen."*

"Professor Moutte, *bonsoir*," Yann said, politely shaking the hand of the elderly, white-haired gentleman.

"Good evening, Doctor," Thierry said, taking his turn at shaking the age-spotted, frail hand. "Thank you for the invitation."

"Not at all. Not at all," stammered Dr. Moutte. "My professors did the same thing for us when I was your age. Besides, you both had good reason to come, no?" He chuckled at his own joke. Thierry smiled meekly, knowing that Dr. Moutte was making a reference to the Dumas Fellowship. Yann quickly decided that he didn't care what Moutte thought. He wanted the fellowship (which he hoped would be a quick ticket into an MBA program) and didn't see any reason why he should hide the fact.

"Mmmm . . . indeed," replied Yann, chuckling, causing Thierry

---

* The oldest member of a group; in this case, the dean.

to roll his eyes toward the ceiling, where they froze on the brightly colored frescoes depicting mythological figures. The floating gods and goddesses were enclosed by an elaborate white plaster framework molded into the shapes of flora and fauna—*gypseries*, he was fairly certain it was called. He turned to see if Yann had noticed the ceiling—Yann not only came from money, but he loved art and was eager to pass on his knowledge at any given opportunity—but Yann was looking over Dr. Moutte's shoulder toward the long wooden table laden with food. Thierry saw that his friend had been correct in his estimations: pizza, cut into little squares; wheels of brie; bread and cold cuts. But the wine was in bottles. Yann then abruptly excused himself and inched his way over to the table, where Dr. Leonetti was pouring herself a glass of wine. She had been watching the young men with a smile forming at each end of her broad mouth—she liked both students but was puzzled as to why they were studying theology. She had a feeling that Yann Falquerho had chosen theology because the funding was better—and admissions easier—than in history, for the simple reason that there were fewer students in the subject. He would probably go into law or business. She had a friend who worked for a financial company in London, who told her that they were now wooing theology and history graduates into the world of stocks and bonds. The shorter one, from Marseille, was more of a mystery. Perhaps she would ask him his future plans this evening, if she could get him to stop looking up at the ceiling.

"Would you like some?" she asked, raising the bottle up to Yann, who now stood at her side with his head tilted toward her at almost a ninety-degree angle. She followed his eyes—worried that perhaps her dress was a little too *décolleté*—and then noticed that his awkwardness was not because of perversity but because he was trying to read the bottle's label.

"A Bandol red!" he finally exclaimed. "Why yes, thank you! Dr. Moutte has gone all out this evening!"

Annie Leonetti smiled. "The wine is my contribution. Life's too short for bad wine, *non*? Get your cohort over here and I'll pour him a glass too." But Thierry was already at their side—he had seen Professor Leonetti with the wine bottle in her hand and had weaved his way through the professors and graduate students toward his friend. He had just picked up a used wineglass off of the table—no time to search for a clean one when the bottled wine might be finished any minute—when Dr. Moutte's voice was heard above the chattering of theologians.

"No, Bernard! It will be as I told you in my office today . . . and my decision will be final!"

Professor Bernard Rodier, a middle-aged man whom many colleagues thought too handsome to be in theology, turned on his heels and walked toward the front door. Annie Leonetti could never understand why people thought that Bernard was *too handsome*— did that mean that one had to be ugly to teach theology? Certainly there were some eyesores in the Philosophy Department; but Law compensated with some very fine, if not beautiful, specimens. And where did she stand in all of this?

Thierry and Yann exchanged worried looks, assuming that the professors had been arguing about the fellowship, and Annie smiled and poured them more wine. "Don't worry," she said. "It's nothing to do with the Dumas." She had rightly guessed that Bernard had unwisely asked about Moutte's retirement, announced the previous week at a faculty meeting. Three names had been put forward to take on the directorship—a post that came with a generous salary, many sabbaticals, and the historic two-thousand-square-foot apartment they were now standing in, located on the square that many Aixois believed held the most beautiful fountain—les Quatre Dauphins. In addition to the frescoes that watched over the apartment's occupants, the walled garden contained a rarity that was, in summer, sometimes heard by Aixois, but never seen, as it was hidden by a ten-foot-high stone wall: a swimming pool.

Such a post was unusual in Provence, but the Theology Department had always managed to distance itself from the rest of the university. In the late 1920s, Father Jules Dumas, a priest as well as a former head of the department, bequeathed his family's mansion and fortune to the university, stating that the new head would live in the antiques-filled third-floor apartment, while the bottom two apartments would be rented out by the university to help pay for the fellowship in his name. A building—now housing offices and classrooms—and a street were named after him. It had been his way of paying back the world. He had lost two brothers in World War I; ironically, his family had made their fortune fabricating machine parts for the tanks that were tested on the muddy fields of Picardie and Belgium in 1917.

As she had hoped, Annie Leonetti's name was one of the three contenders. Although she was younger than her colleagues, and known as a modernist in the department, her PhD from Yale and frequent publications were realities that could not be disputed. Working against her, more than her being a minor radical, was the fact that she came from Corsica. Where she had spent the first eighteen years of her life had a greater impact on her career than she could ever have imagined, and at times she regretted not staying in the United States—where, as a Corsican, she wouldn't have been labeled as either a "peasant" or "terrorist." The irony was that both she and her husband adored the island, and they had moved back to France after Annie was awarded her doctorate so that they could return to Corsica every holiday.

The second name was Bernard Rodier's, a solid if dull Cistercian scholar, and the third, when announced, was met with cackles and hollers: Giuseppe Rocchia—"everyman's theologian," as he liked to call himself—who taught in the Theology Department at the university in their sister city, Perugia, and earned tenfold his university salary by writing books and theology-based articles in fashion magazines and appearing on Italian television, explaining his version of world religions to the masses. For this reason Annie defended him—Rocchia put in plain words what many people believed to be a complicated, overwrought subject—and for his contribution to Italian television, which desperately needed improving. She had read his books—best sellers across the world—and found some value in many of the things he said. On a recent trip to Perugia she had asked one of her colleagues why Rocchia continued to teach, given how much money he made from his books and talk-show appearances. "It gives him respectability," Dario had told her, sipping his Campari in one of Perugia's many stunning squares. "Plus, we Italians love to be called *Dottore.*"

Bernard Rodier set his empty glass down on an Empire-era console made from exotic woods extracted from one of France's former colonies and left the room. *Stormed* out of the room, Annie would tell her husband later that evening. She smiled slightly at the gaffe that Bernard had just made, damaging his chances at the directorship. Annie looked at Yann and Thierry and thought of her own student days—the weeklong celebrations her family had hosted in their Corsican village when she had been accepted into a *grande école* in Paris; the effort and time she had put in to learn English; and her doctoral years in Connecticut—paying part of her tuition by waitressing at a French restaurant in New Haven. And the late hours continued—when she should have been reading to her two young children, or in bed with her husband, she had stayed up late in her study, researching. But the reward would soon be worth it. She could—should—be the next doyen of the Theology Department, able to move her family from their charmless 1970s boxlike apartment into one of the most sought-after buildings in Aix. She felt no pity for Bernard, who hadn't published as much as she had, nor studied at a prestigious foreign university. "Pauvre Bernard," she whispered, grinning.

Chapter Two

✼

The Real Scholars

Annie Leonetti set down her wineglass and looked around the now silent room. Georges Moutte raised his hand to his mouth and coughed, breaking the awkward silence. Could Moutte be announcing his replacement this evening? She tried not to smile at the idea, and suddenly regretted not inviting her husband.

"You may as well all know now," the elderly man said in a loud, clear voice. "I have decided, after all, to postpone my retirement." A low murmur broke out around the room and once again the doyen had to loudly cough in order to speak. "Indefinitely," he added in answer to the silent question most of his guests had been mulling over in their heads. "I'm still good for a little bit," he continued, trying to laugh. "And the Dumas's winner," he said as he looked over in the direction of Yann and Thierry, "will be announced at this time next week. And now, please eat and make yourselves comfortable."

Yann put down his slice of pizza and looked at Thierry. "All of a sudden I'm not hungry."

"I know what you mean," Thierry replied. "I wish that we could share the fellowship."

"No, no," his friend insisted with a seriousness Thierry seldom heard coming from Yann. "You're the real scholar. I only went into theology because there were more spots available and I hoped that it would royally piss off my parents."

Thierry picked up the bottle and poured them both more wine. "Here, we may as well drink. Did it work?"

"Did what work?" Yann asked, taking a sip of wine and helping himself to a petit four. Having made his confession, he was suddenly hungry.

"Pissing off your parents?"

Yann laughed and made a toasting gesture with his wineglass. "Funny, that. My father was in the middle of filming a documentary on the Shroud of Turin and was all of a sudden a reformed, mystical Catholic. He thought me studying theology was great. And much to my surprise, so did my mom. We have a wealthy great-uncle who is a missionary in South America whom she was hoping to impress."

"Well, whatever you say," Thierry said, "I still think that you are a good scholar."

Yann laughed. "I did surprise myself by enjoying studying theology. Dr. Leonetti has been a big reason for that. But fellowship or no fellowship, it's off to MBA land I go."

Thierry poured his friend another glass of wine, but not for himself. Yann noticed Thierry's furrowed brow and said, "What's wrong? Don't worry, even if I do go to the States, we'll still keep in touch, right?"

Thierry shook his head and, leaning in closer to Yann, said, "No, no, it's not that. It's Moutte not retiring. Think of how Professor Leonetti must be feeling right now. I thought she would replace him, didn't you?"

Yann looked across the room at Annie Leonetti, who was sitting on a hard-back dining chair with her hands on her knees, looking up at the ceiling. "I thought so too, but what do we know? It's not like they tell us anything here. Perhaps there are other profs in line for the job. Like Rodier, or that guy from Toulouse who's obsessed with the Norman church. Anyway, Moutte will retire soon—he's ancient."

"How soon is soon? You know how when you're sure to get something, and then it doesn't happen, how hard that is. It could be six months or three years, it doesn't really matter. You still feel like you've been punched in the stomach."

Yann drank some wine and tried to think of the times that this had happened to him, but couldn't think of one. When Laura had told him at the last minute that she couldn't go to Brittany in July with him, and then he found out through a friend that she had gone to Saint-Tropez with some guy who was already working at a law firm? No, he had gotten over that fairly quickly when Suzanne had come back into his life this past summer.

"Look at that," Thierry said, nodding in the direction of the opposite corner of the room. "If I didn't know any better, I'd say that Mlle Zacharie has the hots for Moutte." Yann snuck a glance in the same direction and shuddered.

"Disgusting! What is she *doing*? It looks like she's trying to kiss him! I thought she hated everyone in the department, especially me ever since I pestered her to tell me when they were going to decide on the Dumas."

"No," Thierry said, grabbing a cracker. "I think she hated you long before that."

Yann frowned, choosing to ignore his friend's comment. "Well, you're right, she obviously doesn't hate the doyen right now." Audrey Zacharie, age twenty-seven, had been a graduate in art history and had started working in the Theology Department the occasional afternoon when she was in her last year of university. She graduated, the Theology secretary left, and Audrey's part-time job became full-time. She was eternally dissatisfied and reminded the professors and students daily that she had not meant to take this course in life, that it was the economic crisis that had forced her to type letters and file. At the same time, she was fiercely protective of her new role in the department and proud of her secure job with its excellent retirement fund and vacation time.

"Is she trying to kiss Moutte's ear?" Yann asked while chewing a piece of bread.

"No, she's whispering something. Probably about how much she hates you."

Yann grabbed a piece of cheese, frowning as he put it into his mouth. He made a sour face.

"God, this cheese is crap. I really need to make just enough money to buy good food and wine."

"Here, here!" Dr. Leonetti echoed, now standing beside the two students. "I'm glad you like the wine. Funny that a hilly place so near the sea would produce such hearty, strong reds." Her stomach was in knots since Bernard's angry departure, for she had desperately wanted to succeed Dr. Moutte—but she was also well aware how easily, carelessly in Bernard's case, one could fall from the elderly doyen's graces. What did "indefinitely" mean? Perhaps just another school year? It would go by quickly, but more than that would be hard to bear. Wasn't Moutte nearing seventy? She realized that she had no idea how old the doyen was. Perhaps he was still in his late fifties. Was that possible? Who would know? She was wondering how she could befriend Moutte's secretary, whom she despised, when one of the boys made a comment that brought her back into the now-stuffy room.

"And so strange that Cassis, just down the road, would produce only bright, sparkling whites!"

Annie Leonetti stared at Yann, surprised at her student's knowledge of wine. She was suddenly happy to be with Thierry and Yann and to have the chance to talk about wine, or soccer, or whatever boys their age talked about. "Yes! I've always thought the same thing! Let's open another bottle, shall we?" she asked, bending down and reaching under the white linen tablecloth to grab a bottle she had hidden there before the party began.

Chapter Three

A Really Stupid Idea

Yann stared at Thierry in disbelief, his hand on the cheap metal doorknob and the door open a few inches.

"I don't . . . believe it," Thierry said, hiccuping. "I knew that these buildings . . . were falling apart, but this is just . . . insane that we would be able to get in here so easily."

"Shhh," Yann said, holding up his hand. "Could you try to hiccup a little more quietly? Go on, I'm right behind you."

The two students squeezed through the doorway, neither of them thinking to open the door any wider. The door was at the side of the arts faculty building on the rue Jules Dumas, down a narrow alleyway that was used for garbage bins. Yann had some experience in breaking and entering—his father's apartment building in Paris had a back door that was just of this vintage, and the lock was easy to force open. It helped on those nights when Yann forgot his keys and didn't want his father to catch him coming home at 3:00 a.m. And then there was that other incident, and the cold police cell, and the look of disappointment on his father's face when he arrived the next morning. Yann pulled the door shut without making any noise and motioned at the stairway on their left, shining his miniature flashlight up the stairs. "His office is on the fourth floor. Let's go."

"This is a really stupid idea."

"I already explained to you," Yann said, pushing Thierry up the stairs. "Moutte is obviously off his rocker . . . he proved that to everyone this evening. He's been teasing us all along, changing the deadline, throwing out hints here and there as to who has won. What if he decides to cancel the fellowship? Or change the winner."

"We could get into so much trouble if we're caught," Thierry said, stopping again on the stairs.

"Who's going to find out, eh? We'll slip in and out, as quiet as church mice," Yann whispered.

"What if Moutte is in his office?"

"I already told you, he'll be at home, fast asleep! Old people need lots of sleep."

"I think it's the opposite," Thierry said. "I think they need less sleep than we do."

Yann sighed. "Whatever. He won't be here this late; it's almost 2:00 a.m. You're all red, by the way."

Thierry felt his forehead with the back of his hand. "You know that I break out into a sweat when I'm nervous. It's a sign of how bad an idea this is!"

"Listen: If we find the documents showing who the winning candidate is, I can take a picture of it with my new cell phone, and we can show it to Dr. Leonetti. That way we'll be prepared if he pulls another stunt like he did this evening."

Thierry looked down the dark hallway and tried to imagine

that it was daytime, the hall full of students, staff, and professors. But try as he may, the darkness and stillness of the place—after the loud bars they had just been in—seemed sinister.

Yann saw the concern on Thierry's face and quietly said, "We'll stay for ten minutes tops, okay? Besides, aren't you curious?"

"Yes, all right. That fact that I'm drunk helps too."

"Shhh. His door is the fourth one down on the left. Do you see it?" Yann shone his light down the row of doors, each one made in a light wood and paneled with carved rectangles popular in the 1930s. "Here it is." Yann handed Thierry the flashlight and took his wallet out of his back pocket, pulling his bank card out.

"You should use your university ID card!"

"Shhh! Get serious. Watch this . . . it will open just like in the movies," Yann said, positioning the card to the right of the door knob, in the gap between the door and the frame. "Shine the light in the crack for me. I need to see where the lock is."

Thierry bent down and did what he was told, but he couldn't see any black mass where the bolt should have been.

Yann looked over at his friend and shrugged. He put his hand on the doorknob and slowly turned it, the door opening. He hissed. "I told you! Moutte has lost it! He didn't even lock up this afternoon."

"Should we turn on a light?" Thierry asked.

"Why not? This office isn't on the street side, so who's gonna see? Let's."

The light illuminated the doyen's office in all of its ridiculous splendor. Yann shook his head back and forth in disgust. "I hate this office!" He looked to his friend for an accord, but Thierry was staring at an immense nineteenth-century oil painting of Saint Francis of Assisi. Yann put his hands on his hips and continued, "Why didn't he furnish this office in cool art deco stuff that would have suited the clean lines of the building? This is so tacky!" Yann had spent a large part of his childhood being dragged around antique auction houses and design showrooms with his mother—in the beginning because, as she was recently divorced, she felt guilty spending time away from him—but it quickly became apparent to Mme Falquerho that her youngest child not only loved but had an eye for great art and good design.

Thierry looked around at the office, and while he knew what Yann meant by "clean lines" and "art deco," he quite liked the heavy red-velvet curtains covering the windows, the rows of dark wooden bookshelves lining the walls, even the striped gold-and-cream wallpaper. It was a place where one could, he imagined, work happily all day long. An oasis among the cheaply built, uninteresting buildings that made up the rest of the university campus.

"Where should we look?" he asked, turning away from Saint Francis, ashamed that he was committing a sin and breaking the law. He was cold and wanted to quickly find the papers and leave.

"Well, the best place would be in a filing cabinet, in a file labeled . . . um . . . let me see . . . the Dumas Fellowship? Umm . . . what do *you* think?"

"Okay, okay!" Thierry walked over to the bookshelves, where rows of cabinets had been built in below where the shelves started. He pulled open the doors of the first one, only to see shelves lined with more books. Yann came beside him and opened the next set of doors where paper and office supplies were stacked neatly. They moved along together to the third set and opened the door, Yann whistling. "Bingo," he whispered, as if now that they had found some filing drawers they had been reminded of their purpose there and the fact that they were breaking the law. He pulled out the top drawer and saw that the files were organized alphabetically. Quickly flipping through them, he found the Dumas file and stood up, holding the file and opening it for both of them to see. As Yann held the file, Thierry flipped through the pages.

"These are our submissions. There's mine, and yours after it," Thierry said. "Garrigue?"

"Don't worry! She doesn't have a chance! Have you ever heard her speak up in class?"

Thierry let his shoulders fall, relieved.

"No, you're right. She's really smart though. And pretty, don't you think? You know, if you did one of those makeovers on her, changing her glasses and clothes."

Yann looked at his friend, bewildered. "What are you reading these days? *Elle* magazine?" He picked up the next application himself, frustrated by Thierry's ramblings. "Ah, Claude. No chance. His grades aren't as good as ours, and he's a recluse. Damn! There isn't anything here about who won!"

"Well, that's that. Let's go," Thierry said, grabbing the files and putting them back in the drawer. "I'm getting freaked out." He turned around to see the saint from Umbria, surrounded by animals and birds, smiling at him.

"No! Let's just look on his desk. He may have made a note of the winner, even on a piece of scrap paper." Yann walked over to the desk while Thierry sighed, following his friend.

"I'm going to sit down while you look," Thierry said. As he came closer to the desk he stopped, realizing that something was missing. "Where's his chair?" he asked. He walked around the desk. "Maybe he works on one of those ergonomic stools."

Yann laughed, picking up an unlabeled file that was on the desk. "I hardly think that Moutte shops at Ikea!"

Thierry then gasped and jumped backward, bumping into a

marble-topped console, causing a glass vase to tip and begin to fall over. Yann dropped the file and reached out and caught the vase, crying, "*Merde*, Thierry!" The vase looked like, to Yann, an art nouveau vase . . . from Nancy . . . ? he thought to himself. He tried to remember the name of the turn-of-the-century glass designer who had made the vases his mother bought, with much difficulty, for very, very wealthy clients. The vases were always dark, smoky shades of green and brown and orange, with flowers and plants creeping up the side of the glass.

"Jesus, Mary, and Joseph!" Thierry yelled.

"Shush, dude! They didn't hear you in the *centre-ville!*"

Thierry turned away from the desk and faced the wall, leaning on his forearm, whimpering.

"Hey," Yann whispered, now concerned. He reached out to his friend and patted him on the back. "Okay, we can leave now."

Thierry remained motionless and slowly extended his arm behind his back, pointing to the floor behind the desk. Yann turned away from his friend. "Holy crap!" The doyen was lying on his back, his eyes wide open, beside his desk chair, which had been toppled over and was now lying on its side. "Let's get out!"

Thierry turned around and forced himself to look at Moutte's body for a second, and then at his friend. "Yann! We can't leave him!"

Yann pulled at Thierry's sweater. "Who are we gonna call? He's dead! He must have had a heart attack. But we can't get caught . . . we broke in here, remember?"

"We can call Emergency on the way out!" Thierry pleaded, reaching for the phone. Yann put his hand on Thierry's.

"They'll find him in the morning! Let's go now! Come on!"

"We could call and leave an anonymous tip," Thierry suggested, becoming frantic, his voice cracking.

Yann put his hands on Thierry's shoulders and looked him straight in the eye. "Calm down. There's nothing we can do for the old fart. We need to look after ourselves now and get out of here as quickly as possible. The janitor will find him in the morning. Okay? Let's go!"

Thierry looked at Yann, now convinced of his friend's argument. If they were found in Moutte's office, neither of them would win the Dumas. In fact, they would probably be expelled from the university. He would end up teaching high school French in a rough neighborhood in Marseille, as his father did. He looked down at the doyen again, horrified at the professor's open eyes. Thierry Marchive would remember that stare for the rest of his life. Thirty years on, when he himself would be the chair of the Theology Department of a small American college, his four-year-old daughter would fall off of a swing, and for two or three seconds her eyes would stare vacantly at the big cloudless sky, until she caught her breath and Thierry, almost at the point of fainting, would cry tears of relief. He would see those eyes again, on a too-thin, too-nervous colleague, who, after his daily jog around the campus, would collapse of a heart attack in Thierry's office.

"Let's get out of here," he said quietly.

As they walked toward the door, Thierry stole one last look at the painting and realized why he thought it was so lovely: Saint Francis was smiling, leaning down as if speaking to the birds—not preaching. A large oak tree spread out over the group, protecting the saint and his friends, and tiny colorful wildflowers dotted the foreground. Yann sighed as he held the door open and ushered his friend through.

"Gallé," Yann whispered, frustrated that Thierry would find a kitsch nineteenth-century painting so enthralling.

"What?"

"Oh, it's just that vase that I saved from crashing. It's an Émile Gallé."

Thierry didn't reply. He thought it odd that his friend would comment on a vase when the head of the Theology Department was lying on his back, lifeless. And, unbeknownst to the two young men, the file that had slipped from Yann's hand, now on the floor, did hold the name of the Dumas Fellowship's recipient.

Chapter Four

With Every Job . . .

*T*he rain poured down steadily, as it had been doing since early morning. Bruno Paulik stood at his kitchen window and watched it crush the plants in his small backyard. It hadn't rained in Provence for months—he couldn't remember the last time it had—and now it was making up for lost time. It had just been announced on the radio that the residents of a village in Haute-Provence had been evacuated for fear of flash flooding. He thought of the gravel lane leading to his parents' farm near Ansouis, in the Luberon Sud—far from the flooding, but still, after rains like this it would become a muddy swamp. The Range Rover that he had bought secondhand paid for itself on days like today: bad weather no longer meant that to see his parents he had to park on the departmental road, about three hundred meters from their stone *mas*; and in the four-by-four he could visit his father's, and his wife Hélène's, more isolated vineyards, although his father, now approaching eighty, preferred to walk. "I'll walk while I still can," he would mumble when offered a ride. But Paulik suspected that his father had other motivations—Alceste Paulik had recently found a Roman coin buried between a row of vines and was now obsessed with finding more. He showed the coin to whomever came into the house—from family members to the guy who came to read the electricity meter—and although the inscription was too worn to read, he was fairly certain that the bust, clearly visible, depicted Hadrian: bearded, with a long aquiline nose, wearing a toga and crown of laurel. Alceste Paulik had, overnight it seemed to his son, become a fanatic amateur historian, having Bruno drive him into Aix—his parents had never liked driving in "la grande ville"—so that he could borrow Roman history books from the library.

"Papa!" Léa moaned, holding her small blond head in her hands. Bruno Paulik turned around and faced his daughter. "*Solfège! Solfège!* I hate it! Why do they make us do it? I can read music already!" She took her right hand off her head and shoved aside her papers, some of them sliding across the pine dining table and one or two falling on the floor. Paulik left the window and came and wrapped his arms around her.

"You know that in order to go to the *conservatoire* in Aix, you have to take all of the music reading classes, even if you can already read music," he said. When his daughter didn't reply, Paulik continued, "Léa, you love singing, but with every job, no matter how much we love it, there come some tasks that we don't like doing. But, in order to do our job really well, we also have to do some . . ." He searched for the right word, but the only thing he could come up with was, "shitty stuff."

"Papa!" His nine-year-old daughter couldn't decide if she should laugh or groan. She chose the latter, and Paulik silently agreed with her. He saw the overly difficult but obligatory music theory classes potentially doing more harm than good. What a perfect way to kill a child's love of music, Hélène had once said. And if he, Bruno Paulik, son of Luberon farmers, had been forced to take the same *solfège* classes that his tiny daughter was now taking, he would have, he was sure of it, given up his opera passion. Léa loved to sing— why couldn't she just keep on singing, and take the theory classes when she was older?

He bent down and picked up the fallen papers, and whispered, "Mint chocolate-chip ice cream." Léa beamed and nodded, holding up two fingers, which meant that she wanted two scoops. Paulik got the ice cream out of the freezer and Léa reached up in the cupboard for two bowls. They were just finishing the bright green ice cream when the back door opened.

"Maman!" Léa shrieked. "We're having a *solfège* break with ice cream!"

Hélène Paulik stared at her husband, pretending anger, and then laughed.

"Would you like some?" Léa asked. Hélène couldn't understand how her husband and daughter could eat ice cream when it was cold enough to have a fire in the fireplace.

"No, I think that a hot toddy is more what I need." She leaned her back against the wall and struggled to take off her rubber boots.

"Coming right up!" Paulik said, putting on the kettle. Léa walked over to the liquor cabinet and asked, "Rum, Maman, or whiskey?" The Pauliks looked at each other.

"Do you think that it's a good sign that a nine-year-old knows what goes in a hot toddy?" Bruno Paulik asked his wife.

"Rum, sweetie!" Hélène replied. "Our daughter's brilliant, what can I say?"

"You look tired and wet," Paulik said, bringing Hélène her favorite woolen poncho and draping it over her shoulders.

"Both, but more wet, and frustrated. We had set aside this weekend to plow the vineyards. . . . You know what that's like; you did it plenty enough for your dad."

"Why, Maman? Don't the vines have enough soil?" Léa asked. Hélène moved over to her favorite armchair, beside the fireplace, and sat down. When the Pauliks had renovated their village house in Pertuis, they had kept only the supporting wall and made the ground floor as open as possible, the focus a large contemporary kitchen and a fireplace flanked with two large armchairs. Bruno Paulik's parents had walked around in disbelief the first time they visited the house after the renovations had been completed. "Spécial!" the elderly Mme Paulik kept mumbling, running her hands along the stainless steel cabinets and work surface. She preferred oak.

"In early November it's a good time to move some extra soil over the bases of the vines. It protects them from frost," Hélène replied, looking at her daughter. Hélène rubbed her feet and continued, now looking at her husband, "But with this rain . . . we ended up working in the cellars, racking the wine to be bottled. I think Olivier had just fought with his wife; you could have cut the silence with a knife. And, despite almost twenty years in this business, I'll never get used to the cold, cold, cold of a damp wine cellar."

"Well, with any luck you should be able to do the plowing early next week," Paulik replied. "The rain will be over by then, and the frost is still far away."

"I hope you're right," Hélène replied. "Still, Olivier is completely panicked."

"Olivier Bonnard likes to be panicked. It means he can avoid his wife. All things considered, you have a great boss. He lets you do what you want out there, *and* put your name on the wines. Most winery owners are too pigheaded for that."

"You're right," Hélène replied. "But one day, I'd love to own my own vines."

Bruno Paulik smiled and put a small wool blanket on his wife's knees. With his salary as a policeman and the price of real estate in Provence, his wife's dreams of being her own boss were hopeless.

"Perhaps not in Provence," Hélène continued, smiling. "Somewhere cheaper. Chile?" She shuddered and pulled up the blanket. "Could you put another log on the fire, Bruno?" He nodded and was walking toward the back door to get wood when his work cell phone rang.

"Paulik here."

"Sorry to bother you on a Saturday, Commissaire Paulik," the voice said.

"It's okay, Alain. What's up?"

"A professor has been murdered at the university," Alain Flamant, one of the commissioner's favorite policemen, replied. Paulik walked out of the kitchen and ran up the stairs to his small office. "What do we know?" Paulik asked, closing the door to his study.

"The professor, Moutte, was found this morning by one of the university cleaning staff. She said it looked like a heart attack, but when she looked closer she saw that the side of his head had been bashed in. When the ambulance arrived and the paramedics saw the body, they called the police station right away. I got there as quickly as I could. The professor was hit on the head."

"Thanks. I'll come in right away. Are you still there?"

"Yes. It's one of the humanities buildings, 124 rue Jules Dumas. Fourth floor," Flamant said. "You'll see the policemen . . . we have the whole building roped off."

"Wait for me, then. I'll be there in about thirty minutes."

Downstairs, Léa let out a long sigh, slapping her pencil down on the table.

"Léa!" Hélène said, sitting down beside her daughter.

"But Daddy took the phone upstairs! That means he'll have to go into Aix now!"

"Probably, dear."

"But who will help me with my *solfège*? I'll fail!" Léa said.

"I'll help you," Hélène said, picking up her daughter's music theory book.

Léa looked at her mother quizzically, while Hélène Paulik pretended she didn't see her daughter's raised eyebrow.

Chapter Five

❧

One in a Million

"*L*isten to this," Marine said. "'Napoléon once said that the examining magistrate is the most powerful man in France.'"

"How nice," Verlaque mumbled, reaching across her for his reading glasses. "That makes my day."

"Stop it. I know you see the error!" she said.

"That it was Balzac, and not Napoléon, who said that?"

"Exactly! And why can't my students write well? Napoléon 'once said'? It's not a fairy tale, it's a historical essay! And what sources are they using for their research?"

"The Internet, what else?" Verlaque suggested. "These kids don't go to the library, and no one reads anymore. I see it all the time when I take the TGV up to Paris. Dimwits playing with their cell phones for three hours because they've forgotten how to read." He had a sip of coffee and then added, "But, did Balzac really say that?"

"What do you mean?"

"Well, was it written down? Or did someone just overhear him mumbling that, as he was waiting for, let's say, the men's room at the *opéra*? How can we know for sure?"

"You're a pain in the ass."

Verlaque smiled and pulled Marine down under the covers. "I am ze most powerful man in France," he said, joking, in English.

Marine laughed and threw back the covers.

"And I am an overworked teacher who has grading to do."

"Ah, come on! You knew that this weekend was this 'Verlaque and Bonnet minibreak'! Why did you even bring papers to grade? Is it because you feel guilty over your ten-week summer holiday, ten more days in early fall, two weeks at Christmas, two weeks to ski in February, and then, worn out as you teachers must be, two more weeks off in April?"

Marine sighed. "You know that I work over those holidays, researching and publishing."

"Yes, you do, but I don't see any of your colleagues doing the same."

Marine laughed. "How would *you* know? Oh, I can't believe we are arguing about this, on, as you say, our Verlaque and Bonnet minibreak!" Marine made to get up, but Verlaque leaped up, grabbing her white blouse that was draped over an armchair and waving it about.

"I'm sorry! I'm an idiot!"

"Yes, you are," Marine said.

"Great, we agree on something. Wanna come wine tasting with an idiot?"

"Antoine!" she cried. "We went wine tasting, and *buying*, yesterday!"

"But I only bought one case of that Visan wine, and I can't stop thinking about it. All of my favorite grapes, all in one wine—Syrah, Mourvèdre, Cinsault . . ."

"Yeah, yeah. And Carignan and Grenache."

Verlaque stopped waving the blouse and looked at Marine, blinking. "You were paying attention! I sometimes think you have a photographic memory."

Marine smiled at his compliment. Several of her teachers in high school and university had made the same comment, but she was, in fact, falling in love with wine. Her parents had never had any interest in grapes; it was a hobby that they associated with less intellectual pursuits, or with people who voted conservative. Marine then thought of Verlaque's antique Porsche, and the tiny thing that was a kind of half trunk.

"You only bought one case because we already bought three in Châteauneuf-du-Pape and you have a small sports car. You need to buy a minivan."

"Did I just hear you correctly?" Verlaque asked, throwing the blouse on the bed. "A minivan? Me? Put your grading down and let's go, or else we'll stay in bed all morning, like yesterday. The maid was mad at us."

"Where are you going to put more wine?"

"Delivery, my dear." Verlaque walked over to the window and opened the heavy cotton drapes. "*Mon Dieu*," he whispered.

"What is it?" Marine asked.

"Come over and look at our Provence," he replied. Marine got out of the four-poster bed and shivered, running beside Verlaque, who put his arms around her. They both looked at the five-star view of the Luberon Mountains that were half-buried in fog, their tops, snowcapped, brilliantly lit up by the sun. The valley that ran between their hotel and the mountain was made up of thousands of mist-covered greens, the horizontals broken by the slim verticals of cypress trees.

Just outside their door steam rose and danced around in the

air, and both Marine and Verlaque took a few seconds to realize that the steam was coming from the blue heated lap pool.

Marine looked at Verlaque and asked, "Fancy a quick dip?"

"It's November."

"Yes, but it isn't raining like yesterday. And the pool's heated. We could have a quick swim, come back in here and have a quick you-know-what, and then I'll agree to go wine tasting with you, as long as we can visit the Roman ruins in Vaison."

"Yes to the swim, yes to the you-know-what, no to Roman ruins."

"What? Don't you enjoy Roman ruins?" Marine asked.

"Not really, no. I always find myself yawning, which makes me feel guilty. I understand their importance, but I can never see the beauty, or imagine the beauty, in a few knocked-over columns lying on their side."

"Wow, you've never told me that before. Can I visit the ruins and you visit the medieval church? It's Romanesque, if I remember correctly. My mother did a research paper on it once."

"Romanesque? It's a deal. Then we'll meet in that lovely square and have a coffee and recount our discoveries, having not been together for two hours."

They spent breakfast reading and slowly eating the restaurant's home-baked bread and jams. Verlaque was rereading Hemingway's *A Moveable Feast*, smiling at the writer's descriptions of an obnoxious Gertrude Stein, the sort of middle-aged woman that he often observed at Monoprix or at the post office, who jumped the queue or gave her opinions loudly. His grandmother Emmeline had referred to their kind as "Miss Doggetts," the name of a character in one of her favorite books. He had always meant to ask her what the book was.

"How many times have you read that book?" Marine asked. Verlaque looked up over his reading glasses.

"About a dozen, I would guess. I just bought this new edition when I was up in Paris last weekend."

"How was Paris, by the way? Did you see your parents?"

"No," Verlaque replied. Marine thought he had ended the conversation with that comment, but he continued, "I did see Sébastien." Marine smiled and nodded, saddened by the fact that he would visit his real estate mogul brother but not his aged parents. She did not understand, but knew, from experience, not to ask. She made a mental note to call her parents later in the day—they had just returned from a two-week trek across Sardinia, their sole luxury being the rustic hikers' auberges they were sleeping in instead of their usual tent camping. She looked around the hotel's dining room—the pressed white linens and bouquets of fresh flowers—and was sure that her parents had probably never set foot in such a hotel.

"I've finished my chapter and can't drink any more coffee," Verlaque said. "How about you?" Marine folded her copy of *Le Monde* and put it in her purse. Verlaque leaned forward and took the newspaper from her, seeing that she had marked certain passages with her blue pen. He laughed and said, "Do you always do this?"

"Yes! It's for my students. I like to bring up interesting, newsworthy topics in class, even if it's off topic. I think that's one of our roles as university professors. I only wish I could smoke and make great jokes in class as JP did." Verlaque laughed, knowing how much Marine admired Jean-Paul Sartre, but also how much she detested cigarettes.

"He was one in a million," Verlaque said as he reached across and took her hand.

They left the dining room hand in hand, passing in the hallway a wealthy American entering his room and then saying good morning to a maid, who smiled shyly. As they walked into their room, Verlaque had a sudden longing to be gone from that hotel and to be alone.

Marine, too, suddenly wanted to be out of the hotel. She felt guilty, guessing that the room probably cost per night what many people in the village paid in rent per month. She could feel that Verlaque, too, was suddenly elsewhere, and she was a little peeved at him. When he had said that Sartre was one in a million, it would have been a perfect opportunity to add the line "And so are you."

Chapter Six

The Unloving and Unloved

*V*erlaque maneuvered his car around yet another roundabout of the industrial zone of Carpentras, anxious to be out of that drab town and on the Autoroute du Soleil, which on a Saturday might be busy. After receiving a phone call from Commissioner Paulik he had agreed with Marine—her purse full of postcards of Roman mosaics of birds—that she would spend the afternoon grading and he would return that evening, since Crillon-le-Brave was less than two hours away. He could question the deceased's secretary and then speak with Paulik and Yves Roussel—the prosecutor had decided to proceed with a criminal investigation and had turned the case over to Verlaque by phone—and then be back at the hotel for dinner.

As he smoked his cigar and listened to Gerry Mulligan's baritone saxophone, he thought of Hemingway, his perfect sentences and his sorrow, as an old man—a year away from death—that he had cheated on and quit his first wife. The book was, if anything, a love letter to her. "Hadley," Verlaque said aloud as he slowed down for the *péage*, putting his car in the automatic toll lane, having a Télépéage on his dashboard. His cell phone rang and he answered it, putting it on speaker.

"Yes, Paulik. I just went through the toll at Lançon, so I'm about a half hour from Aix."

"Great. Let me fill you in a bit," Bruno Paulik said, pausing to take a sip of lukewarm coffee that he had purchased out of a university vending machine. "Dr. Bouvet says that Moutte was hit over the head early this morning, sometime between 1:00 and 3:00 a.m. A maid found the body at 8:00 a.m. when she was cleaning. His office door was open and the lock wasn't pried, so the murderer had a key, or was let in by Moutte, or the door wasn't locked in the first place. There were four sets of fresh prints all over the office. One belongs to Moutte, two others we have no record for, and the fourth we've identified as belonging to one of his students, Yann Falquerho."

"Fast work. Falquerho has a record?"

"He was a juvenile offender when he was seventeen, breaking and entering into his father's men's club, on a prank apparently. The charges were dropped, but the Parisian cops scared the pants off of him by throwing him in a prison cell overnight and taking his prints."

"I see. Isn't that normal that this kid's prints were in the office?" Verlaque asked. "He was his student, right?"

"Yes and no. Georges Moutte was the doyen and so had little contact with the students. But Falquerho's fingerprints were on the office doorknob, on files on Moutte's desk, and on the stainless steel arms of his desk chair, which was toppled over when the professor fell. Roussel and I have already questioned Falquerho in his apartment. Another student was there too—Thierry Marchive—

and the two of them immediately confessed to breaking into the doyen's office late last night."

"*What*? Do they realize how bad this looks for them? How did they break into a university building, anyway?"

"I checked the door where they entered. My daughter Léa could have broken in. And yes, the boys were very nervous . . . they couldn't stop blabbing. One of them was going on and on about a painting of Saint Francis, and the other one telling us how he kept a vase from turn-of-the-century Nancy from breaking." Verlaque listened but didn't comment—the innocent were often very nervous under police questioning, but one of them had already broken into a building before. And it was strange that both boys would comment on objects in the office, as if that mattered, when their doyen was lying dead on the floor. Verlaque dragged on his cigar and guessed that the vase was a Gallé. Could a doyen afford one of those?

"What did they say about the professor?"

"That they saw him lying there, and thought he had had a heart attack. They fled, not wanting to be found in the office."

"I'm sure. What were they doing in there, anyway?"

"Looking for the name of the winner of some fellowship award—they both applied for it. That's what Roussel was raking them over the coals about. He accused them of killing the professor over this award."

"*Merde*, Roussel," Verlaque hissed. "What an ass." While there were things that Verlaque respected in Roussel—the prosecutor's hard work and bravery—he was constantly frustrated by the prosecutor's impulsiveness, and he hated Roussel's tasteless jokes and general need to be the loudest in any room. Short man syndrome, Verlaque thought, doubled in a Marseillais. The second thought he tried to erase, wanting to be politically correct. After all, he did know a few men from Marseille who knew what it meant to be discreet.

"Sir?"

Verlaque shook some cigar ashes off of his jacket and answered into the speaker, "Sorry, Paulik. Please continue."

"I have a team going over Dr. Moutte's apartment, and we've been calling all those who were at a party that he gave last night—Moutte's secretary has a list. I've ordered those we've been able to contact to be present tomorrow morning in the school's assembly hall at 9:00 a.m., even if it is a Sunday. Some people seem to have gone away for the weekend and we haven't been able to reach them."

"Tomorrow morning's perfect, thank you. Anyone else we can speak to on Monday. I'll be in Aix any minute," Verlaque said, and he hung up. He realized that he would not be able to return to Crillon-le-Brave this evening, so he would pay for Marine to take a taxi home. He had the sudden desire to go to Marseille, and he pulled the car over to look for the phone number of someone who was a new friend and a die-hard lover of Marseille, Olivier Madani. Verlaque got ahold of the filmmaker and suggested they eat at his favorite Marseille restaurant on the rue Sainte, run by a husband and wife team with, in a rare reversal of duties, the wife in the kitchen and the husband working the dining room as host. Each time Verlaque walked into the restaurant he felt like he was home—or a place he imagined felt like what a home should be: warm, dimly lit, with genuinely friendly owners. The restaurant's patrons all seemed to know each other and hopped up and down, moving from table to table, as if eating could be a game of musical chairs. Verlaque loved the fact that he could walk up to the kitchen, which had a sliding window, poke his head in, and say hello to Jeanne and ask her what she was cooking for him that evening. Jeanne cooked with local ingredients using many family recipes, the food rich and heavy but refined at the same time. "Fancy comfort food," Emmeline had called it when he took her there. Jeanne and Jacques were now old, and Jacques walked from table to table with the aid of a cane. Verlaque imagined that they would retire soon, and no doubt close the restaurant, which saddened him.

The bit of sun he had seen over Mont Ventoux from their hotel room had now disappeared. He drove into Aix and pulled up in front of the address Paulik had given him, seeing that the name of the building matched the street name—Jules Dumas. He squeezed his dark green antique Porsche between two police cars. Three young men—students, presumably—came up to his car and walked around it. "She's a beauty," he heard one of them say. Verlaque got out of the car and nodded to the students, who smiled shyly then turned back to their diversion of watching the police go in and out of their college, the students slightly bored by the entire procedure but for some reason unable to move on.

Bruno Paulik came out of the building's art deco front door and strode toward his boss. The two shook hands and then the commissioner groaned.

"What is it, Bruno?" Verlaque asked. Paulik rolled his eyes and Verlaque turned around to see a middle-aged man in a wheelchair speaking to two female students who were also mesmerized by the police activity.

"Get out of here!" Verlaque said to the man, walking quickly toward him. The girls looked at the judge in horror.

"Just you wait a minute!" the shorter of the girls, with a pierced eyebrow and a nose ring, said. "This man's handicapped!"

"*This man* has spent time in prison. Why don't you two go to a café instead of hanging around here?" The taller girl, wearing glasses and dark, ill-fitting clothes, grabbed her friend's arm and led her away.

"Okay, Lémoine," Paulik said, towering over the wheelchair. "You were given strict orders to stay away from schools and young girls!"

"This is a university! These girls are now consenting adults," Lémoine spat out.

Verlaque walked over. "Do you remember me, Lémoine?" The man did indeed remember the judge who had given him a maximum prison sentence for two counts of misconduct—for verbally and physically offending two teenage girls just outside their junior high school.

Paulik leaned down on Lémoine's wheelchair's armrests and began to shake the chair. He let go, and Lémoine began to furiously turn the wheelchair around. "I'm going! I'm going!"

"I somehow thought he had disappeared from Aix," Verlaque said, standing on the sidewalk so that Lémoine knew he was being watched until he had in fact disappeared, up the street and around the corner. Verlaque thought of Philip Larkin, who once wrote that human beings—rich or poor, beautiful or ugly—were bound to be disappointed by life. The poet cynically separated people into two groups: those unloving and those unloved. Lémoine was both, Verlaque decided. Verlaque's parents were unloving, and his brother? Unloved.

"I'll bet he's heading into the parc Jourdan," Paulik said.

"I hope not." Verlaque thought that with the chill and the grayness of the afternoon there wouldn't be many people—girls—in the park. "Are you coming back into the building?"

"No, I've been here long enough. Dr. Moutte's secretary is waiting for you, up on the fourth floor." Paulik smiled slightly, which Verlaque thought strange, but he didn't comment on it.

"All right, I'll see you tomorrow morning, back here."

Verlaque walked into the building and immediately remembered his university days, which had been good ones—away from all that had happened in Paris. Being a student was a luxury, ironically seldom appreciated by students: being permitted to read and write all day long. He walked up the stairs and crossed, coming down, a tall, blond policewoman with her hair tied up in a tight bun and wearing the faintest touch of pale pink lipstick.

"Judge Verlaque," she said, smiling and holding out her thin hand.

"Good afternoon," he replied, not remembering her name but looking her in the eye. She was not one of Larkin's unhappy ones, surely? He continued up until he reached the fourth floor and walked down the hall, where he saw a policeman sitting in a chair beside one of the office doors. The young policeman, on seeing Verlaque, jumped up.

"Judge!"

"Hello. Sit back down. Has anyone thought to bring you a coffee?"

The policeman looked up, stunned. "Um, well, no."

Verlaque smiled. "I'll arrange it for you as soon as I get a chance. Sugar?"

The policeman looked as if he had been offered champagne. "Um . . . one lump. If it's no trouble."

Verlaque smiled and walked into the office, only to be met with a high-pitched "It's about time!" He stuck his head back around the corner and looked at the red-haired rookie policeman, who lifted his shoulders and smiled, pointing a finger to his forehead, making a circular motion. Verlaque laughed out loud.

"I beg your pardon?" he said as he went back in. The voice had come from a petite woman who was no more than thirty years old.

"I've been waiting forever!" she complained. "On my day off!

My boss is dead—murdered—and here I am, not being told any-thing!"

"You'll be given information soon enough. For the time being . . ."

"Murdered!" she cut in. "And it's a school day on Monday, and with all the work I have to do . . . waiting for midterm grades to come in, certain professors—always the same ones—taking the longest and giving me their grades at the last possible minute! And then the students want their results immediately, naturally. With all that . . ."

Verlaque kept his temper. "Please be quiet." The woman looked up at him, openmouthed. He took this as an opportunity to continue. "As you said, your boss has just been murdered, so have some respect for the dead and keep quiet and do as you're told." For further effect Verlaque leaned down on her desk, pressing his big hands into the cheap wood. He thought of Paulik leaning down on Lémoine's wheelchair, but he knew that he didn't have the same effect as the six-foot-two former rugby player commissioner.

"Yes sir," she replied, barely audible, her sigh accompanied by a nonchalant shrug, as if she understood why she was being rep-rimanded but could care less. She then pretended to flip through some papers and ignored Verlaque, until he said, "I know that you've toured the office with the other policemen, but could you take me through again, Mlle . . . ?"

She sighed again, flipped through a few more papers—of extreme importance, no doubt—and got up from her desk, silently making her way to Moutte's office door.

"Mlle Zacharie, Audrey," she finally answered. She took a deep breath. "Nothing was taken, as I told the commissioner. The Gallé vase is the object of most value, and it's still here."

"You're sure it's the same one?" he asked.

The secretary laughed. "Yes, of course! And besides," she added, rolling her eyes and placing her hands on her hips, "Gallé vases aren't worth so much money that a thief would pay to have it replaced with a phony." She added, uninvited, "I studied art history."

Verlaque said nothing, because he had no idea what a Gallé was worth. He did remember seeing Gallé vases at the Petit Palais in Paris, but would someone go to the effort of reproducing one? He thought, *au contraire*, that they were worth a lot of money.

"Were you at this party last night?" Verlaque asked.

"*Bien sûr*, as I told the commissioner, and I gave him the guest list."

"How long did you stay?"

Mlle Zacharie put her hands on her hips.

"Me? I left around 11:00 p.m." Her voice had slightly wavered when she had answered Verlaque, and he registered it immediately. It could be nervousness, or guilt.

"Did you go straight home?"

"No. I met my boyfriend at the Bar Zola. We were there well past midnight, and then we went home." Again, her voice cracked and she added, "We left the bar around 2:00 a.m., you can ask anyone who works there."

"And the doyen's post . . . how long is it for? Four, five years?" Verlaque asked.

Mlle Zacharie laughed. "Life. But I wouldn't think that he was killed for . . ."

"Good-bye." Verlaque said with a note of severity. Not thanking her, he walked as slowly as he could out of her office. He couldn't stand being in the presence of Mlle Zacharie any longer, and they would have some answers, hopefully, tomorrow morning.

He then turned back and said, "Get my officer a coffee, with one sugar."

She opened her mouth to protest and he added, "Now. And for tomorrow's meeting, I'd like you to make a list of the faculty, staff, and graduate students' contact information—photographs of them would be a big help—and get class schedules."

Mlle Zacharie banged a book on her desk, causing the young policeman in the hallway to grin from ear to ear. What a snob! she thought to herself. It was obvious to her that the judge saw her as a lowly secretary, not someone who had done graduate work in art history. She sighed as she remembered that today was Saturday and she had to make her weekly visit to her parents and watch them fawn over her older sister Lisa's perfect baby, and worry aloud whether Lisa and her husband, both doctors, were getting enough sleep. Her parents never asked her about Michel, her boyfriend, nor did they ask her if she was getting enough sleep, or had enough to eat (no on both counts). At least today she would have something dramatic to tell them. The baby getting a new tooth was nothing compared to a murder.

Her parents regretted that she had not continued her studies, that she knew, but to pass up full-time work in Aix would have been foolhardy. Besides, she needed the money; Michel didn't make much as a waiter, and working at the university at least meant that she was among her peers. Michel was certainly not an intellectual, but they seemed to be destined for one another. It had been advantageous working for the doyen, and she had not been looking forward to his replacement, whomever that would be. Mlle Zacharie sat down and ran her hands over the top of the glass paperweight the doyen had given her for her birthday, and she realized that she would miss that silly old man.

Verlaque walked out into the early evening and it began to drizzle. Mlle Zacharie could be a beautiful girl, he thought, but her sour personality ruined any softness around the edges she might have. Was she unloved, or incapable of loving? The dancerlike policewoman on the stairs? Loving. He forced himself to think of that morning in the hotel room, but he could no longer hear Marine's voice, and he had a gut feeling that he had said something wrong. The bells of Saint-Jean-de-Malte began to ring in the distance, and he walked on, pulling the collar of his coat up around his neck.

Chapter Seven

❧

An Uncomfortable Moment for Sylvie

"*T*his room is bigger than my apartment!"

"Hardly!" Marine answered.

"I'm exaggerating, of course, but the bed is huge. There'll be lots of room for us three tonight!" Sylvie Grassi said, fluffing her pillow and lying on it with her hands behind her head.

"With me in the middle!" cried her nine-year-old daughter, Charlotte. "I'm so lucky!" Charlotte had been raised by Sylvie alone, and for the first two years of her life had slept with Sylvie in her double bed. Marine's parents had been aghast; when Marine had tried to explain Sylvie's reasoning, she had remembered that the subject of babies and sleep was taboo in her family, and so had to quietly listen to both parents complain of spoiled children.

Charlotte hugged her mother and godmother, hopped off the bed, and went into the marble bathroom to explore, and Sylvie gave Marine an earful.

"He is so undependable. You always come last. *Last*. He'd better take you on a replacement weekend."

"Sylvie, I'm not a prima donna," Marine replied, turning on her elbow to look at her friend. "I don't need to be pampered. He has an important job, one of the most important jobs in the region. I understand that he has things hanging over his head all the time. Professors do too . . . always grading to be done, class prep, papers to publish. We choose our careers and then have to make the best of it." Marine wanted Sylvie to lay off Antoine, so she delivered the news. "Besides, today's call came from his commissioner. There was a murder late last night in Aix."

Sylvie sat up and glanced toward the bathroom, where she could hear her daughter humming. "Murder? Who? Where?" she whispered.

"This is the thing. It was at the university."

"*What?*"

Marine nodded. Luckily she didn't have any details, as her friend's love of the macabre and sensational had always irked her. She was sure that it came from the fact that Sylvie got all of her news from the television instead of a newspaper.

"Marine! Details!"

"I don't know any more than that," Marine answered.

"Come off it, Marine! You teach at the university! Where was it?" Sylvie taught art history and photography at the École des Beaux-Arts, which was on the other side of town.

"Okay, okay. Antoine did say that it wasn't at the law school, fortunately, but at the theology school, in the Jules Dumas building."

Sylvie jumped off the bed and rushed to the dresser, where she fumbled in her purse for her cigarettes, only to remember that they were in a no-smoking room, and that Charlotte was there too. Sylvie had strict rules about not smoking in front of her daughter.

"Sylvie?" Marine asked. "What's up? Do you know anyone at the theology school?"

Sylvie shook her head back and forth. "No, no. No one," she mumbled. "Hey! What about your mom?"

"She's fine. I called her right after I spoke with Antoine. She doesn't know any more than we do at this point." Marine thought it odd that Sylvie had a sudden concern for Mme Bonnet. The two disliked each other, Marine's mother seeing Sylvie as promiscuous and selfish. Sylvie regarded Mme, or Dr., Bonnet as a cold and unjoyous mother, busying herself with causes so that she could ignore—Sylvie guessed—unresolved, painful issues.

"So you see why Antoine had to leave this afternoon," Marine said. "Besides, he loves his job."

"Has he ever said that he loves *you*?" Sylvie asked, still playing with her cigarettes and considering the possibility of stepping outside for a quick smoke. If there was ever a time she needed nicotine, this was it . . .

"Nineteen out of twenty!" Charlotte hollered as she ran into the room and jumped back up onto the bed. The women laughed at her generous rating of the bathroom and were in hysterics when they saw that her sweater's pockets were stuffed full of miniature shampoos and hand lotions. Charlotte turned to her godmother and, taking Marine's slender face in her chubby hands, asked, "Marine, do you think they'll have pasta in the restaurant tonight?"

Marine stroked Charlotte's head. She tried to force a smile, happy as she was that Sylvie had insisted on driving up to Crillon-le-Brave as soon as she had heard about Verlaque's canceling, but she couldn't get Antoine's voice out of her head. It was true, and she didn't tell Sylvie this, that he had spoken to her quickly and curtly, as if he was desperate to get off the phone.

"I'm betting that they'll have some kind of pasta," she answered. "But if they don't, this is such a good restaurant that the chef will prepare for you your very own pasta." Charlotte sighed and let her head fall back on the pillow, her eyes staring up at the ceiling.

Sylvie wandered over to the minibar and took out a half bottle of white wine. She pulled a small corkscrew out of her purse (it was permanently attached to her key chain) and opened the bottle, motioning to Marine that she would pour her some too. "I'll pay for it, don't worry!" Sylvie said. She found an apple juice for Charlotte, who was on the floor now, separating her toiletry finds into categories of "Beautiful," "Pretty," and "Ugly." Sylvie took a long drink of wine and looked at herself in the mirror, hoping that neither her daughter nor her best friend could read her mind.

Chapter Eight

⚘

Comfort Food

*I*n the restaurant of a nondescript 1960s hotel near downtown Perugia Giuseppe Rocchia leaned over his bowl of linguine with wild boar sauce and took a long sniff before he sprinkled it with Parmesan. He came here for dinner once or twice a week, comforted by the mellow wood decor and by the fact that there was parking behind the restaurant big enough for his Mercedes. He had taken more time than usual reading the surprisingly extensive wine list, finally choosing a Cabernet from the Alto Adige mountains, the vintner's name sounding more Austrian than Italian. The wine would also go well with the wood-fired carp—freshly caught from nearby Lago Trasimeno, he had been assured—that he had ordered as a *secondo*. An impatient man, he decided to phone Bernard Rodier, having finished the linguine, and while he waited for his carp to arrive. He liked having something to do while dining alone, and by being occupied on the phone, he would ensure that fans and well-wishers would leave him alone.

Rodier answered the phone on its first ring, his normally deep, actorlike voice cracking with excitement. "Giuseppe?"

"Yes, Bernard," Rocchia replied, annoyed that Bernard asked that every time he saw the Italian phone number.

"Have you heard? Georges has been murdered! Late last night or early this morning."

Giuseppe Rocchia set his linen napkin down and leaned forward. "Speak slowly and clearly, Bernard. You do get so excited. I thought I heard you say that Georges Moutte has been murdered."

"That's exactly what I said! Murdered in his office! That's all I know for now, I don't even know how he was killed!"

"In his office? But where is the . . ."

"Don't worry! I have it," Bernard answered.

Rocchia breathed a sigh of relief. "You are to say nothing, Bernard. Understand?"

"Of course; of course. But there's a murderer about! What if he . . . or she . . . is looking for the . . ."

"Shhh! Bernard, where are you? Can anyone hear you?"

"No, I'm at home."

"We'll leave this to the police, *non*? Poor Georges was probably just at the wrong place at the wrong time. It was most likely thieves looking for money and Georges tried to put up a fight."

"But we're murder suspects!" Rodier said.

Giuseppe Rocchia chuckled. "Correction. You're a murder suspect. I'm in Perugia."

Rocchia's carp arrived and he tried to put the whining Bernard Rodier out of his head. With Moutte dead, Rocchia would soon have possession of that lovely apartment on the place des Quatre Dauphins, so convenient for the Aix opera festival. He already had in mind whom he would invite, if she could sneak away from her husband long enough. He took a first bite of fish and leaned back, happy.

Bernard Rodier still couldn't get used to eating alone, especially in the evening. He switched on the television only to see a multi-paneled game show featuring actresses and actors he didn't know. He turned off the television, not even bothering to try the other stations. He walked over to his tiny kitchen radio—his ex-wife had let him take it out of their house—and turned on France Musique. Some classical music would be soothing.

It had been a grueling day, finding out that Moutte was dead, and being told, by that prosecutor with the high-pitched voice, to appear at the university early the next morning, as if he were a suspect. And why didn't the police call Giuseppe? He then realized that Giuseppe did not easily give out his cell phone number; the Aix police probably only had his home number, and Bernard was quite sure that Dr. Rocchia spent little time at home. Rodier decided that it was best to distance himself from this whole affair. He would aid the police, just as Rocchia had advised, but only that, no extra information. And he would keep his appointment at the Bibliothèque nationale for later in the week.

He opened his freezer, knowing that he had little in the way of fresh food in his refrigerator. After being married for twenty-six years, he hardly knew how to do the grocery shopping and was still very much unorganized. He always seemed to think of buying food after the shops had closed, and so a week ago had driven his car to Picard and bought over one hundred euros' worth of that chain's specialty—frozen gourmet food. The choice was rather extraordinary, and he had been careful to buy a good selection of fish, meat, and vegetable dishes. Meat would be too heavy this evening, it was already late. He didn't have any white wine to go with fish, and besides, he felt like something a little more substantial. He turned over one of the many single-serving-size boxes and saw that it was pasta carbonara: an excellent choice for this evening, and he had a half bottle of cheap Bordeaux sitting on the cupboard. Bernard Rodier had no taste for wine and bought Bordeaux because of the name and because he had read that a glass of red wine a day was good for your health. Or was it two glasses?

The microwave rang its now familiar ding and he pulled the plastic container out, slipping the contents into a pasta bowl. The radio was playing Bach's Goldberg Variations, and he sat down, feeling a little more comforted. He had nothing to worry about, and with Moutte dead, the post of doyen was once again up for grabs—the logical choice being that hardworking professor who had published multiple volumes on the Cistercian religious order. He smiled as he pictured himself in Moutte's office, calling Picard and ordering his weekly groceries over the phone to have them delivered to that prestigious address on the place des Quatre Dauphins.

Chapter Nine

Naming Names

"*I*'m starving."

"Tell me something new."

Yann looked at Thierry in surprise. "Aren't you hungry? It's nearly 9:00 p.m."

"I feel sick to my stomach!"

Yann opened their tiny refrigerator and bent down to look inside.

"You feel sick because you haven't eaten."

"No, dude," Thierry answered, sighing. "I feel sick because we're murder suspects."

Yann laughed, turning over a jar of raspberry jam in his hand, frowning when he saw the thick layer of green fuzz on the jam. "That little hyper guy is nuts. But the big rugby player, the commissioner, doesn't suspect us one bit. You can tell by his face. You have nothing to worry about."

"How can you stay so calm?" Thierry asked, looking over at his friend, who was now back on the sofa, the biography of a rock star in his hands.

Yann answered, "All we did was break in . . . that's nothing, compared to murder. Our little mishap will be forgotten about, you'll see."

"So who do you think did it?"

Yann put down his book and got up, walking around their small living room. "Interesting question. I would dismiss theft, since there's nothing to steal in that ugly office. Unless . . ."

"What? The painting of Saint Francis? They were after that, then ran out without it?"

Yann laughed. "No, you jughead. The Gallé vase I saw. No, scrap that theory since the vase was still there, and I don't think you'd murder for a piece of art and then not take it with you. Especially, my friend, some schlock late-nineteenth-century religious painting." Yann walked to the bookshelf, picked up a book and opened it at random, and pretended to smoke a pipe.

Thierry laughed. "Okay. So name me the suspects."

Yann put his forefinger in the air. "Bernard Rodier, my dear Watson; and then our own beloved big-bosomed Annie Leonetti."

Thierry looked at his friend, shocked.

"Look at what they had to gain," Yann said. "An apartment to die for on the best square in overpriced Aix-en-Provence *and* a lifetime, secure job. One that probably pays really well too, given the Dumas endowment."

"Yeah, I see your point. It's the equivalent of the Dumas Fellowship for us," Thierry suggested.

"*Well*," Yann replied. "Not quite. And then there's Giuseppe Rocchia . . ."

"Hardly," Thierry said. "He lives in Perugia."

"Look at a map. Perugia is a day's drive from here. We found Moutte at 2:00 a.m. That means that Rocchia could have murdered the doyen sometime after the party and then driven all night back to Perugia. I can see him now, sitting in his favorite café on his favorite square, at 9:00 a.m. sharp, just as if it was any other day."

Thierry shrugged and scratched his head. "Hey, what about Audrey Zacharie?" he asked. He wanted to make his own contribution to the list of suspects.

"What could she have to gain?" Yann asked.

"Um. Maybe it was a lover's quarrel? You saw her getting cosy with him at the party."

"That's disgusting. She's a third his age."

"Oh, you're an expert, I see." Thierry leaned back on his desk chair and rubbed his stomach. He was in fact very hungry, but nervous too. "Listen, Yann. I really think you should tell the judge that you weren't in the pub with me the whole time."

Yann stared at his friend and then let out a nervous laugh. "Thanks, Thierry!"

"I just think we should be honest!"

"I am being honest. I felt light-headed from all the wine and beer and wandered outside. I walked down the rue d'Italie and threw up into a potted tree, then fell asleep on a bench in front of Saint-Jean-de-Malte. I was gone, what, forty minutes?"

Thierry picked at threads on the old blanket that covered his desk chair. "And you left me all that time alone with those American girls."

"You're too shy with girls. I did you a favor. And when I came back, I was in fine form, right?"

Thierry nodded, rubbing his stomach. "I think there's some dried pasta in the cupboard."

Yann stood up and looked at his friend. "Please tell me it's De Cecco."

"It's De Cecco."

Yann clapped his hands and opened the door, grabbing the familiar blue bag of his favorite pasta. "You do listen to me!"

"It really is superior," Thierry replied, running his hand through his hair in mock pretension.

"Sauce? Do we have sauce?"

"There you're in luck too. No sauce, but there's a bottle of my uncle's olive oil. It's under my bed. I've been saving it."

Yann ran to Thierry's bedroom and fell down on his knees and rummaged under the unmade bed. "Your uncle with the olive orchard in Allauch?" he called.

"Yes! Full of the flavor of Marcel Pagnol's stories, or so my uncle always claims."

After finding slippers and one tennis shoe, Yann found the olive oil and hugged the bottle.

"Just don't ask me for wine," Thierry said, getting up to help.

"Ah. The sadness."

"I'm sorry about the pasta," Marcel Féau said as he cleared away the dishes.

"It wasn't that bad," replied his wife.

"That's very kind of you, but it was overcooked, and I know how fussy Corsicans are about their pasta."

Annie Leonetti rested her head back against the kitchen wall. "I hardly noticed, to tell you the truth. And the kids gobbled it down. Where did they learn to put ketchup on pasta, by the way?"

"My parents' house," Marcel replied, pouring his wife a cup of herbal tea. He braced himself for a discourse on the poor eating habits of his parents, who as retired French civil servants had more money than they knew what to do with. They obviously didn't spend it on food—as Annie complained about regularly—and Marcel often wondered if his father had a secret gambling habit, or if his mother had been a victim of some Internet scam. But Annie stayed quiet for some time, until she finally said, "It is terrible about Professor Moutte's death, but I can't help but not feel too saddened by it. Terrible for a theologian to admit that, isn't it?"

"Theologians aren't immune to impure thoughts," her husband replied, putting a packet of cookies on the table. "Besides, Moutte wasn't the most likeable man in the world. He treated you and Bernard horribly, waiting until the last minute to retract his retirement promise, teasing you the whole time with the suggestion that you had the job. I'm sure he did the same to Bernard."

"Yes, I'm quite certain he did, judging by Bernard's behavior at the party. You don't think . . . ?"

Marcel looked at his wife, surprised. "Annie, I can't imagine *anyone* doing such a thing, and I'm surprised that you would think so of Bernard."

"I'm sorry. You're right. More likely it was Rocchia."

"Annie!"

Annie laughed and took a cookie and dipped it into her tea. "I was feeling quite cocky up until Friday night. I was sure I had the job, and I had mentally moved us into the Quatre Dauphins apartment."

"Ah," Marcel said, frowning. "The kids would have left a trail of water from the pool into the house all summer long. Think of the mess." Annie laughed and reached over the table, taking her husband's face in her large brown hands and giving him a kiss.

Chapter Ten

❧

Dr. Bouvet Delights
in Annoying Judge Verlaque

Verlaque arrived late at the restaurant, having toured each level of the underground parking garage only to find, on the bottom floor, what he was fairly certain was the very last spot. He had then run up the stairs of the garage that emptied into the immense place aux Huiles, then run up more stairs that led to the rue Sainte, the restaurant just on his right. Opening the restaurant's door was always a delight—a haven away from the busy Marseille port and its bars spilling out onto the sidewalks, most of them televising a soccer game at full volume.

Jacques saw him and walked, as quickly as his cane would take him, toward Verlaque. *"Monsieur le Juge!"* he exclaimed, slowly lifting his right hand up to shake Verlaque's.

"M. Jacques!" Verlaque exclaimed. He knew the couple's family name, but had always referred to them as Jacques and Jeanne.

"M. Madani is already seated, with a view of the old port." This was Jacques's regular joke, as the restaurant had no windows overlooking the port, but one long fresco of the port that took up the entire west wall—where the view would have been, had there been windows. The painting was too bright, the perspective all wrong, but Verlaque loved it. He made his way to the table, smiling at two young women as he passed their table.

"I'm dying over this whiskey," Madani said, taking Verlaque's hand and shaking it.

"Jacques has a new one?"

"Bruichladdich," Madani answered. "I'm sure I'm butchering the name. Jacques says it's new—well, it was old, but the distillery closed and so the head whiskey maker went out and raised just enough money to save it. A labor of love, according to Jacques."

Verlaque sniffed the golden whiskey and asked, "Islay?"

"Yes," answered Jacques, who was now at their table.

"Were you Scottish in another life, Jacques?" asked Madani, laughing and looking over Verlaque's shoulder at the dozens of whiskey bottles displayed behind the bar.

"Oh yes, I think so," the restaurateur replied, with a seriousness that surprised the two diners. Jacques stared off for a moment, as if he were imagining the island of Islay, before saying, "Jeanne has grilled shrimp tonight, with an artichoke tapenade, as an entrée. As a main dish she made her daube, which I know you love, Judge, served with pasta."

Verlaque did love Jeanne's beef stew, which she made with Camargue bulls' meat, a generous helping of orange zest, and to-matoes that she had canned over the summer. But he could never understand the Provençal preference for noodles with stews. "Sounds great, but I'd like potatoes instead of pasta."

Jacques smiled. "Jeanne made the pasta, *Monsieur le Juge.*"

"In that case, pasta, please. And I'll start with the same whiskey that my filmmaker friend here is drinking."

Jacques motioned to the barman to pour another whiskey and then looked down at their table, leaning even more heavily on his cane. Madani and Verlaque exchanged looks and Verlaque nodded, winking. Madani understood the cue and said, "Jacques, would you like to sit down and join us for a whiskey?"

Jacques looked around at the restaurant, full but with the other diners already happily eating.

"Well, I think I might! Just for a minute or two!" With surprising quickness he pulled out a chair from a neighboring table and sat down.

Just before Verlaque began to break the golden crust of his lavender crème brûlée, his cell phone rang. He immediately answered it, seeing that the caller was Dr. Emile Bouvet, his coroner. He got up and took his phone into the men's room. "Yes, Emile."

"Sorry to bother on a Saturday night, but I have some interesting news for you."

"Go on."

"Dr. Moutte was hit on the side of the head, as I'm sure the commissioner told you."

"Yes," Verlaque answered quickly, not hiding his impatience.

"The object was wood," Bouvet continued, enjoying drawing out the suspense.

"Go on, Emile," Verlaque said.

"And old."

"An antique?" Verlaque asked.

Bouvet smiled, delighted to hear the impatience in the judge's voice. "You could call it an antique. I'm with an old friend in the lab right now, who specializes in dating these kinds of things."

"So what does your friend say?" Verlaque breathed heavily into the phone. It surprised him that there would be a dating specialist living in Aix, but perhaps, like so many people did nowadays, he commuted from Aix to Paris on the TGV. "You are going to tell me, right? What does he say? Fifty? One hundred years old?"

Bouvet laughed. "*She* says," he answered slowly, smiling as he looked across the stainless steel table at Dr. Agnès Cohen. "Judging from the sliver we extracted from the guy's hair, seven hundred years old."

Chapter Eleven

✌

Meeting Florence Bonnet

*T*hey met at the Quatre Dauphins fountain. "Fancy meeting you here," Paulik said. Verlaque smiled and shook his commissioner's hand.

"I left the car in the garage. Since it isn't raining, I thought that the walk would clear my head."

Bruno Paulik nodded, thinking to himself that Verlaque had probably left his dark green 1963 Porsche in the garage for other reasons—yesterday the commissioner had seen university students walking around the car, peeking inside with cupped hands and whispering with excitement.

"I just dropped Léa off at the *conservatoire* for a Sunday rehearsal, and there was a rare empty parking spot in front," Paulik said, as if needing to explain why he too had been staring at the sixteenth-century fountain whose four fat dolphins spat out water.

"Ah, how is *solfège* going?" Verlaque asked.

"Moments of panic, soothed by mint chocolate-chip ice cream."

Verlaque laughed and the two walked on, talking of the weather, Paulik's father's newfound enthusiasm for ancient Rome, and a banking machine that had been blown up at 5:00 a.m. that morning, giving the thieves easy access to whatever money hadn't been burned in the explosion. Moments of silence were not uncomfortable, Verlaque noted to himself. He was happy to have a colleague with whom he could speak of history or music so easily. Conversations with Parisian colleagues usually began with real estate prices.

After ten minutes of pleasant walking, they arrived at the humanities building. Verlaque looked up at the gray exterior, built in a hurry sometime in the 1930s and in dire need of a paint job. The windows looked as if they hadn't been washed in years, but up on the third floor someone had made an attempt to cheer up their office or classroom with planters, hung crudely to the metal shutters with wires. French *facultés*—unlike the elite, much smaller *grandes écoles*, which both Verlaque and Marine had attended—were open to any student who passed the high school baccalaureate exams. Because of this there was overenrollment and the *facultés* were underfunded, but the bright pink pansies above him, blooming despite their surroundings, reminded Verlaque that many students, underprivileged or otherwise, did benefit from this free-of-charge, nonelitist system. It touched him, all of a sudden, being French, a feeling that usually came over him in restaurants and museums, not in front of a *faculté*.

Two young men, one tall and slim and the other short and stocky, ran past Verlaque and Paulik, both boys trying to squeeze past each other to be the first one in the door, but both getting stuck and then having to step back in order to let out the ballerinalike policewoman Verlaque had seen yesterday. She smiled when she saw the judge and commissioner, and the boys hurried into the building, the taller one pushing his friend through first and following behind.

"Officer Cazal, good morning," Paulik said, shaking her hand. Verlaque and the policewoman said hello and the three walked into the building. "We'll be in room 103, the third door down on the right," she said, smiling at both men but her gaze lingering on Verlaque. "Everyone is here now; we were waiting for the boys to arrive."

As they got closer to the assembly room voices could be heard—some high-pitched, others rapid-fire whispers—but all silenced when the judge and two police officers entered the room.

"Good morning and thank you for coming on a Sunday," Bruno Paulik said. Those gathered—twenty-some-odd who had been present at Professor Moutte's party or who had worked with the deceased—stared at the former rugby player, some of them with half-eaten cookies in their mouths. Verlaque stayed silent, enjoying the impression that his six-two, 210-pound bald commissioner was making.

"We'll begin by talking with all of you together, followed by individual interviews. As Officer Cazal has informed you, you'll be expected to remain here for the day, and if you are planning to leave Aix this week, please let her know where you can be reached."

"I have research to do at the Bibliothèque nationale in Paris later in the week!" complained a well-dressed middle-aged man with chiseled cheekbones and thick white hair.

"Ah, come off it, Bernard, you can do your research anytime!" a woman answered. She looked Italian or Spanish to Verlaque, and like her colleague had also been blessed with abundant, thick hair, all of it still black.

"But my train ticket is booked!"

"Paris is no problem, just leave us a number where we can get ahold of you," Paulik quickly replied before any other interruptions could be made. "Most of you present this morning were at Professor Moutte's party on Friday night. The doyen was murdered sometime early Saturday morning, just a few hours after the party. My first question is, who was the last person to leave the party?"

"I was," the Italian-looking woman spoke, her voice loud and self-assured. "My name is Annie Leonetti. I'm a theology professor. I heard Georges—Dr. Moutte—tell his housekeeper that she could go home and come back in the morning to do the dishes."

"And so you stayed late to help the doyen?"

"No," Dr. Leonetti replied. "I stayed late to help out the maid. I took the dirty wineglasses into the kitchen and helped wrap up the leftovers."

"Okay," Paulik said. "What did you speak of with the doyen?"

"No doubt his surprise retirement postponement," the white-haired professor said, quietly but loud enough for those close to Verlaque and Paulik to hear.

"Certainly not, Bernard!" Leonetti replied. Then, looking at Paulik and then Verlaque, she added, "We only spoke of the merits of cling wrap versus aluminum foil."

"Did he tell you that he was going to the office after cleaning up?" Verlaque asked.

Annie Leonetti paused for the briefest of seconds, Verlaque noted, before replying.

"He did mention it, yes."

"Did that not seem unusual to you? Given the late hour?"

"No, not really," she answered. "He had no family to look after, and he often worked late. But when I left just after midnight he was still in the kitchen. We didn't leave together."

"Thank you," Verlaque replied. He wondered how Annie Leonetti knew that the doyen often worked late. She also sounded resentful of the fact that he had "no family to look after." She was a beautiful woman, with olive skin and thick red lips, but her sparkling brown eyes had dark circles under them. He thought of the modern professor's life—publish or perish—and imagined that she might have small children at home.

"So no one saw Dr. Moutte leave his apartment early Saturday morning? Or did he mention it to anyone that night? The fact that he may have had some late-night work to do?" Paulik asked.

The assembly remained silent, some of them looking at each other in hopes of hearing someone speak, others looking into their coffee cups.

"He did tell me that he was meeting Giuseppe Rocchia, but he didn't say when," the handsome Bibliothèque nationale researcher said, quite unnecessarily, thought Verlaque.

"Bernard!" Annie Leonetti again chastised her colleague. "That could have been anytime!"

"The policeman did ask what we talked about. I'm Bernard Rodier, by the way." He looked over at Annie Leonetti and added, "I too teach theology, but I'm mainly a researcher and writer." Annie Leonetti sighed and rolled her eyes up toward the ceiling. Rodier went on, "You may be familiar with my volumes on the Cistercian order . . . they're in most good bookshops, even on Amazon . . ."

"Thank you, Dr. Rodier," Verlaque quickly answered. "We've been given a list of those of you who have keys to this building and will begin our interviews with you, for obvious reasons." He was already getting tired of the bickering between Drs. Leonetti and Rodier and wanted to remind the professors that their boss had been murdered only two nights ago.

"I'll call you in one at a time to the office across the hall from this room," Officer Cazal said. "There will be sandwiches provided for you at noon, so please don't leave the building until you have been interviewed. We'll start alphabetically."

"*C'est pas vrai!*" moaned the doyen's secretary. "I'll be last! My name starts with a Z! But surely you don't need to interview me? I didn't even stay long at the party."

"No exceptions, I'm sorry, Mademoiselle. You have a key to the building, don't you?" Paulik asked.

"Yes, of course I do!" she replied, her hands on her narrow hips. "But Dr. Moutte could have let in his murderer!"

Paulik stared at the young secretary with something close to disbelief. "We'll still need to interview you. We should be through by six."

The secretary sighed, and Paulik added, "You can work upstairs in your office, right?"

"Yes, I suppose so."

Verlaque imagined that Mlle Z. had either been planning on leaving early or was nervous about being interviewed. He left the assembly room and walked across that hall to a small office that appeared to be the kind that was used by graduate students or for small meetings. The desk was 1960s metal and in a few years would probably be considered vintage and be sold in antique stores in the sixth arrondissement in Paris. Three mismatched chairs had been placed in the room, along with a stack of paper and two pencils. Extra office supplies, most of the boxes half-opened, were stacked on the floor in a corner, as were the parts of a dusty plastic coffee machine.

Paulik came and sat down across from Verlaque. "Does anyone in that room like each other?"

"I was thinking the same thing, although we only heard from the same three people."

Officer Cazal poked her blond head in the room and said, "The first interviewee is ready if you are."

Verlaque nodded. A woman in her late sixties with outdated wire-rimmed glasses and neat, short auburn hair stood in the door and looked at Paulik and then at Verlaque.

"Hello, Judge," she said. "Since I'm here on official business we won't speak of your routine practice of breaking my daughter's heart."

Antoine Verlaque looked up over his reading glasses at Mme Florence Bonnet. She smiled.

"I seem to be a suspect," she said. "By the simple fact that as a semiretired theology professor I have a key to the building. Plus I hated Georges Moutte, but no one has known that until now."

Chapter Twelve

✶

Poor Old Georges

"*P*lease sit down," Verlaque said, motioning to a chair but not returning Mme Bonnet's forced smile. "This is my commissioner, Bruno Paulik."

Florence Bonnet took her seat and looked at Paulik, adjusting her glasses as if to see him better. She smiled—obviously liking what she saw—and then said, "We're a motley crew in the Theology Department, aren't we?" Verlaque hid his smile and liked Mme Bonnet a little more.

"We did get the impression that not many of the theologians actually get along," he answered. "At least those who spoke up during the meeting."

Mme Bonnet made no acknowledgment of the judge's hint and continued. "That was Georges Moutte's fault." Both men leaned forward, interested. "Moutte played cat and mouse with his professors. He left me alone—I think that he was a little afraid of me." She smiled openly at the thought of it. "Both Drs. Leonetti and Rodier are under a fair amount of stress right now," she added, wanting to give the policemen a better impression of her department. "Georges was going to retire at the end of the school year, and Annie and Bernard were up for the post. But Georges would play the other professors off of each other, promising one a full professorship and then giving it to someone else. He even did the same thing with the graduate students, dangling the Dumas prize in front of their noses, hinting at who would win, that sort of thing."

"Was the Dumas that big of a deal?" Paulik asked. What he really wanted to add was *that someone would kill for it?* Mme Bonnet looked at Paulik and then at Verlaque, her eyebrows raised.

"Have you heard of the Prix de Rome?"

Verlaque nodded but it was Paulik who replied, "The prize given to artists and architects to study in Rome?"

"Yes. Well, the Dumas was almost that prestigious. A cash prize of fifty thousand euros to enable a scholar to study; a furnished apartment here in Aix, just downstairs from the doyen's apartment; travel expenses paid in case your research takes you to Jerusalem or to Dublin; and something on your résumé that's invaluable."

"And will no doubt lead to future employment," Verlaque added.

"Almost certainly."

"And the fellowship has been in existence since when?" Verlaque asked.

"Since 1928, when Father Jules Dumas left the family fortune to us."

"Could you explain to me how a French university was allowed to keep a Theology Department going after 1905?" Verlaque asked.

Mme Bonnet peered at the judge and thought twice before answering, not because she didn't know the answer but because he hadn't said *please*.

"In 1905, as you know, a separation of church and state was declared. The university Theology Departments across France were closed, save in Alsace because it was German at that time, and this small department in Aix, thanks to one savvy Dr. Roland Dumas, uncle of Jules. Those wishing to study theology had to do so in a History, or even Law, Department. Fortunately the Dumas family was wealthy beyond belief, and even in 1905 money spoke loudly. The fact that one uncle was a cardinal and another a politician helped. The department was granted autonomy if they could prove to the state that they would be totally self-funded. The family had made enough money and wise investments that this was easy to affirm, and the scholarship has been granted yearly without a break since 1928, except during the occupation of the south of France from 1942 to '45."

Verlaque asked, "And how long will it keep going on?"

Florence Bonnet shifted in her seat. "Ah, with God's will . . . many years to come . . ."

Verlaque cut in. "So there remains quite a bit of money."

"Enough," Mme Bonnet answered, clearing her throat.

"You're the treasurer of the Dumas Committee," Paulik said, looking at his notes.

"Yes. We're having a meeting at the end of the week, as a matter of fact."

Verlaque knew that Florence Bonnet was hiding something, but he wanted to get her to continue talking of the murdered Georges Moutte.

"You said that you hated the doyen," Verlaque said.

"Well . . . 'hate' may have been too strong a word. He wasn't good at his job and I think he knew it—so he used fear and false promises as weapons. I hated that part of him, yes. I didn't value his scholarship either. . . he was a Cluny specialist but he rarely published, and when he went up to Cluny it seemed to me it was more for the Burgundian wine and food than for research. But I suppose I didn't hate the man."

"He would have made enemies treating people like that," Verlaque said. "But enough to be killed for it?"

Mme Bonnet's face became rigid at the word "killed," smoothing out the many wrinkles of her extremely tanned face. Marine's parents were great walkers, and unlike their daughter, they adored the sun.

"Perhaps in a rage?" Mme Bonnet suggested. "You're the policemen. Are people capable of such acts?"

"In a rage, yes," Paulik answered.

"Well, Bernard Rodier was certainly in a huff at the party, but not in a rage," she offered.

"Tell us more about the party, Dr. Bonnet," Paulik said.

"I couldn't hear what they were saying—Georges and Bernard, that is—the harp was ringing in my right ear. We all heard Georges yell at Bernard, 'And my decision will be final!' and then Bernard left, slamming the door. But we've all slammed doors on Georges Moutte, myself included. And then Georges made his announcement that he was not going to retire just yet, or anytime soon. This must be what he told Bernard, which is why, we all assumed, Bernard left the way he did. But you should ask Dr. Rodier himself."

"What time did you leave the party?" asked Verlaque. Mme Bonnet raised her eyebrows but did not question why she was being asked for an alibi.

"Early, right after Bernard left. I was home by ten-thirty, and my husband—Marine's father," she said, as if wanting to remind the judge of his ties to the Bonnet family, "was waiting up for me. We drank some herbal tea, read for an hour or so, and then turned out the lights and slept until 8:00 a.m."

"Do you think it odd that Dr. Moutte would leave his apartment so late, after a party, and walk across town to his office?"

Florence Bonnet crossed her arms and thought for a moment, looking down at her cream-colored skirt. "No, knowing Georges, it wasn't that odd," she answered. "He may not have been tired. Or maybe he wanted to get his mind off of the argument. Or, and possibly this is the best reason, he wanted to go to the office to work on his real passion, which you may have gathered is not theology."

"I beg your pardon?" Verlaque asked.

"Didn't you look around his office? Georges Moutte had one true passion, and with the arrival of the Internet—another useless American invention we've all become dependent on—I am told that Georges was becoming rather addicted."

"Antiques?" Verlaque guessed, remembering the Gallé vase and the seven-hundred-year-old object that killed the doyen.

Florence Bonnet nodded up and down, tilting her head to one side and smiling shyly, as her daughter often did. "Art nouveau glass, to be specific."

"Do you have any idea, then, given his hobby, why Dr. Moutte would have postponed his retirement?"

"A number of reasons came into my head the night of the party," Mme Bonnet mused. "To anger Bernard Rodier and Annie Leonetti, for one. While Bernard drives me mad with his stupid questions, and Annie Leonetti is an Ivy-League show-off, they are both passionate historians and thinkers and deserved better treatment from the doyen. But I think the real reason is the money."

"*Ah bon?*" Verlaque asked. He couldn't imagine that the doyen's civil servant salary was that high.

"Yes, the doyen is generously paid, thanks to the endowment," she answered, as if reading the judge's mind. "And whoever the doyen is, they live rent free, in what is, if you haven't seen it already, a fabulous apartment. The apartment alone would be worth murder, in my opinion."

Paulik shifted in his chair and cleared his throat.

"Do you know who the doyen dealt with when buying antiques?"

Mme Bonnet laughed, and Verlaque immediately remembered Marine's descriptions of her parents' 1960s home, devoid of charm not because of its era but because neither of her parents had any flair for decorating or how to make a home warm.

"No, I've no idea," she replied.

"And Dr. Moutte was a bachelor with no family," Verlaque stated, wanting confirmation from Mme Bonnet, who seemed to know, or be willing to reveal, a great deal.

"That's right. He had an older brother, also never married, who died two years ago of cancer."

Paulik crossed his thick legs and put down his pencil. "We were told by Dr. Moutte's secretary that there is an Italian also in the running for the doyen's job."

"Ah," Mme Bonnet said, laughing. "How Giuseppe Rocchia ever earned a doctorate, I'll never know. But yes, he was also a candidate for the post. I'm not sure why Georges chose Rocchia, possibly to anger the other two, or possibly because of their shared hobby."

Paulik looked at Verlaque and then back at Mme Bonnet. "Rocchia collects antiques too?" he asked.

"Yes," Mme Bonnet answered. "Glass as well, but more than early twentieth-century French. Anything from Roman to contemporary American, so I've heard."

"Did either of them collect wood?" Verlaque asked. Mme Bonnet looked puzzled by the question.

"No, no. Only glass as far as I know, although I've never been invited to any of Giuseppe's many houses."

Verlaque thanked Mme Bonnet, who then stood up, straightened her skirt, and picked up her all-purpose mesh carrier bag, full of books and papers and what appeared to be a sandwich wrapped in plastic.

"You've been most helpful, Dr. Bonnet," Verlaque said. This was the longest he had ever spoken to either of Marine's parents, and while he didn't really like Mme Bonnet, he appreciated her straightforwardness, and he now knew where Marine's strict work ethic came from.

"You are welcome," she answered. She stopped at the door and said, "I hope I wasn't too harsh on poor old Georges. While I didn't think he was the best person to be the doyen, he certainly didn't deserve to die, or be murdered, as you seem to think he was."

"We know he was murdered, Dr. Bonnet," Paulik said.

"Well, well, now," she answered, shaking her head and bringing the carrier bag up to her chest. Paulik got up and opened the door for her and she walked out into the hallway and then paused and stopped, as if she wasn't sure where to go next.

Chapter Thirteen

✌

A Really Humble Guy

"Your mother-in-law is quite a character."

Verlaque looked over his reading glasses at his commissioner and laughed. "Are you teasing me?"

"Yeah, just a bit. Sorry, sir. Dr. Bonnet reminds me of one of my cousins, who runs the post office in Lourmarin and terrifies all of the other workers and villagers. She tells it like it is, which some of our family members appreciate and others don't. Hélène thinks she's a hoot."

"I get what you mean. Mme Bonnet was a good source of information. She has some strong opinions, which we'll have to sift through. But the antiques-collecting angle is interesting, don't you think? Collectors will do anything to add to their collections. Do you remember that attempted murder in Bordeaux a few years ago?"

"Yeah, I'd kill for some old Burgundies, but not for Bordeaux wines."

Verlaque laughed. "I agree. That reminds me, I think that guy is being released in a couple of months."

Paulik nodded and then said, "But a thief who knew about art would have taken the vase from the office. Unless there was something in the office even more valuable than art nouveau glass. Like a seven-hundred-year-old wooden sculpture?"

"Let's try to find out Moutte's most recent purchases. And if there have been any thefts or sales of wooden medieval statues recently, especially in France."

Paulik crossed his arms and said, "The real motive, it seems to me, is still that job, and the apartment." Verlaque looked at his commissioner but didn't reply.

"I know that we still have to speak to the rest of the party guests, but I think that the primary suspects are those three professors who stood to get . . . and still do, now that Moutte is dead . . . the job," Paulik continued. "Imagine you have been promised that you'll be the next doyen, and then Moutte announces at a party that he won't be retiring just yet? That would explain why the murderer didn't take any art from the office. What they wanted was that apartment and tenure. What's an apartment of that size and history worth in Aix? A couple of million. Okay, they can't sell it, as it belongs to the school, but they're still living in it. And the post is for life."

Verlaque thought of his commissioner's suggestion and knew that it had some validity: his brother Sébastien was a realtor in Paris and had, at their last dinner together, entertained Verlaque with stories of wars between families—husbands and wives, siblings, nieces and nephews—over the inheritance of such apartments.

"All right," Verlaque said. "But what about the wooden object? What was it? And where is it now?"

"It was just the murder weapon. It's probably in the sea by now.

Okay, it's a fancy murder weapon, which happened to be in the right place at the right time. It could have been a recent purchase and so that's why the secretary didn't know about it. Or the murderer may have brought it with him, but that's pretty far-fetched."

Verlaque nodded in thought and was about to reply when a knock was heard and Officer Cazal opened the door.

"Ready for the next interview?" she asked.

"Yes," Verlaque replied.

A tall, ill-dressed girl in her early twenties stood in the doorway as if frozen. Officer Cazal gently put her hand on the girl's shoulder and nudged her into the small office.

"This is Garrigue Druon," the officer announced. She smiled at the girl and said, "This is Judge Verlaque and Commissioner Paulik. They're speaking to everyone who was at the party on Friday night. After you've answered their questions you're free to go. Okay?"

The girl quickly nodded, and not looking at the judge or the commissioner, sat down, staring at her long, thin, pale hands.

"Garrigue?" Verlaque asked. The evergreen low-lying shrubs that covered Provence's limestone hills—among them lavender, rosemary, and thyme—were collectively called *garrigue*. Verlaque knew that the sweet-smelling honeysuckle and Scotch broom also made up the garrigue, as did juniper bushes and olive trees. He imagined that Bruno Paulik would be able to list all of the other garrigue plants, ones that Verlaque may only know by sight, if that.

"My parents were hippies," the girl whispered, used to explaining her name.

"It's a lovely name," Verlaque said, trying to get the girl to look up at him. When she did, he recognized her. "You were outside of the school yesterday, weren't you? With another girl?" he asked.

"Yes," she replied, looking up at Verlaque and then over at Paulik. "That man . . . in the wheelchair," she continued. "He's nasty, isn't he?"

"Yes, don't go near him," Verlaque answered. "Did he bother you?"

"Not really," she whispered. "But I was glad you came when you did."

"So you were at this infamous party on Friday night," Paulik said, wanting to change the subject away from Lémoine.

"Yes."

"Did you know Professor Moutte well?"

"Oh no," she answered, surprised by the question. "He was the doyen. That was the first time I had been invited to his apartment, and only because I was nominated for the Dumas."

"Well done on that," Verlaque said, wanting to make the girl feel more at ease. She continued to play with the frills on her cheap flowered blouse, but did manage to look the judge in the eyes and smile slightly.

"Who else was up for the Dumas?" he asked.

"Four of us. Myself, Thierry Marchive, Yann Falquerho, and Claude Ossart. Claude wasn't at the party. He seldom leaves the library."

"And the other graduate students don't have keys to the building, right?" Paulik asked.

"No, only those of us who are teaching assistants. That's myself and Claude."

"You're Dr. Leonetti's assistant?" Verlaque asked.

"Yes."

"Who, or what, are you researching?" Verlaque asked.

She sat up, her voice now clear and happy. "I'm researching Saint Ambrose, Augustine's teacher." Verlaque smiled, now out of depth in his knowledge but wanting the girl to feel at ease. It was Paulik who continued the conversation by saying, "I had a great-uncle Ambrose. He too was a priest."

Garrigue Druon looked at the commissioner and smiled.

Paulik continued, "My uncle was always telling us stories about Saint Ambrose and about his life in Milan. What I remember most was that Ambrose was a saint of the people, a really humble guy, where Augustine was the scholar."

"Exactly," Garrigue replied, leaning forward. "Ambrose baptized Saint Augustine, but was known more for his passionate sermons, whereas Augustine is still widely read for his letters and confessions."

"My great-uncle kept bees, too, just like Saint Ambrose!" Paulik added, now sitting forward, almost cutting the girl off.

"Really?" Garrigue exclaimed. "Saint Ambrose is the patron saint of beekeepers!"

Verlaque glanced, slightly annoyed, at his commissioner, who was now leaning back in his chair, as if remembering this great-uncle. It then briefly crossed Verlaque's mind that Paulik may have invented the story to make Mlle Druon more comfortable, but he was never sure with Bruno Paulik, who seemed to know half of Aix and almost all of the Luberon.

"What time did you leave the party, Garrigue?" Verlaque asked.

"Latish," she answered quietly, now remembering why she was here. "I felt out of place, but for some reason felt too shy to leave." Verlaque pictured the girl leaning awkwardly against a wall, alone. "Wallflower," he thought the expression was in English. Garrigue went on, "I helped Dr. Leonetti gather up some of the dishes and then left just before midnight."

"Did you notice anything strange that evening, apart from the argument between Dr. Rodier and the doyen?"

The young student thought for a moment and then said, "No, not really, except that Dr. Moutte received a phone call really late, just before I left."

The commissioner and judge looked at the girl, trying to hide their surprise.

"Go on, Garrigue," Verlaque said softly.

"It's none of my business, but we always had a rule in our house: no phone calls after 9:00 p.m. And the doyen was an old man."

"And so he took the phone call?" Paulik asked.

"Yes, but in another room," she confirmed. Verlaque thought Garrigue very wise for her age—he realized that her answer to the question was her way of saying that she couldn't hear the conversation, and that she probably would have listened had she been able.

"Did the doyen seem nervous after the phone call?"

"Nervous? Not really, more like impatient. It was clear that he wanted us out of the apartment, but Dr. Leonetti kept chatting on and on, so I just slipped out without saying good-bye."

"Did you go straight home?" Verlaque asked. Garrigue Druon was visibly surprised by the question.

"Well yes! It was almost midnight! I share a flat on the rue de Tanniers with a law student. I woke her up when I came in. She had put her purse right in front of the door and I tripped over it."

"Fine. Thank you, Garrigue. If you could just leave your address and the name of your roommate with Officer Cazal before leaving, that would be great. And good luck with the fellowship," Paulik said.

Garrigue nodded and quickly got to her feet, looking relieved that the interview was over, but also looking much more confident than she had when she had first entered the room.

"Thank you," she added before closing the door behind her.

Paulik turned to Verlaque and said, "She's a clever girl, isn't she?"

"Yes," Verlaque answered. "She knew that we were asking for an alibi and gave us a sure one. Tell Officer Cazal to talk to the roommate as soon as possible."

"Do you think that the shy, good-girl stuff is faked?"

"It's impossible to tell, isn't it? But Officer Cazal can ask Garrigue's roommate that same question."

"Was that true about your uncle?" Verlaque asked.

Paulik looked surprised. "Of course."

"He made honey and the whole bit?"

"Yeah," Paulik answered defensively. "Lavender honey, mostly, but my favorite was chestnut. You couldn't believe how that tasted in my mother's madeleines."

"Spare me the Proust," Verlaque said, smiling.

Paulik smiled and said, "Before Léa was born, I wanted to call her Garrigue."

"Really?" Verlaque said. "I love those hearty plants. I sometimes miss them when I go to Normandy. So why didn't you?"

"Hélène thought that Garrigue sounded like a hippie name."

There was a knock on the door and Officer Cazal came in and introduced Yann Falquerho, who stood awkwardly behind her. "Come in, Yann," the commissioner said.

The tall, thin student sat down quickly and Officer Cazal softly closed the door.

"You're in big trouble," Paulik said.

"I know," Falquerho replied, looking steadily at the commissioner.

"Thanks to a Parisian policeman who was doing his job, we have your fingerprints on file. You were caught breaking into a private club, *non*?"

Yann Falquerho winced. He hated to think of that night and had since avoided that street in the eighth arrondissement where his father's automobile club was located, which was most inconvenient as it was on the same street as one of his favorite bistros.

"I was afraid you'd find out about that," he finally answered.

"It certainly doesn't help your case," Paulik said. "It will be up to the university to decide whether they are going to proceed with pressing charges."

Yann closed his eyes and remained silent.

"Dr. Leonetti's on our side," he finally said.

"That's neither here nor there. You must realize the importance of what's happening right now. You break into an academic building, and the same night your doyen is murdered."

"We didn't do it!"

"So how about telling us what happened, step-by-step," Verlaque ordered. He looked at Falquerho's thin blond hair, straight and neatly kept, but as he turned, Verlaque saw a gray patch on the left side, about the size of a large coin. It reminded him of something, or someone—he couldn't put his finger on it yet. Perhaps someone he had known in Paris? The gray patch of hair was distinctive and made the boy look older; without it Yann would have looked more like a high school student than a doctoral candidate.

"Well, as you know, we were invited to Moutte's . . . I mean Dr. Moutte's . . . party. We had a fair bit to drink, as it was a boring party and there was this really decent red from Bandol . . ."

Verlaque looked down at his paperwork and tried not to smile.

". . . and then we left around 11:00 p.m. to go and try our luck at the Anglo pubs."

"Try your luck?" Paulik asked.

"Girls . . . American students. They're nuts for the French

guys. Or so we're told, but we've never been that successful, to be honest, that night included. So we had a few beers, and that combined with the red wine . . ."

"You were drunk," Verlaque finished Yann's sentence. He then remembered the gray patch: Holden Caulfield from *The Catcher in the Rye*. Verlaque's grandmother Emmeline had given the book to him the year he lived with her in Normandy, when he was fourteen. "You should be reading books like this, instead of . . ." she had quietly said, and then she had hugged him.

"Yes, sir. Even more than drunk. And it was my idea . . . I take full blame . . . to break into the humanities building. The Dumas means a lot to us, you may not understand . . ."

Paulik was tired of being instructed by opinionated theology students, professors, and the secretary.

"I think we do understand its importance . . ."

"I had it in my thick head that I just had to know who had won the fellowship," Falquerho continued, cutting Paulik off and not seeming to pause for a breath. "I don't know why. I get these ideas in my head sometimes and I can't stop myself."

"And so you broke into one of the side doors, in the alley."

"Piece of cake, way too easy, sir."

"And then?"

"We walked upstairs, and when we got to Moutte's office we found the door open . . . I mean, not locked."

"And the file?"

"We didn't find the right file, and we were just about to look around the desk when we saw the doyen lying there, eyes wide open, but dead."

"Why didn't you call the police? Or an ambulance?"

"Totally my fault, again. Thierry is a real scholar, please don't blame him. I just want to get an MBA . . ."

"You're off topic, Yann," Verlaque said.

"Right. Sorry. We didn't call an ambulance because we thought the doyen had had a heart attack, and it was obvious there was nothing to do for him. And we didn't want to get caught in the building."

"Do you have witnesses who saw you and Thierry in town? After the party and before you . . . broke into the *faculté*?"

Yann Falquerho smiled for the first time.

"As luck would have it, we do. Claude Ossart, a fellow grad student, was coming home from the gym when we were leaving the party, and we talked for about five seconds. That's all you ever get out of Claude. Five seconds . . ."

"Anyone else? I'm sorry, Yann, but five seconds isn't quite long enough to establish an alibi. No one in town, at one of the pubs?"

Yann Falquerho paused, and then continued, "Well, the bars were really busy, so I'm not sure that any of the barmen would remember us. I can't say I even remember any of them, you know, the wine . . ."

"Bandol," Paulik said.

"Yeah. Hey, wait, we did manage to talk to two American girls for about an hour, or two-beers'-length time. But I have no idea what their names are and I can't remember which of the foreign programs they're in." He shrugged. "They wouldn't give us their cell phone numbers."

"Do you remember what they look like? In case you saw them again in town?"

Falquerho smiled. "Yeah. The small blond one I do."

"Keep your eyes peeled for them, then. That will be all, Yann, and if you think of anything that may be important, will you call us?"

"Yes, sirs." Falquerho stood up and looked at both Verlaque and Paulik. "What's going to happen to us?"

Verlaque stayed sitting but answered, "As I said, it's more up to the university than to us. If you cooperate and tell us the truth, that may help your cause. But I can't promise anything."

Falquerho nodded. "Thank you."

Chapter Fourteen

❧

Rue Saint Lazare

Marine sat down on a bench in her apartment's front hall and laced up her running shoes and put her high heels in a market bag. She then stepped out onto her terrace to check the weather. It was cold, as she had thought it was, with a slight wind. She took a few seconds to look at the steeple of Saint-Jean-de-Malte, gray on this November morning, as were her plants. It was always hard to imagine the riot of colors the plants would produce in the spring and summer, and she already longed to see the bright pink oleander flowers and the purple lavender.

She had returned in the early afternoon from Crillon-le-Brave, much to the whining of Sylvie, who begged to stay longer; but Charlotte had a Victor Hugo poem to memorize for the next morning, and Marine had promised to visit her mother for afternoon tea. Verlaque hadn't called the night before. She left the flat and walked down her street, turning left on the rue 4 du Septembre. Sunday afternoons were the quietest time in Aix, the best time, she thought, to walk the streets. Saturdays had become so busy that she now strolled about on Sundays. She stopped and gave a *bise* to a colleague who was on his way into town, seemingly just strolling as she liked to do, and she apologized that she didn't have time to talk to him as she didn't like to be late for anybody, especially her mother. Her colleague laughed, appreciating the joke. He had never met Dr. Florence Bonnet but knew of her reputation.

In a few seconds Marine was at the bottom of the street, waiting for the light to change so that she could cross the busy *périphérique*, the ring road that circled the old town. The wall that had once been there in the Middle Ages was long gone, but a section still survived north of the *vieille ville* near the Roman baths. It was hard to imagine that Aix had been a fortified town and the 1950s apartment building across the street was sitting on land that had been farmed less than two hundred years ago. The wall had been defensive, protecting Aix from invaders or *la peste*, including one particularly devastating plague in the early seventeenth century that had arrived in Marseille by boat and had killed thousands there. The town fathers of Aix had been warned and the city gates were closed, no one allowed in or out until the plague ran its course or went somewhere else. Since Aix's citizens were instructed not to leave their homes, even for Mass, over ninety oratories were built, religious statues placed in niches that were carved into the corners of the buildings' facades. The oratories enabled the faithful to pray by leaning out of their windows, without having to leave their house and perhaps get infected, or infect a neighbor. The plague passed, and Aix was saved, not a soul lost.

The city celebrated, and in thanks a local baker invented a sweet made from almond paste and candied melon, coated it with glazed sugar, and called it a *calisson*. The lozenge-shaped candy was to Marine's parents, and many Aixois of their generation, venerated, and much debate went into which baker now produced the best.

She was still thinking of the plague when she walked past the *rectorat* that housed the region's education offices. The building was one of Aix's supreme eyesores, built in the 1970s using cheap materials that were now showing their age and poor quality. Marine thought it sad that the institution that made decisions about children's education should be housed in such a building when other agencies, like the association of notaries and the bureau of *commerçants*, were located in seventeenth- and eighteenth-century architectural gems. Her mother was on a committee—one of her many—hoping to demolish the building and open a competition to contemporary architects to design and build a replacement, but after years of meetings the city still hadn't accepted their proposal.

She passed under the railroad tracks and then turned left onto her parents' street, Saint Lazare, and walked past the houses that she knew by heart. When she was growing up the families had been mostly civil servants; the housing was cheap and conveniently located near the university, *rectorat*, and downtown. Now the neighborhood, and especially this street, was a desirable one, and her parents had new English neighbors who were both physicists trained at Oxford and employed at a nuclear research center north of the city. She walked by and saw a newer model Audi parked in the driveway and then arrived at her parents' house, their car recently purchased as well, but a Citroën. Her mother opened the door before Marine had rung the bell. "*Bonjour, chérie,*" Florence Bonnet said, holding out her cheek for the *bise.*

"*Bonjour,* Maman."

"Come in, I've just made a pot of coffee and I'm heating up some croissants left over from breakfast."

Marine smiled and took off her jacket and placed it on the coatrack. The sight of the coatrack piled with her parents' coats and scarves made her miss them, and she was happy to have arranged this snack with her mother, despite the fact that the coffee would be too weak and the croissants would have been purchased yesterday, or even the day before, at a supermarket. Marine's mother, the oldest of six girls, was of a generation that rejoiced at the emergence of the supermarket, or the gigantic *hypermarchés*, in France. Antoine had told her it was called "one-stop shopping" in English, and although she understood why people went, she hated it. The few times she had been to a *hypermarché*, the store was so big and the lines so long that she suspected her multistops along the rue d'Italie were actually quicker. But she was spoiled too: she was an only child—no five siblings, or four like her father had— and she had no children and worked close to home.

"Come in, *chérie*, I have lots to tell you," Mme Bonnet said, pulling out a chair at their kitchen table. "The shit has really hit the fan at the university."

Marine almost laughed, surprised to hear her mother cuss. "Yes, it's been terrible. Dr. Moutte's murder, right in your building on campus."

"Your . . . Antoine . . . was asking me lots of questions this morning."

"He had to ask everyone questions, Maman. Did he ask you if you had any idea who might have done this?"

"Yes, but I told him I couldn't imagine anyone killing Georges, or anyone killing another person, period. He kept going on and on about the Dumas, without saying 'please' or 'thank you.'"

"I'm sorry. He gets a little serious, I would imagine. It *was* a murder. Could it have been love gone wrong, Maman?"

Florence Bonnet dropped her spoon loudly on the table and

then picked it up and set it on her plate. "Why would you ever think such a thing?"

"Dr. Moutte was a handsome man; he may have had a lover? *Non?* Someone his age, perhaps divorced but elegant. Lovers' quarrels can lead to murder."

"No! Get your mind out of the gutter! That's your friend Sylvie's influence!"

Marine set her coffee down and sighed. She had wanted to come here and for once not have an argument about Antoine or Sylvie. Florence Bonnet saw the frustration on her daughter's face and decided to divulge some information, although normally such gossiping was against her nature.

"During the party on Friday evening," she said, leaning over the wooden table, "I did see Georges's secretary, a mousy little know-it-all, flirting with him."

"Really?" Marine asked. She highly doubted her mother knew what flirting looked like. "Go on," she said, pretending to be only half-interested.

Mme Bonnet spread more apricot jam on her croissant and continued. "Yes, she was whispering in his ear, with her eyes half-closed, and then laughing. She did it a few times."

Marine thought that did in fact sound like flirting. How odd. Moutte must have been in his seventies.

"Could Mlle Zacharie have been cozying up to Dr. Moutte to win him over, perhaps get something out of him? Money?" Marine asked.

"What would she need money for?"

"To live!" Marine regretted that her voice was raised and tried to speak more calmly. "She must make minimum wage, Maman." The elder Bonnets were blissfully unaware of the soaring cost of living, low wages, and the price of real estate. They were thrifty too, and had a hard time imagining that others were not—that people could desire things they thought frivolous: nice cars, meals out, designer clothes. "I highly doubt she would be sexually interested in such an old man," Marine said.

"You said earlier that Georges may have been murdered because of a lover's quarrel," Mme Bonnet reminded her daughter.

"Yes, by a lover of his own age and social background, yes, it's highly plausible."

"Well, there's more to the story that I should tell you. Wait till you hear. Let me pour you some coffee."

Marine moved her chipped coffee cup across the table. Her mother was being uncharacteristically diffident, and nervous. "More to the story? Did you tell Antoine this?" Marine asked.

"I have only just found out. Besides, he . . . your judge . . . I can only stand him in small doses. I could smell the stale cigar smoke on him. *Frimeur!*"

"Maman, Antoine's not a show-off just because he smokes cigars. There are some guys in his cigar club who are not at all rich, nor are they show-offs. Anyway, I don't want to have this argument. What's your news?"

"We just had an emergency Dumas committee meeting, to discuss the next recipient—I'm pleased to report it's someone I like very much—only there are a few problems," Mme Bonnet reported, dipping her croissant into her coffee and then biting into it. Marine watched the butter slip off the croissant and into the hot coffee, leaving an oily slick on the surface. "We, as a committee, can only recommend the Dumas recipient. This final decision has always been the doyen's. And with Georges dead . . ."

"I see the problem," Marine said. "And the other problem?"

Mme Bonnet sipped some coffee and again leaned over the table, whispering. Marine listened to her mother's story.

"This does sound odd. I'll look over the accounts if you want a second opinion," she said.

"I have the paperwork here," Mme Bonnet said, handing Marine a yellow folder that looked like it had been reused about a dozen times.

Marine looked at her mother, who had jumped up and was now busy washing the coffee cups. The Bonnets had never bought a dishwasher, something that amazed Marine but shocked Mme Bonnet's five sisters. And could it be that her mother was as afraid of Antoine as he was of her? Marine smiled at the thought of it and got up to leave. She grabbed the folder on the kitchen table labeled "Dumas" and said, "I have a busy week ahead, Maman, but maybe I could see you and Papa next weekend?"

Mme Bonnet continued to face the sink but called out over her shoulder, "Oh, yes, we'll see what we can arrange. Your father will be back from his medical conference by then."

Marine nodded, not surprised that she needed an appointment to visit her parents. She walked to the front hall and put on her jacket. She saw her father's old green quilted coat that he wore when the Bonnets took long walks in the country, and she missed him, as she was sure he missed her. Did her mother ever miss her? She doubted it; even in retirement Florence Bonnet busied herself with committees and theology and church projects, as she always had done.

Chapter Fifteen

❧

Broken Promises

*P*aulik and Verlaque were discussing the possibility of the murderer being someone not at all involved with the university when Annie Leonetti came in for her interview, her arms piled high with thick hardcover books.

"How are you two doing? Can I get you anything?" she asked.

Verlaque looked up, surprised. "We've been looked after, thank you," he said curtly.

She set her books down, the top one sliding off of the pile and toward Paulik. He put out his thick hand and stopped the rest of the texts from following suit, and Annie Leonetti gave him her famous wide smile. Verlaque noted that she had recently touched up her deep red lipstick.

"Hot on the trail of Sainte Dévote," she said, still smiling. "Thought I could get some work done while waiting for the interview."

Paulik held out a chair for Dr. Leonetti and she sat down.

Annie Leonetti was very self-assured, Paulik thought, especially given the circumstances.

"So you left the party after helping in the kitchen," he said. "Do you know what time exactly you left?"

"Yes," she answered. "I looked at the kitchen clock. It was ten minutes after midnight."

"How long did it take you to get home?"

"About ten minutes on foot," she answered. "We live in a cheap apartment on the boulevard Winston Churchill, near the university. Very close to the humanities building, actually."

"And your husband was still up when you got home?" Verlaque asked. He silently noted the word Leonetti had used to describe her apartment—"cheap."

"Yes. We stayed up for a bit and talked . . . I told him about Bernard's temper tantrum, and how charming I thought the boys, Yann and Thierry, were, and how Garrigue, my own assistant, said absolutely nothing the whole evening, *comme d'habitude*."

"Are you close to Garrigue?" Verlaque asked.

She leaned forward, her eyes bright. "I think so, yes. It's not like she confides in me or anything like that . . . she's far too proud. But I respect her intellect, and modesty, tremendously. Garrigue's going to be a bright star someday, which makes her shyness all the more frustrating."

"Thank you," Verlaque said. "That will be all."

Annie Leonetti looked at the judge in surprise. "Really?"

"Yes, an officer will speak to your husband to confirm your alibi."

She quickly got up and gathered her books. She appeared to be annoyed. Verlaque wondered if she perhaps thought that she deserved more attention than three minutes? Or perhaps she had wanted to give her opinion of what happened to Dr. Moutte.

She put her hand on the doorknob and said, "Her head was bashed in."

"I beg your pardon?" Verlaque asked.

"Sainte Dévote. Her head was crushed by stones, in 304 AD, by Romans. Somewhat like Georges's." She opened the door and left.

"I was waiting for her to point a finger at someone," Paulik said after Leonetti had gone. "Romans equals Giuseppe Rocchia, *non?*"

"Perhaps," Verlaque answered. "But perhaps it wasn't meant to be a reference to Dr. Rocchia."

The door opened and a young man with a short, thick build quickly and quietly sat down. Paulik and Verlaque's eyes turned to the young man, who had already begun perspiring.

"And you're . . . " Paulik said. Officer Cazal seemed to have disappeared.

"Thierry. I mean Thierry Marchive, sir."

Verlaque looked at Marchive with curiosity. He wore a green woolen sweater over a T-shirt, and clean, pressed jeans. He wasn't fat, but had the rounded cheeks and stomach of a gourmand. His thick black hair and blemish-free olive skin reflected his Provençal origins . . . Italian, thought Verlaque, or pure Massalia, the city established by the Greeks in 600 BC on a Phoenician settlement. Verlaque imagined a mother and grandmother somewhere, doting on Marchive.

"So, Thierry," he said gently. "Could you take us through Friday night's events?"

Marchive coughed and began. "Well, we got to Dr. Moutte's party just after 8:00 p.m. I remember that it was after eight because Yann was worried about being late, and it ended up not mattering at all as lots of guests arrived after us."

Paulik stared at the young man and stifled a yawn. The university's coffee was terrible. "Anything unusual happen at the party?"

"Well, just that argument between the doyen and Dr. Rodier. I couldn't hear what they argued about. We were all surprised by the doyen's announcement."

"Really?" Verlaque asked.

"Yeah, because, well, he was old, and seemed tired. Tired even that night. So you'd think that he would have wanted to retire. Plus he told me so." Paulik and Verlaque leaned forward and looked at Marchive.

"When? What did he say to you, Thierry?"

"Well, it was the day before. I was in his office . . . did you see his office? Nice, eh?"

Verlaque said, "Yes, we saw it. Please continue."

"Well, I was in there getting him to sign some paperwork for my housing loan, and he just started talking to me, sighing, and asking me questions about what I wanted out of life. And I told him that after I finished my doctorate I hoped to teach theology and maybe someday be head of the department, just like him. I wasn't making it up to schmooze . . . I really do hope to become an academic. A small department somewhere, maybe not even in France. And he said that sounded like a fine idea and that he was really looking forward to retiring himself, and maybe traveling a bit. I felt sorry for him. I mean, he seemed like a real person, not just the doyen." Thierry now realized that he hadn't told Yann about this meeting with Dr. Moutte. Perhaps this was why, when they found the doyen on the floor of his office, Thierry had been more shaken than Yann. Or maybe he was just more sensitive? He then chastised himself for thinking ill of his best friend. Yann was a good scholar and deserved the Dumas just as much as anyone else. But would the fellowship, or a graduate degree in theology, be of any use in banking?

"And what time would this have been?" Paulik asked.

"Um, well, let's see," Marchive answered, scratching his thick hair. "After lunch, because I went to the snack shop across the street with Yann for a *croque-monsieur* and was worried I'd be late or that Dr. Moutte would still be out at lunch when I got back . . . so I'd say between 2:00 and 3:00 p.m. Does that help?"

Verlaque nodded. They spoke for a few more minutes on the details of the break-in, which matched almost word for word Yann Falquerho's report, except that Marchive began each sentence with "well." Marchive didn't remember the American girls' names, but did remember their faces.

Marchive rose to leave and Verlaque said, "I hope you get that wish, Thierry, to become an academic."

Marchive managed a slight nervous smile. "Thank you, Judge. If I can stay out of trouble."

"Yes, just stop breaking into buildings. All right?"

"Yes, sir!"

When Marchive had closed the door behind him Paulik turned to the judge and said, "You're compassionate today, sir." Paulik thought that Verlaque had been even too kind; they were interviewing suspects over a murder, not job candidates. But he found it hard to believe that Thierry or Yann could hurt anyone, and in his career as commissioner he had never been wrong. But there was always a first time, and this was a crime of passion.

Verlaque managed a smile but his thoughts were elsewhere. "I hate to see lost youth. It would be such a shame . . ."

"Yes, it would . . ."

Verlaque broke in. "He seems so innocent, doesn't he? He hasn't been tainted yet."

Paulik didn't know what to say and was relieved of his response by Officer Cazal, who opened the door and announced the next visitor.

"Claude Ossart, sirs."

Where Marchive, Falquerho, and Garrigue Druon still looked young, Claude Ossart looked tired, aged. He had a receding hairline; his eyes were a pale gray framed by dark circles. Verlaque thought that could come from worries or from spending too much time in the library. Ossart was of medium height but thin. He wore an oversize polyester sweater and baggy jeans, so it was impossible to tell if his time spent at the gym gave any results. Ossart sat down, neither smiling nor frowning. His was, as Verlaque stared at it, a face that gave nothing away.

Verlaque asked, "You weren't at this party at Dr. Moutte's. Why not? You were invited, *non?*"

"I was invited, yes, but why go to an event where you know no one will speak to you," Ossart answered with a half question.

"Is that your usual experience at the university?" Verlaque asked.

"Yes."

Paulik looked at Verlaque and then at Ossart. "Surely you speak to Professor Rodier, your adviser?"

"Our conversations are limited to our mutual studies—Saint Bernard and the Cistercians."

"When did you find out about Dr. Rodier's argument with the doyen?"

Claude Ossart paused for the briefest of seconds before replying. "The next day, Dr. Rodier phoned me. He told me about their argument and the doyen's decision to postpone his retirement."

"Even though your conversations are usually limited to Saint Bernard," Paulik said.

Ossart smiled despite the severity of the commissioner's tone. "I guess not all the time. Dr. Rodier is recently divorced, and I think he just wanted someone to talk to. I think he felt guilty too."

"Guilty?" Verlaque asked.

"Yes. Guilty for secretly hoping that with Dr. Moutte dead, he might get the post of doyen."

Verlaque noted the very mature way in which Claude Ossart spoke, so different from the shy mumbling of Garrigue and the nervous chatter of Thierry and Yann. "Are you hopeful as well?" he asked.

"Of course. I've worked hard to get where I am in my studies. I've recently coauthored a paper with Dr. Rodier. Dr. Rodier is by far the most qualified scholar to be the next doyen, and he deserves that post."

"It would help your career too," Paulik said.

"I can assure you that I had only Dr. Rodier in mind," Ossart replied with a seriousness that both men noted. "But you're right, it would help my career, and the continuation of the study and promotion of the Cistercian order."

"Thierry Marchive told us that he and Yann ran across you late Friday evening."

"Yes, I was coming home from the gym. I was just about to cross the cours Mirabeau and they were on their way to some pub. They were drunk, of course. They wanted me to go to a pub with them to pick up girls, but they weren't being sincere. They know I don't go in for that kind of thing, I don't drink nor do I 'pick up girls,' as they call it. And I know they don't even like me, so the invitation was hardly genuine."

"Do you think that anyone saw you go home? A neighbor, perhaps?" Paulik asked.

Ossart shook his head back and forth. "No. I took the small back roads home and I live on the ground floor, so I rarely pass anyone in my building, unless we're coming or leaving at the same time. There are a few restaurants on my street, but they were already closed for the evening."

"I need to know more, Claude. Why *exactly* didn't you go to Dr. Moutte's party?" Verlaque asked. "And what did you do instead?"

Claude Ossart paused. "I was invited, as were the other grad students, but I don't like those social events." Again there was a brief silence, and then he continued. "I'm working on a paper with Dr. Rodier on the Cistercian order in Provence, and in the afternoon we had made an interesting discovery, and I was anxious to get to the library and look it up. That seemed a more pleasant way for me to spend a Friday evening, than to pretend to like my fellow students."

"What about the professors?" Verlaque asked.

"What about them?"

"Do you like them?"

"No. I'm afraid I'm biased . . . I've worked for two years now alongside Dr. Rodier, and I see that his scholarship, his dedication to his subject, greatly excels that of the other professors."

Verlaque said nothing, but he doubted that Dr. Leonetti was not a fine scholar.

"Dr. Moutte included?" Paulik asked.

"Especially him."

Verlaque looked at Paulik and then at Claude Ossart.

"Go on, Claude. What do you mean?"

"Dr. Moutte's research was unoriginal. He was more interested in the Cluny order's love of art than any theological issues."

"When was the last time you saw Dr. Moutte?" Verlaque asked, intigued that someone so young would be confident, or bold enough, to find fault in his elders.

Ossart looked up at the ceiling, as if trying to remember. "Last week, he called me into his office. It was before I was about to lead a seminar class for first-year students on the Old Testament, so Wednesday, just after lunch."

"Why did he want to see you?" Paulik asked.

"To wave the Dumas prize in front of my face," Ossart replied with no trace of hostility. "He liked doing that, making hints about the fellowship and then changing the subject. He was also supposed to sign off on a research grant I was applying for, but then when I got there he had forgotten the paperwork at home. It was a total waste of time, and it made me late for my seminar class." Ossart had raised his voice for the first time during the interview. "I hate being late," he finally added.

"I understand," Verlaque said. "That will be all for now. Could you please leave us your key to the building?" Ossart reached down into his front jeans pocket and pulled out a large silver key and laid it gently on the desk.

"I of course could have made a copy," he said.

"We will have to trust that you didn't," Paulik answered, taking the key. "You may leave now."

Ossart stood up and carefully placed his chair back under the desk before leaving.

"Thank you," Verlaque said.

"You're welcome," Ossart answered. "If you need me, I'll be in the library. Second floor, last desk at the end, facing the window."

Officer Cazal came in with lunch for Verlaque and Paulik, said, "*Bon appétit!*" and closed the door behind her.

"It's funny, I mean odd, that we should interview Claude Ossart and Bernard Rodier back-to-back, given that Ossart is Rodier's assistant," Paulik said, checking the list, finishing his tea and tossing the plastic cup in the wastepaper basket. Their lunch had consisted of tuna sandwiches, grated carrot salad with an industrial-tasting dressing, and then surprisingly good and oily brownies that a caterer had delivered to the university. The university coffee was so bad that Paulik had resorted to drinking tea, which suited the unusually gray weather. Verlaque skipped both and drank sparkling water.

"Yes, we'll be able to compare mentor and student," Verlaque answered. He was about to ask Paulik what he thought of the interviewees so far when the door was opened and Dr. Bernard Rodier quickly walked in and sat down.

"Terrible, terrible news," he said, looking from the judge to the commissioner.

"Yes," Verlaque answered. He looked at the professor, handsome enough that he could have been a leading actor on one of the American television shows that Sylvie Grassi watched on DVD. He was about six feet tall, broad shouldered, lightly tanned even in November, and had thick white hair. His face was perfectly chiseled, a large square jaw and large mouth, perfect teeth, and dark eyes.

"You've no doubt heard of the argument I had with Georges on the night of the party," Rodier quickly said. Before Paulik or Verlaque could reply, he went on, "Georges had made an announcement last week that he would be retiring within the year, either at the end of this term, at Christmas, or in May. On Friday night, at the party, I simply asked him if he had decided yet if he was leaving after Christmas or in May." Rodier looked from commissioner to judge as if to double-check that they were still listening and then continued.

"I begin a year's sabbatical in January, and I simply wanted to know when Georges would be announcing his replacement. If I was fortunate enough to be offered the post, and if the job began in January, that would mean I would have to change my travel plans, as you can imagine."

Verlaque nodded and quickly said, "Yes, I see that. And that was when Dr. Moutte raised his voice?"

"He shouted, yes! He told me that he was, in fact, not retiring just yet, or anytime soon. I was most affronted! To be treated like that, in front of my colleagues and the students. I left immediately."

"Where did you go?" Verlaque asked.

Once again, the words came quickly and easily, and Verlaque wondered if they had been rehearsed. "I went and got my car out of the public parking garage and drove home, naturally. I live in an apartment on the avenue Philippe Solari, just north of downtown."

"What time did you get home?" Paulik asked.

"It was just before 10:00 p.m., because I watched the news at 10:00 p.m. on television. Nothing else seems to be worth watching. I then read for a bit, then turned off the lights at 11:00 p.m."

"Do you live alone?" Verlaque asked.

"Yes, I've been separated from my wife for over a year now. She kept the house, in Puyricard."

"Did anyone see or hear you come home?" Paulik asked.

Rodier seemed surprised by the question, as if he only now realized that he was being asked for an alibi.

"Well, no," he answered, this time slowly and awkwardly. "My apartment is on the ground floor, in the back of the building. My neighbors who live above, a young couple, came home late, after I had already turned in for the evening. I heard them laughing in the hallway."

Paulik silently noted that both Rodier and his assistant lived in ground-floor flats and neither had an alibi.

"Were your dealings with Dr. Moutte usually this confrontational?"

"No, not at all! We get . . . oh, I mean got . . . on quite well, considering . . ."

Verlaque turned from Paulik to Rodier.

"What do you mean?"

"Well, that Georges and I are on opposite sides of the history of Catholicism in France. He's a Cluniac specialist, and I research the Cistercians." Rodier smiled for the first time. "He lived very opulently, like the priests he studied."

"Are you saying that you have a problem with that?" Verlaque asked.

"No, no," Rodier answered, stammering. "What I meant, no judgment intended, was that I live very differently."

"But surely not in a cave or a remote monastery?"

Rodier chuckled, falsely, Verlaque thought. "No, but not as austerely as I should. Simply, let's say."

"Do you know a lot about art?" Paulik asked. "The doyen was a collector, was he not?"

"Yes, he was. But I have a very basic, undergraduate-level knowledge of the history of art," Rodier answered. "That was the one thing we disagreed on. I thought his art collecting . . . frivolous. That aside, we normally get on quite well, and he had all but promised me the . . ."

"Post of doyen?" Verlaque finished Rodier's sentence for him.

Rodier nodded. "Yes. Drs. Rocchia and Leonetti seem to think they were destined for the job, but just last week Georges said to me, 'When you're in this office . . .' So you see why I was so upset, and surprised, at his outburst and announcement on Friday evening. I was so confident that I even had Claude, my graduate assistant, pack up the bookshelves in my office!"

Rodier suddenly let out a long sigh that sounded to Paulik like the same kind of sigh Léa released when she wasn't permitted a second helping of Nutella: overly theatrical.

"Your assistant, Claude, he wasn't at the party . . ." Verlaque said.

Rodier smiled. "Oh no, a party is not Claude's cup of tea, I'm afraid. He was at the library, following up on something we had come across in our research earlier that day."

"And you didn't tell Claude on Friday night what happened at the party?" Verlaque asked, double-checking Claude's answer. "Did he know that the doyen had canceled his retirement?"

"No, I didn't call Claude. I don't have a cell phone nor does Claude. I called Claude from home later the next day. But I did stop at a phone booth and called my ex-wife on my way to get my car after the party."

Verlaque raised his eyebrows. "Really?"

Rodier shrugged. "We were married for thirty years, and she knew Georges. She had always complained about him, telling me that he was two-faced and that he was more interested in his glass, and in women, than in the university. I called her to tell her what he had just done. She was furious!"

"And then you went home?" Paulik asked.

"Yes. The streets in the Mazarin were oddly quiet. I went home, watched the news, read, and then went to bed."

When the interviews were finished for the day, Dr. Rodier walked the three miles back to his apartment. The latter bit was up a steep hill, but he didn't like using his car every day. Bruno Paulik went to hunt down stronger coffee and Verlaque sat in silence, doodling on his notepaper. It had been interesting to interview student and teacher back-to-back, as Paulik had suggested. Something was bothering Verlaque during Rodier's interview, and he now realized what: the student had been the more mature and better spoken of the two. If Verlaque had been an undergrad and had to pick between a class given by Ossart or Rodier, Verlaque knew that he would choose Claude Ossart's class, hands down.

Chapter Sixteen

❧

Home Is So Sad

*P*aulik and Verlaque agreed that on Monday morning they would take a look at Georges Moutte's apartment and continue any interviews necessary. They still needed to speak to the cleaning woman who had discovered the doyen's body on Saturday morning. A refugee from Rwanda who had seen too many murders as a young girl, she had been given sedatives by a doctor and had been sent home to rest. She, unlike the boys, had been worried, or curious enough, to lean in close to the body and discover that the doyen had been bludgeoned to death.

Verlaque was exhausted and drove home and parked his car in the garage just north of the ring road that looped around Aix's old center. He walked home past the cathedral, its sculptures lit up. Surprisingly most of the saints still had heads, unlike other churches in France whose saints' heads were removed during the Revolution. It was a Sunday night and the town was still, and although Verlaque regretted the fact that his refrigerator was empty and he wouldn't be able to cook, he loved Aix when its streets were empty, a rarity. He turned left into the empty place de l'Archevêché, which in the summer would be full of operagoers, turned right and walked to the end of his street, the tiny rue Adamson. He decided that he would, as he did two or three times a year, call for a pizza to be delivered. He forced himself to run up the five flights to his apartment and was relieved to open the door and be among his treasured books, paintings, and objects. Plugging his cell phone in to charge, he checked the landline for possible messages from Marine, whom he had abandoned in the Luberon. There were no messages. He ordered his pizza, grabbed a cold beer from the fridge, and then walked to the bathroom in the back of his apartment, where he undressed and showered. The pizza arrived just as he had sat down with a book of poetry. He ate three quarters of it and put the rest in the fridge. He thought of Bruno Paulik, who would be home with a hot meal and his wife and daughter at his side.

The telephone rang and he crossed the living room to answer it, flopping down in a leather club chair. Seeing that it was Marine's number, he said, in English, "Hey."

"Hello, Antoine," Marine answered. "How did it go today?"

"Well, it's always the same with a day of interviews—the day goes by quickly, but when you get home you realize how exhausting it all was. No one confessed, as you may have guessed."

Marine paused, waiting for Verlaque to continue speaking, but he did not. "I had day-old coffee with my mother," she finally said. "And day-old store-bought croissants."

"Yum. Remind me to swing by there tomorrow morning for breakfast."

Marine laughed. "Antoine," she softly said. "Where is this all going?"

He looked down at the coffee table where his book of poems was lying, as if the poets of England would offer him some advice.

"You've been so patient, Marine," was all he could say. It was Marine who stayed silent this time, forcing Verlaque to continue speaking. "You're always a bit sad after a visit to your parents' house."

"Especially when my papa isn't there," Marine answered. Verlaque thought it endearing that she referred to her parents as *Maman* and *Papa*. He used the polite *vous* with his.

"But I'm used to it," she continued. "What I'd like to straighten out, or understand, is our relationship. I don't want to say something corny in the vein of 'my clock is ticking,' but I'm getting tired of the uncertainty. I'd like to see you every evening, to know that you'll be there for me when I get home at night. That's where I am in the relationship, but I think you're miles behind."

Verlaque's eyes watered. "Not miles, Marine. I may be closer than you think. Can you come over for dinner tomorrow night?"

It was the second invitation to dinner Marine had had from a handsome man that week. She had run into Eric Bley, a fellow lawyer, in a café, Le Mazarin, and he had asked her out. A simple, direct invitation as he looked her in the eyes. Sylvie had sat, with her back against the wall, speechless. "He's *so* hot," she had whispered when Marine sat back down.

"Yes, he is," Marine answered. "But I turned him down."

Sylvie raised her hands up to the all-seeing yellow ceiling of the café. "Please, send my friend some common sense."

"All right," Marine finally answered to Verlaque's invitation. "I'll come over tomorrow. Sleep well."

And Verlaque did sleep well that night, a dreamless solid eight hours, and he awoke without the alarm. He walked over to the window and pulled aside the dark gray linen drapes and looked at the cathedral's spire, still lit, although a bluish morning sky had appeared.

He made himself an espresso. Leaving the apartment, he walked quickly, head down, and avoided the streets that would take him past Le Mazarin. He got to the Pâtisserie Michaud just after 9:00 a.m. but cursed as its blinds were still drawn—it was closed Mondays, and since he had worked over the weekend he had forgotten what day of the week it was. He walked down the rue Laroque and turned left on the rue Cardinale, which would take him to the doyen's apartment.

"Home is so sad," Verlaque said once he'd joined Paulik and they slowly walked around Georges Moutte's living room.

"Pardon me, sir?" Paulik asked, turning from a nineteenth-century oil painting of a stormy sea.

"Sorry, it's the first bit of a poem," Verlaque said, and continued in English, "'Home is so sad / It stays as it was left, Shaped to the comfort of the last to go / As if to win them back.'"

Bruno Paulik frowned and then said, "I think I understand it, although I was rotten in English at school. The home, when no one is in it, is sad. Right?" Paulik looked around the apartment and added, "But this room would be sad even with someone using it, wouldn't it?"

"Very much so. Look at these chairs . . ." Verlaque said as he smacked the back of a stiff armchair, identical to its neighbors, all with cane seats and wooden armrests. "It doesn't exactly invite conversation or a good time, does it?"

"And they're spaced so far apart . . . any conversation would be awkward," Paulik added.

"Yes, what's unsaid becomes more important than what's said."

Bruno Paulik looked at the judge and nodded, intrigued.

"My parents have the same kind of rooms in Paris," Verlaque continued, sighing. "So sad."

Paulik opened his mouth to comment but then decided against it. He knew bits and pieces about the judge's family—most of the information coming from fellow policemen: that the Verlaque family fortune came from a business begun by his grandfather, but nobody knew quite what the business was—the ideas most frequently suggested were car manufacturing, a supermarket chain, or publishing. Paulik knew that Antoine Verlaque had been raised in Paris very close to the Louvre and that he had an English grandmother. The commissioner continued walking around the room and then stopped in the doorway and said, "Look at this. These old apartments are *en enfilade*. You can see all the way through the apartment. That's a bedroom down at the end, five . . . no, six rooms down, I would guess."

Verlaque walked across the room to join his commissioner. "It's a huge apartment for one person, isn't it? I guess if you lived alone you'd keep all the doors open, just as he did, wouldn't you? It seems even bigger when you can see from room to room. And the service rooms? Kitchen, bathroom . . . they're all on the other side?"

"Yeah, on the garden side of the building. There's probably a *cafoutche* too, which we should look in."

"*Cafoutche?*"

"Oh, sorry, sir. It's a Marseillais word for a storage room." Paulik turned toward the window that looked over the square below. He could hear the fountain's water gurgling, and the voices of walkers below. "Hey, look at this," he said.

Verlaque looked out the window.

"No, sir, look at the window itself."

"The wood's rotting," Verlaque said.

"Yeah. The first thing Hélène and I did when we bought our place was put in new windows. You'd think that a single man with a good income would do that. But then he didn't pay for the apartment, did he?"

"No. It's part of the foundation."

"So is the foundation running out of money?" Paulik suggested.

"More likely Moutte couldn't handle the red tape at city hall. This is a registered building, as my apartment is, and I had to pull strings to get my windows replaced, even with windows the same size and style as the originals. It took forever, even with connections," Verlaque said as he watched some boys from the junior high school down the street get dropped off for school, shifting their heavy backpacks onto their backs. It was the same school that Cézanne and Zola had attended, inseparable best friends before they had their famous falling-out as adults. As teenagers the soon-to-be painter and writer would exchange ideas at Les Deux Garçons, still Aix's most celebrated café. Verlaque loved its faded and elegant interior, its gilded mirrors and yellowed walls, but he rarely went, a combination of too many white-haired locals and too many tourists causing the waiters to be surly and the service slow. "Let's go into the dining room. I haven't seen any of these famous glass vases yet," he said.

They turned away from the window and Paulik led the way into the next room, reading a message on his cell phone that had just come in. "Message from Yves Roussel," he said. "Another bank machine was blown up early this morning in Calas."

Verlaque frowned. "Calas is tiny."

"I know. But big enough to have a bank, apparently. Wow," he said as he stepped into the dining room, its walls sadly lined with dull floral wallpaper, awkwardly competing with the frescoed ceiling above.

"More frescoes?" Verlaque asked. "Oh, I see now. Wow is right," he continued, looking in the same direction as Paulik at a three-foot-high glass vase that sat in the middle of the dining table. The vase was one and a half feet wide at its thickest point in the middle. Its dark brown base was covered with bright red foliage that came from oak trees that spread around the vase. The vase's painted sky was bright yellow, most likely a sunset.

"This is a Gallé, I take it?" Bruno Paulik asked.

"Yes, I think so," Verlaque said, leaning in and slipping on his reading glasses. "Look, it's signed at the bottom. I had no idea glass could be so beautiful."

"Neither did I. Here's another one." On the fireplace's black marble mantel was a smaller vase, two feet high. Immense pale pink flowers with yellow centers covered the smoky-white glass vase, their long spiky petals reaching toward the top, which had a gold ornamental trim, also in a floral motif. "What kind of . . . ?" Verlaque asked.

"Chrysanthemums, sir," his commissioner answered.

Verlaque smiled. "Thanks. Can you put a call into the Petit Palais in Paris and ask to speak to the decorative arts curator there? We need to price these things."

"Sure, I'll take some photos later. Look . . . here's a lamp with a base that looks like it was made from a Gallé vase."

The lamp had a gold body with orange and red tulips, and a bronze base and handle. Paulik reached down and turned the light on and off, curious to see how the glass looked under light.

"What do you think you're doing?" a familiar high-pitched voice rang out from the doorway of the dining room. Verlaque whirled around and saw his commissioner openmouthed, and before Paulik could say anything Verlaque said, slowly and with as low a voice as he could muster, "I beg your pardon?"

"That's a Gallé lamp! Circa 1914!"

"Mlle Zacharie, you need to lower your voice when speaking to a commissioner and an examining magistrate. Secondly, you are, as a member of the general public, not supposed to be in this apartment. How did you get by the officer downstairs?"

The doyen's secretary shrugged. "I told him who I was and that I needed some papers from Dr. Moutte's home office." Verlaque and Paulik exchanged looks, Paulik knowing that whoever the officer was, he wouldn't be having a good evening.

"What kind of papers couldn't wait?" Verlaque asked, staring at the young woman with a mixture of contempt and disbelief.

Audrey Zacharie sighed. "It's for Claude Ossart. After speaking with you he came into my office practically weeping. He's frantically trying to find a research grant that the doyen was supposed to sign for him. It needs to be mailed by tomorrow at 6:00 p.m."

"And what makes you think you'll find it here?"

"Well, I'm not allowed to even go into Dr. Moutte's office at school, am I?" she asked with a good dose of sarcasm. "Buuuut, I did have a peek through the doorway from my office into his and I didn't see his briefcase, which makes sense, he would have brought it home with him Friday night. Righto?" Verlaque heard Paulik whisper something under his cough, but the secretary continued unperturbed. "I hoped I could just quickly look in his office here."

Having finished her explanation, she looked away from Verlaque and toward the open door that led to the next room. "Wait a minute! Who opened all these doors? They're always closed!"

Verlaque looked at Paulik and sighed, so the commissioner answered Mlle Zacharie. "They were like that when we came in."

"No, no, no," she said, walking through the dining room into the next room, a smaller, cozier sitting room. "Dr. Moutte always closed the doors! Especially his bedroom door!" She walked on, Verlaque and Paulik behind her. The three of them quickly moved through the sitting room into an office and then through a good-size guest bedroom with twin beds and more floral wallpaper, some of it peeling. At the entrance to the master bedroom Verlaque and Paulik tried to go through the door at the same time, their big bulky shoulders getting stuck in the doorway. Verlaque, despite his mounting anger, almost laughed, remembering Thierry Marchive and Yann Falquerho doing the same thing the previous morning.

"Wait, Mlle Zacharie," Paulik said, managing to get through the door before Verlaque. "Don't touch anything . . ." But before the commissioner could finish his order, Audrey Zacharie screamed.

Chapter Seventeen

To Catch a Thief

*S*hards of colored glass covered the floor of the bedroom like confetti. Paulik instinctively put his arm across Audrey Zacharie to keep her from going any further into the room. The three looked around the room in silence until Verlaque asked, "Mlle Zacharie, how many Gallé vases are lying at our feet?"

"Only one, I think," she answered, still looking around. She pointed to a dresser and said, "There was a very tall, fat vase that sat on the dresser. That's it on the floor now. Dr. Moutte had talked about getting the bedroom carpeted exactly for this reason. Nothing withstands a fall onto these *tommettes*."

Verlaque looked down at the red hexagon-shaped ceramic tiles, common in Provence, and saw that despite the chipped paint and peeling wallpaper elsewhere in the apartment, these were sparkling. "The other vases are fine, I see," he said, looking up and seeing two vases, one on each of the nightstands, and another on a small desk that sat under the window. The three of them looked around the room at the open dresser drawers and the desk's open drawers and scattered papers. "The intruder seems to have only been in this room," he continued. "How could someone have come in here with the building being watched by a policeman down-stairs?"

"*Le toit,*" Paulik said.

"Of course, the roof," Verlaque said, sighing. "This apartment's on the top floor." He turned to Mlle Zacharie and said, "Show us the rooms on the courtyard side. I don't think a thief would have risked coming in through a street-side window. Besides, they're all firmly shut; we checked them as we walked through the rooms."

"Why don't you call the maid up?" Paulik suggested, looking at the young secretary. "She lives in the building, right?"

"Yes, all right. I'll go down and get her . . . she's lived down-stairs for years . . . in a small apartment on the ground floor."

Verlaque looked over at Mlle Zacharie and saw that her face was white, her eyes wide, and instead of her usual hands-on-hips stance, she was almost doubled over, her shoulders rounded and her back bent. "Are you all right?" he asked her.

"Pardon? Oh, yes. I'm fine. Just shocked."

"I'll go downstairs," Paulik offered.

"Thanks, Commissioner Paulik," Verlaque said. "Why don't you sit down in the living room, Mlle Zacharie?"

Verlaque led her to the living room, and as she sat down in one of the stiff chairs he noticed that she seemed to have forgotten about Claude Ossart's papers. He left her and walked out the rear door of the living room and into a hall. He opened the first door he saw, this time using a handkerchief, and seeing it was a broom closet, he worked his way down the hall the same way, opening doors with his right hand as he got to them. A bathroom came next, then a pantry, both windowless. He had just entered the small kitchen, built in the days when kitchens were only used by staff, when Paulik came in with the doyen's maid.

"Hello, Madame . . ." Verlaque said, extending his hand.

"Mme da Silva, Rosa," she answered, shaking the judge's hand with a strong grip. She was short and was thick around the middle but wasn't fat—just thick and strong. Her wavy black hair was kept short and she wore a gold baptismal necklace that shone against her olive skin. He liked the look of her; she reminded him of the Verlaque family maid in Paris, who had worked for the family for years and had died when he was in his early thirties.

Rosa da Silva, who couldn't have replaced the wallpaper or fixed the rotting windows by herself, could keep the floors cleaned and waxed, which she obviously did with pride and gusto. "Porto or Lisbon?" he asked.

Mme da Silva smiled and proudly tilted her head back. "Porto!" she exclaimed.

Verlaque remembered the shock he had had visiting the city a couple of years previously, stunned by its modest prosperity, evident not only in its well-preserved historical center but also in its many contemporary buildings designed by avant-garde architects. "Ah, Porto! The workers of Portugal," he answered.

"That's right!" she replied, smiling.

"We think an intruder came in through a window on this side of the building," Paulik explained.

"Via the roof."

Mme da Silva wrung her hands, then suddenly looked down at her flowered apron, remembering the severity of the occasion. "I've heard of thieves doing that, here in Aix, and in Paris." She crossed the room and looked at the kitchen window. "It's locked," she said. A look of worry crept up on her face and she continued, "I think I know how they got in. The *cafoutche*."

"The storage room?" Verlaque asked.

"Yes, the window has been sticking for a few months and you have to give it a really good bang to close it, otherwise it looks shut but isn't really." She left the kitchen and the two men followed her, past a bathroom and another smaller guest room, which they quickly looked into, those windows firmly closed and both rooms in desperate need of renovation. "There's a second bathroom here," Mme da Silva said as she opened the door for the men to look in. The doyen's white housecoat was hanging on a peg affixed to the wall and his toiletries still crowded the small 1960s-era pink sink. The bathtub had a small window above it, much too small for any human to enter, and it too was firmly shut. The maid looked around the bathroom and made the sign of the cross before closing the door.

"This is it," she said before opening the last door in the hallway. The *cafoutche*, lined on two sides with shelving filled with boxes, had a window at the far end, overlooking the garden, and it was wide open. Verlaque looked out as the maid quietly sighed and made "tsss tsss tsss" sounds. He looked up at the roof of the neighboring building to the north, the only one that shared a wall and roof with number 11 place des Quatre Dauphins. It would have been impossible to scale up the building, for there were no trellises or balconies. He looked down at the large rectangular swimming pool, covered for the winter, and the immaculate green lawn that he imagined no one enjoyed. He could hear Paulik and the maid speaking but couldn't hear what they were saying; all he could hear was a voice, "Come here, Antoine." He couldn't see her face beneath the large sunglasses that she so frequently wore, even in winter, but he saw her long tanned legs and thin arms. He knew it was summer, for he could smell the coconut oil, forever a reminder of that summer in Saint-Tropez and why he had never set foot back there.

"Sir?"

Verlaque turned from the window, banging it closed and firmly turning the handle. "Sorry, Bruno."

"Mme da Silva has had to leave . . . pie in the oven. She confirms that there was just the one vase broken. She claims that the dresser has always been unstable and she repeatedly told Moutte not to put it there. The thief must have accidently knocked over the vase. I'll call headquarters and have them send a team over all the same."

"Thanks," Verlaque said, then lowering his voice, he whispered, "Do you see any connection? Why would Moutte put a valuable vase on an unstable dresser?"

Paulik whispered, "Because he didn't care about it? I once did that with a present one of my brothers gave me. It lasted a week on a rickety table in our front hall."

"So why wouldn't the doyen care about it? He collected the stuff . . ." Verlaque said.

Paulik scratched his bald head. "He didn't like that particular pattern? Didn't like the color? Didn't like . . . come on, Judge, help me here."

Verlaque smiled. "I'm as confused as you are. Did he like this vase *so* much that he kept it in his bedroom?" Verlaque knew when he spent far too much money on a Pierre Soulages painting that it would not be hung in his living room but in his bedroom, closer to him, his own private joy.

"That's possible," Paulik answered. "He may have meant to get it fixed but never got around to it. Still, it seems like an enormous risk."

Verlaque nodded, afraid that Mlle Zacharie might hear. He then said, "I have a hard time imagining any of our suspects, especially the professors, walking on steep roof tiles and then lowering themselves into a smallish window by their forearms."

"I agree. The break-in might be a coincidence, which is my guess as to why nothing large was taken. Those rooftop thieves are looking for small objects: cell phones, gold jewelry, and cash. They could have been watching the building, knowing somehow that the doyen wasn't present."

"Why only in the bedroom?" Verlaque asked.

"Either they were scared off and only had time for the bedroom, or they knew that what they were looking for was in that room. People often keep their valuables in their bedrooms; you know, in the underwear drawer."

"Let's go and see Mlle Zacharie," Verlaque suggested. "I left her in the living room."

They walked down the long dark hallway—like the kitchen, it had been only ever meant for servants—until they got to the wide double doors of the living room. Laughter could be heard from the square below and a car was honking its horn, a noise that Verlaque was finding more and more irritating as he got older. But the chair that Mlle Zacharie had been sitting in was now very much empty.

Chapter Eighteen

Wall-to-Wall Brown Carpet

Sylvie was already seated inside Le Mazarin when Marine arrived at just past 1:00 p.m. Marine was late so used the café's side entrance, avoiding the front terrace and main room where she would have run into people she knew. She ran up the stairs to the café's small, intimate dining room and remembered a girlfriend's tenth birthday that had been celebrated there. When Marine stepped into the room, she realized that nothing in it had changed in twenty-five years, and she suddenly remembered many details from that day: what she wore, the presents her friend had received, and what she had eaten. M. and Mme Genzana were very unlike her parents—the father was an entrepreneur and the mother a painter. It had been one of Marine's first meals in a restaurant, and she had never forgotten it. This small room, with its chandeliers and the oval gallery that opened down onto the café below, was still one of her favorite rooms in Aix. She realized, as she saw

Sylvie checking her phone messages, that although she could remember what she had eaten that day—steak au poivre and pro-
fiteroles for dessert—she could no longer remember her childhood
friend's first name.

"It's about time!" Sylvie said, sighing as she put her cell phone
back in her purse. "I was going to call you."

"I'm not that late, Sylvie. It was short notice too. You called me
at 11:00 a.m. for a lunch at 1:00 p.m., remember?"

"Yeah, well, it's urgent. Here, have some wine," Sylvie said as
she filled Marine's wineglass.

"Whoa!" Marine cried, trying to stop her friend from filling
the glass to the rim. "I have to give a lecture at 3:30!"

Sylvie poured more wine into her own glass, which had been
emptied in the ten minutes she had been waiting for Marine. "Believe me, you'll need it."

"What's going on?"

Sylvie leaned in and whispered, "You know that theology
professor who was found dead in his office?"

"Yes. Georges Moutte. I didn't know him, but my mom did,
quite well." Marine took a sip of wine and took a small slice of
salami from a glass dish that sat between them. As she ate she
watched in curiosity as her friend folded and unfolded her napkin.

"Yeah, well, me too. I knew him too," Sylvie finally said.

Marine, distracted by a couple who were squeezing into their
seats at the table next to them, asked, "Really?" She took another
sip of wine, recognizing it as Château Revelette.

"Yes. I was sleeping with him."

Marine choked on her wine, bringing the white linen napkin
up to her mouth, coughing. A waiter whom she didn't recognize
came running to her. "Was something wrong with the wine,
Madame?"

"No, no, it's lovely," Marine answered, still coughing and her eyes watering. "I'm fine, thank you." The waiter nodded and moved away. Marine leaned in closer to Sylvie, who looked as if she had just been caught shoplifting. Marine took a sip of water and said, "Let me get this straight. We're talking about the same man, right? An elderly theology professor, le doyen."

"He wasn't that old."

"Ah! Come on, Sylvie! He was so! How in the world did you ever meet him? How long did this go on?"

"One question at a time!" Sylvie cried. Both women had to sit back, giving them time to gather their thoughts, as their plat du jour arrived, baked tomatoes and zucchini stuffed with beef and rice. "I met him at an art opening. He was charming. Older, yes, but not that old."

"When was this?" Marine asked, not able to eat yet.

"About a month ago. It was an art opening at the château in Lourmarin. It's usually dreadful stuff, local art, way too many oil paintings of poppy fields and mont Sainte-Victoire, but we were both jurors. He was really very charming, and there was free-flowing champagne on the opening night." Sylvie smiled and began vigorously eating.

"Oh, man. When did you stop the . . . relationship?"

Sylvie put her fork down and thought for a few seconds. "We didn't, really. Stop, I mean. The last time I saw him was a week ago last Friday. He was really quite good at—"

Marine cut in, saying, "Too many details! Stick to the facts! So you didn't see him after that night?"

"Saturday morning, actually . . . a week before he died. Charlotte was at your place, remember?"

"Oh, yes, I remember that night. You told me you had a hot date. Why didn't you tell me who it was with?"

"Because you would have been shocked, as you are now! You haven't even eaten!"

Marine lifted her fork to her mouth and began eating, not tasting the food.

"He told me we wouldn't be able to see each other for a few weeks . . . he had a busy week ahead and some party for faculty to give this weekend."

"Yes, that was Friday night, and he died that same night. You need to talk to Antoine, you realize."

"No! You can do it for me!"

"No, Sylvie," Marine said, setting down her cutlery. "Listen, you're very good at getting me to do things you don't want to do, but this I can't. The man was murdered. You can help."

Sylvie pushed her plate away. "I can't! Antoine will judge me! I'm not hungry anymore."

"Eat up," Marine coaxed her friend. "And stop gulping the wine. You'll have a headache this afternoon. How about this . . . I'll talk to Antoine before you see him, and prepare him for your news."

Sylvie nodded. "All right. What should I say?"

"Again, stick to the facts. How many times you went out with Dr. Moutte and where. Did you notice anything peculiar? Did he seem nervous or anxious? Did he mention enemies or friends angry with him? You'll also have to tell Antoine where you were early Saturday morning."

"An alibi? Are you serious?"

"Yes! You were sleeping with the victim!"

"I was with Charlotte Friday night, when you were in Crillon-le-Brave with rich-boy. So my alibi is my ten-year-old daughter."

"Who was asleep the whole night," Marine answered, shaking her head back and forth. "Did Charlotte wake up at all?"

"No, she sleeps like a rock."

Marine smiled, picturing her goddaughter asleep. Charlotte, like Marine, barely moved while she slept. Both Sylvie and Antoine Verlaque were thrashers. "Since we're on the subject of sleep," Marine said, "where did you sleep with the doyen? At his place? Did you notice anything weird or unusual there?"

"Stop calling him 'the doyen,'" Sylvie answered. "I never actually saw his apartment. And I wanted to, believe me. I've been walking by that place for years."

"What? You never set foot inside his apartment? Then where did you . . . ?"

"Ah, where did we sleep together? That's the part that bugged me and why I was going to subtly drop him. The first hotel he took me to was that beautiful Sofitel in Marseille, right on the water. You know it?"

"With the nice restaurant on the top floor?"

"Right. Drinks, dinner, champagne, the whole thing. The second hotel was a step down. Also in Marseille, on the *vieux port* but with no view, and dinner in an unremarkable brasserie."

"And the last time?" Marine asked, predicting the answer. "It was worse?"

"Yep. A hotel on the outskirts of Aix, really drab. Wall-to-wall brown carpet, a saggy bed, and no dinner."

"Did you ask to visit his apartment? My mother told me that the doyen collected art glass."

"Glass? How dull. Sure, I asked him. But he kept avoiding the subject, or he'd say that his cleaning woman hadn't come by. So I dropped the subject. It was obvious he didn't want me there. He *was* single, right?"

"Oh yes. Never married, don't worry."

"So now I have to retell all of this to Antoine?" Sylvie asked.

"Yes. But I could arrange it that you speak to Yves Roussel instead."

"Oh God! That short prosecutor who rides up and down the cours Mirabeau on his Harley?"

"Yes."

"I prefer Antoine Verlaque."

"So do I."

Chapter Nineteen

✢

Le Cha-Cha

Marine stopped between the third and fourth floors, as she usually did, to catch her breath. She was thankful that most buildings in old Aix stopped at the fourth floor and not the sixth like in Paris. She had picked up a small roast beef at Antoine's favorite butcher, a place so small that she usually passed it before having to double back down the narrow rue du Maréchal Foch. The butcher did not flirt with her as other *commerçants* did—he took his job seriously; he was polite, but did not chat or tell jokes. It was obvious that the meat came first, and a poster on the wall confirmed that. It depicted a stone barn with a steep slate roof and flower boxes, below that the name of the farmer and his address and phone number in the Salers region of the Auvergne, inviting the patron to visit and see his herd of strong red cows. The farmer's invitation almost read like a poem, and Marine read it over a few times to be able to repeat it to Verlaque: "Venez-voir mes belles vaches aux poils frisés et aux cornes en lyre, et leurs robes cerise et acajou . . ." (Come and see my beautiful cows with their curly fur and lyre-shaped horns; and their cherry- and mahogany-colored coats . . .)

Her stomach was doing flips as it sometimes did in the seconds before she saw Antoine. Sylvie had told her that this was a bad sign—that the relationship was a false one and was doomed. Marine liked to think of it as love, and that even after a year of on-and-off-again dating she was still excited to see him. It wasn't boring or something she treated lightly, and that was the way she had always assumed great love was. Her parents used to listen to a Jean Constantin song from the 1960s, "Le Cha Cha du Coeur," with the refrain, "C'est un bon signe quand on a un coeur qui bat . . ." That's what she had, le cha-cha du coeur, and she agreed with the song: a pounding heart was a good sign. She knocked twice and then opened the door, calling out Verlaque's name.

"I'm in the bedroom, I'll be right out," he answered. A fire was lit in the fireplace and a pile of wood lay neatly beside it.

"Hey, how do you lug wood up here?" she hollered.

Verlaque came out of the bedroom wearing Levi's and a navy-blue polo shirt, his feet bare, his usual at-home look, whatever the season. "I made a deal with Arnaud, that kid downstairs on the first floor."

"The skinny one?"

"Lanky, more like it, but yeah, that's him. He knocked on my door one night a month or so ago, asking if I had any odd jobs that he could do. He's saving money for a gap year before going to university . . . so I have him picking up my dry cleaning, buying stuff at Monoprix . . . Anyway, come here, you," and he wrapped his arms around her narrow waist and kissed her until he felt her back relax and her body move toward his.

"Will you call your mother for me?" he whispered.

Marine quickly drew away and laughed. "Antoine!"

"I'm afraid of her," he said, walking toward the fridge and taking out an open bottle of white wine.

"You're not afraid of anyone."

"Neither are you, Professor Bonnet."

"I'm afraid of you," she said, quicker than she meant to.

"I wish you weren't." He stopped pouring the wine and took a glass over to her. "There's nothing to be afraid of. I'm just a guy. Why are you nervous around me?"

Marine didn't want to tell him how much she loved him, and that's what made her nervous.

She had no idea what he wanted from her. She had to protect herself and so she laughed. "Don't let it go to your head."

Verlaque smiled and kissed her again, and she could taste the crisp white wine on his lips and tongue.

"What do you want to know from my mother?" she asked.

"During the interviews, I found out that not only do many of the professors dislike each other, but Dr. Moutte was a specialist in the wealthy Cluniac order of clergy while Bernard Rodier is a Cistercian specialist. Two extremes, right? I wanted to know if your mother thought that Rodier could have detested Moutte because of their opposing studies, in addition to envying him the post of doyen."

Marine sipped her white and leaned against the kitchen counter. "Just because the Cistercians were austere and at Cluny they drank out of gold chalices? Doesn't that seem like a stretch?"

Verlaque shrugged. "I'm trying to think of all the possibilities. Plus, your mother seemed nervous during the interviews, especially when I asked her about the Dumas."

Marine nodded. "She told me; she also gave me something for you, which I have in my briefcase. Can I ask her about your Cluny versus Cistercian theory tomorrow?"

Verlaque smiled. "You're afraid of her too?"

Marine laughed and threw a kitchen towel at him. "It's her bridge night!" Marine took another sip of wine and helped herself to a handful of peanuts. "In answer to your question, I think it's more likely that Dr. Moutte was killed for the post and for the apartment. Everyone at the university talks about that apartment. It's a real coup just to see inside that place, let alone live in it. What's it like?"

"Grand, as that kind of bourgeois apartment in the Mazarin usually is. The pool and garden are huge; I don't know how many mature chestnut trees there are . . . five, maybe six," Verlaque said, smiling, knowing what a fan Marine was of gardens and swimming pools.

"You're killing me!"

Verlaque salted and peppered the roast and began inserting slivers of garlic into it with the tip of a sharp knife. He continued, "The apartment was broken into last night, from the roof."

"Do you think the break-in was related to the murder?" Marine asked.

"I'm not sure. A Gallé vase was broken but nothing seems to have been taken."

Marine finished the last peanut and Verlaque watched her, amused. "Tell me more about the interviews," she said.

"Well, there seems to be a fair amount of bickering among the faculty, and the grad students were terrified. We interviewed the staff too, but have pretty much ruled out all of them . . . no motives and they all had alibis that stick. The doyen had a telephone call late at night after his party, so we're having that traced to see where it came from. Everyone denies having made it. What are people saying over in the Law Department?"

"Most of us are avoiding the subject, oddly enough. We're all a bit freaked out, I think. Robbery has been mentioned, but that seems unlikely, doesn't it?"

"Yes, nothing was taken. Just like the apartment break-in."

Marine walked over toward the front door and bent down to get her briefcase. "My mother just found out some news about the Dumas. I have the paperwork here in my briefcase."

The intercom buzzed and Verlaque looked at Marine, surprised.

"I forgot to warn you!" she quickly said, grabbing his sleeve. "I invited Sylvie over!"

"What?"

"Sylvie has something important to tell you . . . about the doyen."

Verlaque walked over and pressed the buzzer to open the front door, saying, "Come on up, Sylvie." He turned to Marine and took a sip of wine. "What's going on? Did she know him?"

"She was his lover," Marine quickly said, pacing back and forth in front of the apartment door.

Verlaque laughed out loud. "Are you serious?"

"Don't laugh! Be nice to her!"

"*Salut*, Sylvie," Verlaque said as he opened the door to his apartment.

"*Salut*, Antoine," Sylvie said, leaning forward so that he could give her a *bise*.

"Coucou," Marine said as she embraced her friend. "Come in! Antoine has a roast beef in the oven."

"Good! I'm starving! Listen, Antoine, judging from your laughter that, by the way, I could hear all the way down the stairs, I'm guessing Marine has just told you that I was sleeping with Georges Moutte. Let me clarify that it was only three times," Sylvie said, holding up three fingers in his face. "And, I was going to break it off. And before you ask, no, I didn't see inside of his apartment or his office."

Verlaque poured Sylvie a glass of wine and handed it to her. "What did you talk about? Did he talk about retiring, or not retiring? Of his glass collection?"

"He tried to tell me about his collection, but when he said that it was turn-of-the-century decorative arts I cut him off. Had he collected Robert Mapplethorpe photos, that would have got my attention."

Marine winced and Verlaque raised his eyes to the ceiling, smiling despite himself.

"He didn't mention retiring or not retiring, as you put it," Sylvie continued.

"So what did you . . . ?"

"Talk about? Wines . . . he had some impressive knowledge, and we both really enjoyed drinking them. Italy too, we talked about Italy."

"Ah. Did he mention Giuseppe Rocchia?" Verlaque asked.

"Rocchia? No. Who's he?"

"One of the possible successors. He lives in Perugia," Marine offered.

"Perugia? That he mentioned. He loved Perugia and seemed to know it really well."

Verlaque looked at Marine and raised his eyebrows. "What did he say about Perugia, Sylvie?"

Sylvie finished her white wine and Verlaque quickly poured her some more. "Let me think . . . I seem to remember it was food related. Yeah, that's it. Do you remember when we went to Perugia, Marine? And we had a so-so lunch on the main square?"

"Yes. It was overpriced, but we chose poorly. The main square was our first mistake."

"So, I asked him where to eat in Perugia. He told me that his favorite restaurant is in town, but not in the old center—in a 1960s-era hotel. It sounds cool, Marine. Sixties decor and art, with a killer wine list."

"Did he give you its name?" Verlaque asked as he washed the arugula.

"Yeah, he did, but I don't know if I can find it. I wrote the name down on a scrap piece of paper and put it in my purse but I can't remember which one. I'll look though. It might be in the pink Fendi," Sylvie said, winking at Marine. Sylvie made a very good living from her art photography. She was represented by a gallery in Paris and one in Berlin. Besides putting money aside for her Charlotte, she also had a passion for handbags.

Verlaque didn't tell the women what Giuseppe Rocchia had said on the telephone earlier that day: Commissioner Paulik had asked Rocchia if he had seen Georges Moutte recently, and the Italian said that they had only met once, at a conference in Munich. If Moutte knew the city of Perugia well, then it was very likely that he had met with Rocchia there. And Marine's mother had told Verlaque that both of the scholars were glass collectors. At any rate, Rocchia was now on his way to Aix, at Verlaque's request.

"By the way, Sylvie, thieves are making their rounds on the roofs of Aix, so make sure you close your windows at night and when you're out," Marine said. Sylvie also had a top-floor apartment, just around the corner from Verlaque's.

"*Merde!* Charlotte's with a new babysitter tonight! I'm going to phone him right away."

"Him?" Verlaque and Marine asked in unison.

"Yeah. He put a flyer in my mailbox, looking for part-time work. He's saving up for his big Che trip around South America."

"Arnaud!" Verlaque and Marine shouted at the same time.

Sylvie tilted her head toward the ceiling. "You two are so annoying." She helped herself to the red wine that Verlaque had just opened. "Wow," she said, looking at the label of the 1998 Châteauneuf-du-Pape. "You know, I do feel terrible for Georges."

Marine and Verlaque looked at each other but neither spoke.

"Really I do!" Sylvie insisted. "In the end we didn't have that much in common, but he was nice to me, if a little silly."

"*Who* was the silly one?" Verlaque said.

Sylvie and Marine looked at Verlaque in surprise. "I beg your pardon?" Sylvie asked, setting down her wine.

"You heard me," Verlaque answered. "Sleeping with an old man?"

"That's none of your business!" Sylvie yelled.

Verlaque stayed calm despite how much he, at times like this, detested Sylvie Grassi. "It's now my business, since he's dead."

"At least he was *kind*!" Sylvie answered, glancing at Marine.

Verlaque sighed and looked at Marine too. "Yeah, I'm a mean bastard, but you always come back."

Sylvie grabbed her purse and Marine followed suit, picking her briefcase up off of the floor. She saw the yellow envelope that her mother had given her and shoved it back into the case. "I'm going with Sylvie," Marine said. Before Verlaque could speak both women were on the landing and then heading down the four flights of winding stairs. He heard the front door bang as the oven timer went off.

Chapter Twenty

❧

The Dancing Hours

Verlaque was asleep when the telephone rang. He had been dreaming of his mother and of Monique, and the telephone rang in his dream. "It's Monique," his mother told her thirteen-year-old son. "She needs you." And so the young Antoine quickly got out of bed, throwing on his jeans, a polo shirt, and a pair of moccasins. A taxi would be waiting downstairs to take him across the Seine, from the Verlaque family mansion—not yet cut up into apartments—through the gates of the Louvre and around the place du Carrousel, long before I. M. Pei's *Pyramid* would grace the square, across the pont du Carrousel into the sixth arrondissement to Monique's apartment. It would have been a short walk for a thirteen-year-old, but Monique was impatient.

He quickly sat up, relieved that he could see his Soulages painting glowing in the moonlight despite its color—black—applied in thick strokes across the immense canvas. It was the first thing he had bought when his grandmother Emmeline died. The art gallery had been on the rue de Seine, curiously across the street from Monique's former apartment.

"*Oui*," he grunted into the phone, unhappy to be woken from a deep sleep by a telephone but relieved that he was no longer thirteen.

"Apologies, sir," Bruno Paulik said. "Bad news."

Verlaque got up and took the phone with him, walking down the hallway toward his kitchen and flipping on the lights that lit up the white marble kitchen counter.

"What happened?" he asked.

"Mlle Zacharie, sir. She was hit by a car about two hours ago. Hit-and-run . . . no witnesses."

Verlaque drew a deep breath and then asked, "Is she dead?"

"Yes. It was instant, so they tell me . . . it happened on the boulevard Roi René, beside the retirement homes."

Verlaque thought of how many times he had crossed that part of the ring road that circled Aix's *vieille ville* and of how cars raced up three lanes of traffic after rounding the corner of the avenue Victor Hugo. "Are you at home?" Verlaque asked.

"Yes. Do you want me to come in?"

"No, no; there's no point. Try to get some more sleep, and I'll see you at the Palais de Justice later this morning."

At 9:00 a.m. Verlaque almost collided with Paulik in the lobby, who jumped back, trying to steady his coffee, which swirled around in its white plastic cup, narrowly escaping his white shirt.

"Sorry! Why don't you dump that stuff and I'll have Mme Girard make us a real coffee in my office?" Verlaque suggested.

Paulik didn't say anything but replied by pouring his light brown coffee into a potted palm tree. "No one has come forward yet about the hit-and-run. It happened around 11:00 p.m., which isn't so late," he said. "You'd think there would have been people around."

Climbing the stone stairs that led to the upstairs offices, Verlaque suggested, "If it was intentional, the driver could have been waiting at the side of the road for a moment when there were no other cars. Plus the residents of that old folks' home on the south side of the boulevard were probably all tucked in for the night."

"As were the residents in the old folks' home on the other side of the street," Paulik added.

"There are two retirement homes?"

"Yes," Paulik answered. "But the one on the south side is decidedly more upscale."

"Don't tell me you have a great-aunt or -uncle in one of them."

Paulik laughed. "No, sir. I don't."

Mme Girard was at her desk when they walked into her office. She stood up, as was her habit, when she saw them. "Good morning," she said. "Prosecutor Roussel has just been here, and Officer Flamant left a message. I took it down for you," she continued, handing Paulik a piece of paper.

"Thank you, Mme Girard," Verlaque said. "Would you mind making us two espressos? We'll try those new Brazilian capsules I ordered, the light brown ones."

"Certainly," she answered. Verlaque watched her walking away, so self-assured and in her usual office uniform of a short skirt, silk blouse, and Chanel-like wool jacket. He knew that her husband was a well-off real estate agent who owned his own firm and that Mme Girard—somewhere in her late fifties or early sixties—didn't have to work. But she loved her job and once told Verlaque that if she didn't work she would spend too much time at her tennis club. He admired her for that—his own mother had never worked but always seemed tired and anxious. His grandmother had busied herself with painting, volunteering to teach English at the local primary school, and hosting simple but elegant parties for the family business. Verlaque sat behind his desk as Paulik silently read Flamant's message, and he thought of the family business and its head office, which had been near the parc Monceau, and was now an embassy for a small Middle Eastern country. How he had loved to visit his father and grandfather in that building, greeted with a huge smile and flourish of his hat by Roger, the concierge who had watched over the premises for over forty years. Roger's wife doted on the young Verlaque brothers, serving them slices of warm apple tart from her kitchen that looked onto the cobbled courtyard.

"The phone call we think enticed Moutte to go to his office late Friday night can't be traced," Paulik said, looking up from the note.

Verlaque looked away from the window. "What do you mean?"

"All we can determine is that it came in on a trunk line from Italy," Paulik said. "But the caller ID was blocked."

Mme Girard brought in two espressos on a tray, with a bowl of sugar and two tiny silver coffee spoons. The cups and spoons Verlaque had brought from Normandy, but he suddenly remembered that they had been used at the family business. Emmeline must have taken them with her when the company was sold. He put the cup up to his mouth, glad to feel the unusual but comforting sensation of the matte, almost rough-textured porcelain against his lips.

Verlaque swallowed and leaned back in his chair, eyes closed.

"This wasn't an accident, was it?" Paulik asked.

"I doubt it," Verlaque answered. "Mlle Zacharie was really high-strung, wouldn't you say?"

"Yeah. Nervous about something? Did she know who killed her boss?"

"Let's interview her family. Did she live with her parents?"

"No. Flamant has written down the name of her boyfriend. They lived together on the rue . . ." Paulik grabbed the paper from Verlaque's desk and read, "Bédarrides. Number 17. Her boyfriend is a waiter, Michel Gasnal."

"Let's go and talk to him . . . at their apartment."

"Right. I'll get Flamant to contact him and arrange a meeting for today." Paulik finished the coffee and held the cup, tiny in his big, thick hands, and looked at the dancing women that surrounded the cup, their garments flowing in white porcelain relief against a cobalt-blue background. "Are these from Greek mythology?" he asked.

Verlaque smiled. "Yes, they're the dancing hours. It was a favorite Wedgwood pattern. The cups came from our family business; they were used when we had important guests at the Paris office. I've only just remembered that now."

Bruno Paulik smiled. He loved families and stories about families. "Does the family business still exist?" he asked, although he knew that it didn't.

"No, it was sold seventeen years ago, when my grandfather died."

Paulik took a sip of coffee and gently put the blue cup down on its saucer. "What was the family business, sir?"

"I wish you'd call me Antoine, Bruno. Flour. We owned flour mills."

The commissioner looked at his boss, thinking of the importance, and money, behind a family that owned flour mills, in a nation that adored—no, worshipped—bread and pastries.

"Oh, I see," Paulik said. "That explains why you're such a gourmet," he added, smiling.

"And gourmand," Verlaque said, laughing. "Yes, the importance of good food, and good ingredients, was drilled into us at an early age."

"How big was the company, if you don't mind me asking?"

"Second. We were the second biggest."

"In France? Wow," Paulik replied, whistling.

"No, Bruno. The second biggest in the world."

Chapter Twenty-one

❧

Only Italian Coffee, Please

*M*me Girard knocked twice on Verlaque's office door. "*Oui,*" he called out. She opened the door just wide enough to slip her elegantly coiffed head in the door. "Dr. Giuseppe Rocchia is here, Judge Verlaque."

"Great. Please send him in."

Both Verlaque and Paulik rose to their feet as Mme Girard led the theologian into the room and made introductions. "Would you like a coffee, Dottore?" she asked before closing the door.

Giuseppe Rocchia held up his hand. "I never drink coffee outside of Italy, but thank you, *chère Madame.*" She smiled and quietly closed the door, and Verlaque could only imagine the grimace she was now making. He thought the Italian's comment offensive but wise. When he drove to Italy, especially along the Ligurian coast with Marine, they would only stop the car once they had crossed over from France into Italy, celebrating by standing at the bar in a highway gas station, reveling in the good coffee.

"Did you just arrive in Aix this morning?" Verlaque asked the dottore.

"*Sì*. I left my hotel in San Remo at 7:00 a.m. in order to be here by 10:00 a.m. The hardest part was finding parking in this town." Rocchia added to the parking drama by brushing some imaginary lint off of his blue striped woolen pants, which matched his vest and jacket. His French was very good, if heavy with a thick Italian accent, and he wore the tan and dyed-red hair of a man who was afraid of getting old. Verlaque estimated Rocchia to be in his midsixties.

"It's Tuesday, market day," Verlaque said to explain the lack of parking.

Rocchia sneered. "Yes, I saw the price of your olive oil as I walked by one of the stands. Scandalous."

Paulik shifted in his chair and resisted reminding the dottore of a recent scandal in Italy, not France, where cheap Spanish olive oil had been bottled and sold as Tuscan. "When was the last time you saw Dr. Georges Moutte, Dr. Rocchia?" he asked.

"As I told your officer, it was at a theology conference in Munich last spring. I was the keynote speaker," he added unnecessarily.

"And you never met at the university?" Verlaque asked.

Giuseppe Rocchia looked at Verlaque with the slightest hint of annoyance. "Yes, of course, once or twice, but I didn't have much reason to come to Aix during the school term." He paused and then said, "Ah. You must be wondering how my name came up in the search for the next doyen. I submitted my candidacy, quite simply, when Georges told me of his plans to retire."

"Why Aix? You're right, I was wondering."

"Aix's Theology Department is renowned in Europe."

Verlaque leaned forward. "I'm sorry to have to ask you this,

Dottore, but we've been asking all of the faculty and staff the same question. Where were you on Friday evening between midnight and the early morning?"

Rocchia let out a small laugh. "I was in Perugia, in bed, with my wife of forty years sleeping beside me."

"Thank you, Dottore. You realize that your wife will have to be prepared to confirm that fact."

"It would not be a problem for her, Judge."

"Did you hear about Dr. Moutte's announcement that he was postponing his retirement?"

"Yes," Rocchia answered. "Annie Leonetti phoned me on Saturday morning to tell me—I can't think why, as we've never been that friendly. Bernard Rodier informed me later that day of Georges's murder."

"Thank you," Verlaque said. "One last question, and I'm sorry if this is off topic. I'm planning on going to Umbria this Christmas . . . fewer tourists than in Tuscany. Can you recommend a good restaurant in Perugia?"

"Around the corner from the Piazza IV Novembre is a good trattoria. I can write it down for you, but normally the restaurants in the countryside are better."

Verlaque passed the dottore a piece of paper and a pen. "A friend of mine suggested a restaurant just outside of the old town, a 1960s place that's part of a hotel."

Rocchia opened his mouth as if to speak and then closed it again. "No. Doesn't ring a bell, sorry."

"Ah, I must be confusing Perugia with another town. Perhaps Orvieto." Verlaque stood up and Rocchia and Paulik followed suit. They shook hands and Verlaque asked, "You will be in Aix for the next few days?"

"Yes, I thought I could get some research done here. You can contact me at the Villa Gallici."

"Thank you," Verlaque said as he held open the door.

Paulik waited for the judge to close the door and then said, "He's from Perugia, so he would know about this 1960s restaurant, even if he didn't like eating there. I mean, if you're from a city that size, you know all the restaurants, good and bad."

"I agree. He knew I was quizzing him."

"What's up with this restaurant? Do you really know it?"

"Dr. Moutte talked about eating there. He told a friend of Marine's about it." Verlaque then told the commissioner of Sylvie Grassi's short affair with the doyen. Bruno Paulik had a reaction that at first surprised Verlaque: a blank stare, as if he had just been told the sun was shining, or the coffee was bad. Verlaque now realized that he had overreacted that night at his apartment, and felt ashamed.

Paulik said, changing the subject, "Moutte went to Perugia? So we can assume he ate at this place with Rocchia. And as far as Rocchia wanting to teach in Aix, I think I suspect a motive other than Aix's Theology Department being renowned."

"What is it?"

"For such an important man, he didn't complain about having to come to Aix on such short notice."

"You're right," Verlaque said. "Perhaps he has other business here? I find it hard to believe that he'll be doing research here in Aix. Someone of his fame always has a string of research assistants."

Paulik continued talking as if he hadn't heard Verlaque's comment. "I recognized Rocchia when he walked in, and I think he recognized me. He's at the Aix opera festival every July, front row center . . . I've sat behind him a few times. He attends all the gala parties and hangs out with the singers and musical directors. I'd say he wanted to be doyen just to have that apartment for the festival. We know that the doyen didn't even have to teach, right?

Just research, which he could have done from Perugia." Bruno Paulik took holiday time to attend operas in France and Italy whenever he could.

"Bruno, it doesn't seem like—" A knock on the door interrupted their conversation and Mme Girard poked her head in the door.

"Excuse me, gentlemen," she said.

"No problem," Verlaque replied.

"I noticed in my calendar that you both have a meeting with the mayor scheduled today."

Verlaque and Paulik jumped up. "Thank you, Mme Girard! What time is it for?" Verlaque asked, reaching for his coat.

Mme Girard looked at her thin Cartier watch. "It started, oh, about ten minutes ago."

Chapter Twenty-two

✣

A Pint of Guinness

"*I* feel like we wasted the afternoon," Paulik said as they left the Palais de Justice and walked along the tiny rue Fauchier. "It's almost 5:00 p.m."

Verlaque stopped to light his preferred cigar of the moment, a Bolivar Belicoso, which smelled like chocolate, making him salivate even before he tasted it. "It couldn't be helped," he replied. "Some days are like that, plus our meeting with the mayor had been planned for months. Did Flamant manage to find out anything?"

"Yes. The car that hit Mlle Zacharie was painted blue, but a special-order paint job, a sparkling midnight-blue that BMW owners seem to like."

"Good. Do we have the list of car thefts in the region last night? A blue BMW should narrow it down."

"You would think. But as you know, BMWs are the thief's favorite prize. There were five blue BMWs reported stolen last night from Marseille to Nice, and going west we checked as far as Montpellier."

"Montpellier? That's two hours away."

"Yeah, but coming to Aix with a hot car seems to be the cherry on the cake. And the thieves around Toulon tend to show off the cars in Saint-Tropez, I'm told."

"So we need to hope that the killer did one, steal a car, and two, that he or she ditched the car somewhere, otherwise it's on a boat to Africa right now."

"Quite honestly I don't see any of the faculty or staff being able to steal a car."

Verlaque nodded. "Although two of the students managed to break into the humanities building. But you're right, we'll have to ask all of our suspects what kind of cars they own."

Paulik doubted that any of the theologians owned midnight-blue BMWs. "I'll put Flamant on it," he said. He stopped at the top of the rue Bédarrides to send a text message to Alain Flamant, and Verlaque leaned against a metal post that stopped cars from double-parking and smoked his cigar. It was silly to have lit it, he thought, as they would be at Mlle Zacharie's apartment in under a minute. He stopped puffing so that the cigar could slowly burn out.

They arrived at number 17 and Verlaque leaned back and looked up at the windows, their broken shutters giving away the poor condition of the apartments inside.

They rang the bell and were buzzed in, for Audrey Zacharie's boyfriend was expecting them. The building's entry hadn't been cleaned in weeks, the dirty white-tiled floor littered with fliers for pizza and Chinese fast-food joints. They headed up the narrow stairs single file and then knocked on the second-floor door labeled "Zacharie-Gasnal." A shuffle was heard and the door was opened by a tall, thin young man whose red, swollen eyes revealed that he had been crying. He said nothing, and stepped aside to allow the men in. The apartment was already dark, the curtains pulled shut. The air was stale and smelled of cigarette smoke.

"You'll have to excuse the mess," Michel Gasnal said in a deep voice. "Audrey did the . . . cleaning." He slumped down in an armchair.

"I'm so sorry for your loss," Paulik said, sitting opposite Gasnal on a small sofa. "I'm Commissioner Bruno Paulik, and this is Judge Verlaque."

Verlaque shook hands with Gasnal and pulled out a chair from under the dining room table and sat down beside the young man. Gasnal put his head in his hands and began to quietly weep. "Do you have anyone who can be here with you?" Verlaque asked, surprising himself with his empathy.

"My parents are on their way down from Rennes," Gasnal replied. "Audrey's parents live here in Aix."

"Good. I'm glad you'll have company," Verlaque replied. Even had they left Rennes in the morning, M. and Mme Gasnal still wouldn't be in Aix until well after midnight. He pictured the Gasnals, driving through rain across France, but he couldn't bear to think of M. and Mme Zacharie.

"Michel," Verlaque said, leaning forward. "Your girlfriend was hit by a car that didn't stop, which is a crime. We have reason to suspect that her death may not have been an accident."

Michel Gasnal looked up at the judge in wonderment. "What are you saying, that she was murdered?" he asked, choking on his words.

"We have to consider it, since her boss was murdered this weekend."

"And now you're going to ask me if she had any enemies,

like they do in the movies?" Gasnal asked. "Well, the answer is no."

Verlaque nodded and Paulik stayed silent, and so Gasnal continued. "Audrey wasn't the easiest person to get along with . . . she was bossy and people thought she was arrogant. But she never hurt anyone, and no one would ever hurt her. It was a hit-and-run, *non?* The driver panicked, *non?*"

"Perhaps," Paulik answered. "Do you know where she was going last night?"

"No. She was high-strung and so liked to go out walking when she was upset or needed to think," Gasnal answered.

"Upset?" Paulik asked. "Did you have an argument?"

"No. We were watching television together and then she just announced that she wanted to go out for a walk. But like I said, she often did that."

"Did she receive any phone calls last night?" Verlaque asked.

Michel Gasnal looked worried. "No."

"And the night of Dr. Moutte's death, you were both at the Bar Zola?" Paulik asked.

"Yeah. I was in the bar from around 10:00 p.m. on and Audrey met me there after Moutte's fancy party. We left around 2:00 a.m."

"And last night?" Verlaque asked as softly as he could.

Gasnal again buried his head in his hands. "I thought you would ask me that. I was here alone, watching television, like I said. No one called, so I have no one to back me up on that."

"And you didn't call the police when your girlfriend didn't come back after her walk?" Paulik asked.

"I fell asleep on the sofa," Gasnal answered. "If you must know, I smoked some pot. It helps me to fall asleep, and I sleep very soundly when I take it. I was woken up by the police at the door this morning." He began sobbing again and Verlaque and Paulik got up.

"Thank you, Michel," Verlaque said. "We'll let ourselves out."

Verlaque and Paulik stayed silent as they walked down the stairs. Once out on the street, where it was getting dark, Paulik said, "Did you see the stereo on the way out?"

Verlaque shook his head back and forth. "No, I didn't."

"It was a newer-model Bang and Olufsen," Paulik replied.

"You're kidding? On a waiter and secretary's salary?" Verlaque relit his cigar and asked, "Care for a pint at the Bar Zola?"

"You're on. My girls aren't at home tonight. Hélène has been working really long hours at the vineyard so she took the day off, took Léa out of school, and they've driven up to her sister's place in the Drôme."

"Well, Guinness doesn't exactly count as dinner, but come on," Verlaque said.

"It's dinner for the Irish, isn't it?"

They retraced their steps up the rue Bédarrides, turning right on the rue Fauchier, until they could hear the bar, noisier than it had been when they passed it earlier. They walked in and squeezed their way to the bar, and the barman, one of the rare Aixois who wore a beard and long hair, recognized the judge.

"A pint of Guinness?" he asked.

"Two," Verlaque answered.

Verlaque watched the barman slowly pour the beers. Tattooed on his arm was a verse from Rimbaud. It made Verlaque smile and almost forget why he had come. He leaned over the bar and asked, "You have a client who comes in here regularly with his girlfriend, Michel Gasnal."

"What if I do," the barman replied, not looking up.

"His girlfriend's boss at the university was murdered late Friday night, and they claim they were here."

"They were. He came around 10:00 p.m. and she came later,

toward midnight. But I told that to the cop that came in here yesterday."

"Audrey Zacharie was hit by a car last night. She's dead."

This time the barman stopped pouring. "Audrey? Dead?" He leaned his muscular forearms on the bar and hung his head. "Who hit her?" he asked, finally looking up.

"We don't know. Hit-and-run."

The barman turned to his colleague and asked him to finish pouring. "Can we talk outside?" he asked.

Outside there were green plastic chairs and small tables that the bar used for when there were too many patrons. "They were both here on Friday night, that I can assure you. But what I didn't tell the cop this morning is that they had a big fight, right at the bar, we all heard. Michel had been in here too long, I should have cut him off."

"What did they fight about?" Paulik asked.

"I was trying not to listen, so I didn't get the details. But he accused her of having a boyfriend on the side. He was madder than hell. He has a wild temper . . . we had him work a few nights here, but he got into an argument with a customer, so we had to let him go. On Friday night he threatened to clobber Audrey if he found out that she had a lover. That doesn't mean that he was behind the wheel of that car, but I think you should know about their fight." The barman got up, signaling that he had said all he had to say, and they walked back into the bar.

An old Rolling Stones song was playing, and Verlaque looked around at the people in the bar, a mixture of liberal arts students and older men who could actually remember buying *Beggars Banquet* when it had come out. Verlaque paid for the beers and they found a table in the back, under a black-and-white photograph of Jacques Brel, Georges Brassens, and Léo Ferré, three giants of French music, sitting around microphones as they did a radio talk show sometime in the 1960s, bottles of beer and ashtrays piled high with cigarette butts covering the table. "I'll go and repay Michel Gasnal a visit tonight, before his parents arrive," Verlaque said after he had taken a sip of his Guinness. The first sip was always bitter, the second less, and by the third, all the bitterness was gone.

Chapter Twenty-three

~

Payment for Services

Verlaque rang the doorbell for the second time that evening at number 17. Michel Gasnal answered, letting out a weary *"Oui?"* and Verlaque presented himself. The door buzzed open and he walked up the stairs to the second-floor landing, where Michel Gasnal was standing in his doorway. "Again?" he asked.

"I'm sorry, but I have a few more questions that I'd like to ask before your parents arrive."

Gasnal said nothing but moved aside so that the judge could enter the living room. This time Verlaque took the time to look around, spotting the expensive stereo that Paulik had seen, and on the floor beside an armchair, a new pair of Swiss leather shoes. Michel Gasnal once again sank down into the sofa, too tired to care why the judge was paying a second visit. Verlaque looked above the young man's head and saw a framed poster of a Cézanne still life. Audrey Zacharie had studied art history, he remembered, and it saddened him to see that she had tried to make the dark apartment a home.

"The barman at the Bar Zola has confirmed your presence on Friday night," Verlaque said.

"I told you," Gasnal whispered.

"But he also told me that you and Mlle Zacharie had a terrible fight and that you accused her of having a boyfriend and then threatened her."

Gasnal closed his eyes and breathed deeply. "That doesn't mean I ran her over."

"I know, Michel, but I need to know everything I can about Audrey's last days. Do you understand?"

The young man leaned forward and rubbed his fingers through his hair. "You're right. Sorry." He slowly sat up, like a bored student who has been accused of not paying attention in class.

Verlaque relaxed and sat back in the armchair. "Why did you accuse Audrey of having a boyfriend, Michel?"

"She was acting even more erratic and uptight than usual," Gasnal answered, sighing. "She would get phone calls during the evening and then rush out and be gone for hours. I didn't know who it was until she started receiving, or buying, these really pricey items. I saw you looking at the stereo . . . that was one of her gifts. She said that it was on sale. Have you ever seen them do sales at Bang and Olufsen? And these shoes," he continued, picking one of them up and then letting it fall back to the ground. "They must have cost her two hundred euros." Verlaque looked at the brand; he knew that they cost over four hundred.

Gasnal continued, "She told me that a great-aunt had died and left her money, but I didn't believe her. She had never talked about any aunts, great or otherwise. When she started talking about buying this apartment, I got worried. How were we going to do that, with no down payment? So I started putting two and two together, right? She adored that boss of hers, Moutte. He couldn't do anything wrong, and was brilliant, had such good taste, blah blah blah. She told me a few months ago that he had made a pass at her and that she shrugged it off. We had a good laugh about it and went to the Bar Zola and had a couple of beers. But it became obvious to me that she took him up on his offer, and that he . . ."

"Repaid her in gifts? Or money?"

"Yeah. I mean, wouldn't you have drawn the same conclusion?"

On his way home Verlaque got a text message from Yves Roussel. He waited until he was in his living room, with his shoes and socks off and a glass of chilled Meursault in his hands, before calling the prosecutor.

"Yves," he said when Roussel answered the phone. "Am I disturbing your dinner?"

"No, I'm still waiting for it! My wife was busy spending all my money at the shops in Marseille today and dinner's late!"

Verlaque closed his eyes and took a sip of wine. "I just came back from a visit with Michel Gasnal."

Roussel jumped in. "No alibi, right?"

"That's correct. He was asleep in front of the television." Verlaque then told Roussel of the argument between Michel Gasnal and Audrey Zacharie in the bar.

"Ha!" Roussel said. "Gasnal is known for his temper; he threatened her in front of witnesses; let me see, what else is working against him?"

"They'd recently come into some cash," Verlaque said. "A Bang and Olufsen stereo; handmade shoes . . ."

"Oh, so he's a thief too? How do a waiter and a secretary get stuff like that? And who would even buy a stereo that's made in Sweden?"

"Denmark. Gasnal claims that Mlle Zacharie had the money;

she said it was an inheritance, but he didn't believe her," Verlaque said.

"Yeah, well, I don't believe her, or him! I've put more officers on the stolen car search, and when we find it I'll bet you ten-to-one we'll find M. Gasnal's fingerprints all over it. Ah, the little woman is finally home. I'll talk to you tomorrow."

Chapter Twenty-four

❧

The 7:43 to Paris

*M*arcel Dubly watched the TGV race by in the distance. He hadn't minded the trains' appearance in the early 1980s in his more distant pasture, as some of his neighbors had. The SNCF had given the farmers money, which had allowed him to fix the roof of his barn, buy more cattle, and renovate his kitchen and bathroom, much to the delight of his wife and four children. More important, he found some sort of reassurance in the train's passing every few hours; the same kind of reassurance he got from his white Charolais cows giving birth each spring, the changing of the seasons, and the weekly cattle auction in nearby Saint-Christophe-en-Brionnais, where he either participated as a seller or as a judge. There would be pastis in a bar afterward and then a long drawn-out lunch with a few of his fellow farmers, some wine growers, and one or two politicians, every Wednesday, rain or shine. He watched the train racing up to Paris, imagining its passengers working in front of their laptops and then rushing off in taxis to meetings, and then rushing back down south, eating a sandwich on the train for dinner. He had been south once, somewhere near Avignon, when a childhood friend had married a girl from a Provençal village. He and his wife had gone to the wedding, and while he found the people friendly enough, the food was a bit too light for his tastes and he left the wedding hungry. "Stop exaggerating," his wife had told him, laughing. They had laughed in the car all the way back to their hotel, he remembered now. He leaned on his walking stick and turned to head back up to the house. It wasn't that he needed a walking stick—at fifty-two he was in great shape—it was just a habit, and he liked tapping the ground, his ground, the ground of his ancestors, with the end of the stick as he walked. There was less laughing in his house these days; his wife seemed tired, and anxious for the children—none of them were proving to be good students, nor did they show any interest in staying in Burgundy—and he thought that over lunch he should try to make her laugh.

Verlaque awoke at 6:30 a.m., hungry. He realized that he had had only two pints of beer the night before and nothing to eat. He threw back the duvet and walked into his bathroom. When renovating the apartment, he had asked the masons to destroy the wall between the bathroom and master bedroom and replace it with glass. He had never regretted the decision, although it had been a fight with his general contractor, who thought the idea insane. The toilet was in another room, with a small sink, and the bathroom had a pedestal sink and old-fashioned bathtub that the interior architect had bought in L'Isle-sur-la-Sorgue. They had kept the nineteenth-century floor—another fight—and Verlaque loved the leafy pattern of green-and-gold glazed earthenware tiles. He ran the bath and went into the kitchen, turned on his espresso machine, and checked his phone messages. There was a text message from Marine: *bonne nuit . . . we'll talk later*, and another from Paulik confirming their rendezvous in front of Verlaque's apartment at 7:10 a.m.

At 7:08 a.m. Bruno Paulik rang the buzzer on the street and in less than a minute Verlaque was downstairs and in Paulik's Range Rover. "Good morning," the commissioner said as he maneuvered his way off the cobblestone square. "I have good news. Léa got sixteen out of twenty on her *solfège* test and has been admitted to the next music grade."

"Hey, that's great!" Verlaque answered, turning to look at Paulik. "With sixteen she gets a special mention, right?"

"Yeah, but she's been so turned off by the whole thing that I'm not sure the special mention will mean anything to her. And here," Paulik said, handing Verlaque a bag. "My mother left these on my doorstep yesterday."

Verlaque opened the bag and peered inside. "Cannelés!"

"You went to law school in Bordeaux, right? I thought you might miss them."

"I love these! Thank you, I do miss them and I sometimes buy them in Aix, but they're never as good as when made by a Bordelais." He tore open the cannelé and bit into the soft inner cake made of rum and vanilla. Crusty and caramelized on the outside and soft and gooey on the inside, it was perfect. "When did your mother move from Bordeaux to Provence?" Verlaque asked.

"Just after the war. Her father was a vineyard specialist, and land in the Luberon was dirt cheap back then. He could have stayed in Bordeaux, always working for others, or have his own vines. When they saw the barren land they had purchased with all of their savings, on the day of a mistral, my grandmother cried and started walking back to the closest village, Ansouis, hoping to catch the next bus back to Bordeaux. But they settled in, with lots of ups and downs, as most immigrants do. And now our family is one of the old Luberon families. But my grandmother always cooked Bordelais specialties, my grandfather planted cabernet sauvignon despite sneers from the locals, and my mother goes on baking cannelés."

Verlaque smiled at the image of Paulik's grandmother walking up a dirt road, head down, fists clenched; and at the thought that Paulik's family considered themselves immigrants. "Did you go to university, or straight into the police force?" he asked.

"Straight in," Paulik answered, steering the car onto the highway while eating his cannelé. "I would have liked to have gone to university, but it was never an option in my family. It never would have occurred to my parents, God love them, nor to anyone at my high school. I was too impatient then too . . . I just wanted to work . . . to support my habit."

Verlaque laughed. "Opera is almost as expensive as drugs but at least it won't kill you."

"Why is Moutte's lawyer in Paris?" Paulik asked. Verlaque took this as a cue that he no longer wanted to talk about himself or his family.

"Moutte was born in Paris. The lawyer seems to be an old family friend, a certain Maître Fabre. He has an office in the seventeenth arrondissement, Batignolles, very close to where my grandparents used to live, near the boulevard de Clichy."

Bruno Paulik nodded but didn't say what he was thinking: that Antoine Verlaque had always seemed like a *rive gauche* kind of guy, one of those Parisians who rarely crossed north over the Seine. And the boulevard de Clichy was the last place he thought Verlaque's grandparents would have lived. It was a noisy, dirty street, full of cheap clothing shops and kebab stands. Paulik veered the car off of the highway, and as they approached the newly built Aix TGV station, Verlaque sighed. "It's discouraging to see all of these illegally parked cars," he said.

"I know, but I can't say that I blame them," Paulik answered. "The new station is a beauty, but there isn't enough parking, and it's too expensive."

They parked in the day parking lot, lucky to find one of the last spots, and Paulik took the parking ticket and put it in his wallet. As they walked into the station Paulik asked, "Do we need to buy train tickets?"

"No, Mme Girard had already left the office for the day so I bought some on the Internet. I wanted to be sure to get seats, and in first class."

The train pulled up from Marseille after a few minutes and the passengers, mostly business people at that hour, calmly got on, found their seats, and pulled out newspapers or their laptops. They were halfway, somewhere in southern Burgundy, around 9:00 a.m., racing by too quickly to see Marcel Dubly, when Paulik received a phone call and quickly got up to take the call in between cars so as not to disturb his fellow travelers. Verlaque looked out at the green hills—his face almost pressed against the glass—where vineyards and pastures were divided by hedgerows and each village had its own Romanesque church. It was easily the most beautiful part of the voyage, and it annoyed him to see his fellow passengers with their window shades drawn.

"That was Roussel," Paulik reported when he came back about five minutes later. "No leads on the cash machine explosions, but that old train station on early Tuesday morning had a janitor inside. He had gotten there after 10:00 p.m. to clean as he's moonlighting . . . he has a day job cleaning the junior high school."

"Was he hurt?"

"Just a broken arm . . . he fell back from the force of the explosion but luckily wasn't next to the machine when it happened."

"Did he see anything?"

"No. He scared the pants off of the thieves, who were more surprised than he was to find someone in the station. He cried out as they were digging around in the rubble for cash . . . he said it took him a few minutes to realize what was going on, and it pissed him off that they steal money while he has to work two jobs. They took off when they realized they weren't alone, and he heard a car but by the time he had dragged himself off of the floor and run outside, they were gone."

The Gare de Lyon seemed about twenty degrees colder and damper than the Aix train station had. Both Verlaque and Paulik pulled their scarves up around their necks. They stood in the queue for a taxi and jumped quickly in when it was their turn, anxious to get warm. The taxi raced along the Seine, heading west to the seventeenth arrondissement, and both men silently looked out the window onto the gray beauty of a Parisian morning.

"I've never been in the seventeenth," Paulik said as they drove through the elegant eighth arrondissement.

"Most people haven't," Verlaque said. "That's one of the reasons I like it so much. There are no monuments or museums, so the only reason to go is if you live, or have business to do, there. Take the rue des Batignolles," Verlaque instructed the cabbie. "I'd like my colleague to see the church."

The taxi drove along the neighborhood's main street, Paulik noting that the street was full of the kinds of businesses that made big city living manageable: food shops, wine merchants, pharmacies, the occasional clothing or shoe store, and the practical shops too: cobblers, hardware stores, dentists' and doctors' offices.

The rue des Batignolles ended at the small white neoclassical church that sat on a semicircular cobbled square that was lined with a few cafés and small shops.

"Nice," Paulik muttered. "It feels like a village."

They drove around the church and turned right up a street and then left, finally dropping Verlaque and Paulik off at 17 rue Nollet. "Thanks," Verlaque said, paying the driver and giving him a generous tip.

The offices of Maître Fabre were surprisingly dingy. Verlaque and Paulik didn't have to wait in the small dark waiting room as they seemed to be either the first, or the only, clients so far that morning. A thin, white-haired man opened his office door when Paulik coughed.

"Judge Verlaque?" he said, peering out of his door as if frightened or surprised at having visitors.

"Yes, Maître Fabre. And this is the commissioner of Aix-en-Provence, Bruno Paulik."

They shook hands and he stepped aside, allowing them into his office. The large, high-ceilinged room had been decorated in the late 1940s, and for Verlaque it suited the old-fashioned feel he got whenever he was in this neighborhood. Two leather club chairs, both ripped in places, faced the maître's large oak desk. A ceiling light made of what looked like Murano glass, more appropriate in a widow's dining room than in a law office, hung above the desk. There were yellowed framed prints of Paris hung on the walls and thick flowered curtains on the two tall windows that looked over the rue Nollet. The walls had that yellow patina that Verlaque knew interior decorators envied, and when he saw the crystal ashtray piled high with cigarette butts, he knew where the patina came from.

"I have the will here," Maître Fabre said as he opened the file with his aged, spotted, shaking hands.

"You were childhood friends with Dr. Moutte?" Paulik asked.

Fabre looked at the commissioner with yellowed, sad eyes. "Yes. We grew up in this neighborhood together. This was my family's apartment . . . my father ran the pharmacy downstairs. Georges grew up on the rue Batignolles. We were altar boys at the church and, when we were sixteen, were both accepted at Louis le Grand."

Verlaque smiled. "I went there too." Maître Fabre looked at the judge and tried to smile, but it seemed as if the effort to smile hurt. Paulik looked over at the judge and he smiled in place of the lawyer. He hadn't known that Verlaque went to the most prestigious *prépa* in France.

"Who killed Georges?" Maître Fabre asked, looking at Verlaque.

"We don't know yet," Verlaque answered. "Do you have any ideas?"

Fabre shrugged. "No. I hadn't seen Georges for quite some time. We used to dine together when he would come to visit, once a year or so. But my wife died last year, and I haven't been too well since."

Verlaque nodded and said nothing. Maître Fabre seemed to be grieving and it made a knot in Verlaque's stomach that surprised him.

"Well, his will is very straightforward," Fabre said, pulling out the first of the typed papers. "Georges has donated all of his assets to the theology school in Aix. He has requested that the scholarships continue but that the name be changed to the Dumas-Moutte Foundation. I don't yet have all of the financial information, as my old friend seemed to have bank accounts in Paris, Aix, Geneva, and Boston, and various investments, but in his accounts in Paris alone there are over two hundred fifty thousand euros."

"Thank you," Verlaque said. "Two hundred fifty thousand

euros sounds like a lot of money for a college doyen to have in a Parisian bank account."

"So it would seem," Fabre answered. "But Georges had been the doyen for a long time, and he told me that his rent was paid for by the foundation. He never was a spendthrift, so if a man of seventy-two puts his earnings in a bank account, or invests them, over a fifty-year career, it would easily add up to even more than that amount."

Verlaque frowned and said nothing, forcing the maître to add, "You seem to believe that Georges was up to no good."

"I'm trying to understand why he was murdered," Verlaque answered, leaning forward. "He must have spent a lot of money on his glass collection. What do you think? Did he buy his glass legally, to your knowledge?"

Fabre paused. "I couldn't say."

Verlaque couldn't tell if the lawyer was protecting his boyhood friend, or he really didn't know.

"He told me over dinner once that he bought some glass at auction houses here in Paris, and that he often sold it to Americans, where a revival of French art nouveau glass has emerged," Fabre said. "It seems like an awful lot of money to spend on flowered vases, but there you are."

"Do you know if Dr. Moutte made trips to Italy, perhaps to buy glass? Near Perugia?" Paulik asked.

"That I can answer in the affirmative. Georges spoke specifically of Perugia, and Umbria in general. He loved a small town that makes majolica . . ."

"Deruta," Verlaque offered.

"Yes, that's it. And he mentioned another town, specifically with a glassworks. I remember at the time thinking it odd that he would visit a modern glassworks, but he said that an Italian colleague did business there and once took Georges along with him."

"Can you remember the name of that town?" Paulik asked.

Fabre frowned and rubbed his long hands together. "I'm sorry, I can't. I want to say that it begins with an 'F,' but I'm just not sure." Fabre leaned back and closed his eyes, clearly exhausted from his first meeting of the day. As there was no secretary in the front office and the place was deadly still, Verlaque imagined that Georges Moutte may have been Fabre's last client.

Fabre suddenly opened his eyes and slowly leaned forward, handing Verlaque a photocopy of the doyen's will. "I'll let you know as soon as the rest of Georges's financial holdings have been released to me."

"Thank you," Verlaque and Paulik said in unison as they got up to leave.

"We'll let ourselves out," Paulik added, handing the lawyer their business cards.

"If you would," Fabre said, leaning back once more. A shaking hand reached for an engraved silver lighter and he lit up a cigarette.

Chapter Twenty-five

✿

The Little Dog under Their Feet

"*F*ancy a short walk before lunch?" Verlaque asked Paulik when they were out on the street.

"Sure. It's not yet noon. Where to?"

Verlaque pulled a cigar out of his leather holder and snipped the end off and then lit it. He began walking. "Just up the rue Brochant and then we'll cross over Clichy and go see my grandparents' place."

"Sounds great," Paulik said. He was curious to see a street on the other side of Clichy where the wealthy Verlaque grandparents had lived. He couldn't imagine it in a neighborhood north of Clichy.

When they arrived at the avenue de Clichy, Verlaque pointed to an elegant café on their left. "Coffee here, €1.20. In the sixth, where my brother lives, €4.50."

They crossed the busy avenue and it looked as Paulik thought it would: kebab shops, what seemed to be too many cheap luggage stores, a fruit and vegetable stand, and hairdressers that specialized in wigs and hair extensions. They walked along Clichy for a block, Verlaque happily puffing on his Cohiba, until they arrived at a small crepe restaurant.

"We turn right here," Verlaque said. Paulik followed the judge and saw a large green metal gate, the center big enough to allow a car to pass through, which was closed, but on either side were smaller pedestrian gates, which were open.

"A private street!" Paulik exclaimed. "I've heard about these existing in Paris."

Both men passed through the gate and looked up the cobblestoned street. It was lined on either side with elegant houses, each one fronted with mature trees and gardens. The street went on for what looked like two city blocks.

Paulik stood with his hands on his hips. "I've never seen anything like this."

"It's an oasis, isn't it? The land was given to the city of Paris in the mid-nineteenth century. The only stipulation from the land donor was that houses be built, not apartments, each one with a large front garden that would be planted with at least three trees."

Paulik looked up and saw that most of the houses still had at least two trees. The small metal gates that fronted each house, and the antique street lanterns, made the street look like it belonged in a wealthy town in Normandy, or Poitou, at the turn of the century. "Sheer Marcel Proust," Paulik said.

Verlaque smiled, took a puff of his cigar, and began walking. "Isn't it? That's why my grandmother wanted to live here so badly."

The noisy avenue de Clichy was far behind them. Birds raced around their heads and cats chased each other from garden to garden. Verlaque stopped halfway up the street and smoked his cigar, reading a marble plaque before a small delicate white house.

Paulik stopped beside him and read—the residents had been killed during World War II for forging passports.

"Notice how they specify that the men were shipped off to their deaths," Verlaque said, "but that the sole female forger, Colette Heilbronner, was killed here, on the spot."

They walked on a few meters and Verlaque stopped at what was so far the most beautiful house on the street. Made of a golden stone, the house was three stories with large multipaned windows and a simple front garden that sloped down to the front door.

They looked at the house for a few minutes, Verlaque hoping to see one of its current residents and Paulik pondering the fact that a wealthy Parisian couple—who could have lived in the sixth or seventh arrondissement—would choose to live in an unfashionable neighborhood in northwest Paris, albeit on a street with distinction and cachet. It made him understand the judge a little more.

"Lunch?" Verlaque asked, smiling.

"Starving. Breakfast was a long time ago."

They walked back down the street and through its green gates, out onto the avenue de Clichy. Crossing where they had crossed before, they entered the Batignolles neighborhood where the shops and cafés became chic at once. After a block Verlaque walked into a small restaurant with freshly painted glossy black trim. Inside a fire was burning in the fireplace, something Paulik had never seen in a city restaurant. The owner, a slim man their age wearing designer eyeglasses, grabbed Verlaque by the shoulders and gave him a *bise*. "Antoine!" he hollered. "It's about time!"

Verlaque laughed and introduced Paulik, and they were given a table for two beside the fireplace. Both men chose an entrée of a duo of rillettes—one pork and the other duck—served with a mustard sauce and caramelized tomatoes. "I'm tempted by your vegetable mille-feuille, though," Verlaque said, stubbing out his cigar.

"It's cold out," Paulik reminded him.

Verlaque laughed. "All right, the rillettes followed by the roasted veal with the garam masala crust and lentils . . ."

"And spinach," the owner, Didier, answered.

Paulik ordered the steak, which the chef had marinated in Indian spices. He sat back, happy that they had ordered and that a bottle of one of his favorite reds, a Pic Saint-Loup, was on its way. "The lawyer was sad, wasn't he?" he said. "He seemed to be grieving, and not at all well himself. And he was protecting his old friend. No university professor has bank accounts all over Europe and one in the States."

Didier came back with the wine and showed the label to Paulik, who nodded, smiling.

"Hey Didier, we just visited Maître Fabre, who works, and I think lives, around the corner. Do you know him?" Verlaque asked.

"Of course," Didier answered, about to pour a little wine in Verlaque's glass but halting when the judge quickly motioned that Paulik should be the taster. Without flinching, Didier poured a small amount into Paulik's glass and continued speaking. "He came at least twice a week for years. He and his wife would sit at this table every Friday night with their little dog. They had no kids."

Paulik sniffed the wine. "It's fine." Didier smiled and poured, impressed to have someone who looked like a rugby player, complete with scars on his bald head, who sniffed a wine, without tasting it, to see if it was corked.

"His wife died recently, *non*?" Verlaque asked.

"Yes, she died early in the year, of breast cancer. And now he has cancer too."

Verlaque gave Paulik a "you were right" look. "Lung cancer?"

"Ah, no, believe it or not. Cancer of the pancreas. They were as thick as thieves . . . it was always a pleasure to see them. She was real bubbly, and he was too, back then. Soon they'll be side by side." Didier finished pouring the wine and left just as a young waiter brought the first courses.

Verlaque and Paulik began to eat, spreading their rillettes on thinly sliced brown bread, neither talking. Paulik was thinking of Hélène and Léa, neither of whom he could live without. Verlaque was thinking of Didier's words "soon they'll be side by side." He thought of one of Larkin's most well-known poems, "An Arundel Tomb," whose opening stanza was,

> *Side by side, their faces blurred,*
> *The earl and countess lie in stone.*

A faithful dog lies at the countess's feet, much like Mme Fabre's dog, whom Verlaque pictured sitting, patiently, under the restaurant's table. And the poem had one of his favorite last lines, "What will survive of us is love." He looked over at Paulik, who was quietly eating his rillettes without his usual excitement. Verlaque imagined that the commissioner was thinking of his wife and daughter, but perhaps married men no longer thought of their spouses in that way. He would go home this evening, make a surprise call on Marine, and apologize for his idiotic remarks.

Chapter Twenty-six

❧

The Black and the White

*T*hierry Marchive was a good twenty minutes into his presentation and feeling more confident with each passing minute. He had secretly worried that using visuals in a theology lecture might be seen as cheating by some of his peers, but he had been invited to speak on the Cluny order's contribution to art history and that could hardly be done without slides. Having Yann sitting in the front row, giving him the occasional grin or thumbs-up, helped enormously as well. Yann had beamed, looking to his right and left, when Thierry had referred to the Cluniac order's eleventh- and twelfth-century building craze as "the boom to end all booms," and Thierry had backed that declaration up with a quick succession of slides showing only a small sampling of the eighty cathedrals and five hundred churches—from large to small—the order had built. It was a subject that Thierry was comfortable with—he loved ecclesiastical art and Cluny had given Europe some of its greatest treasures. He was particularly excited to have found slides showing the clever medieval reuse of Roman bricks—long, thin, and red—in the facades of their churches, one church even using Roman columns, now sunk into its thick outer medieval walls.

"Thanks to Burgundy's excellent river connections—long before the canals were built—materials were easily transported from neighboring countries," Thierry said, clicking to a map of then-Burgundy. He had added, spontaneously, the bit about the canals, and was feeling very pleased. "This formidable location allowed droves of artisans to come to Burgundy," he continued. "Bands of masons, glassmakers, and painters came across from Italy to work here." He then moved on to his best set of slides—the tympanum at Autun. "Such were the frequent and well-paid commissions coming from Cluny, that artisans began to sign their works almost for the first time, save for this sculpted bronze chest from the fourth century BC, which is signed, 'Made by Novius Plautius in Rome.' The carved tympanum at Autun's cathedral is signed, we can clearly see, 'Gislebertus.' That one signature alone could be significant enough to warrant us studying, and praising, the Cluniac order for centuries to come. It encouraged a free-flowing exchange of ideas from all neighboring countries, which would be lost during the French Revolution and only found again in the twentieth century. Thank you."

Polite applause filled the small room as Garrigue Druon quickly jumped up, knocking over an empty chair, and turned on the room's lights. She had agreed to help Annie Leonetti with the technicalities of this symposium only because her own paper hadn't been ready for today's lectures—she still had a few more weeks' work on it before she would send it off to Perugia in hopes of being published in their quarterly journal and perhaps being invited to present, which she dreaded, at their own upcoming symposium in February.

Thierry collected his notes off of the lectern and Annie Leonetti came and took the microphone—hardly needed as there were only two dozen people in the room—and announced that there would be a short coffee break before the open discussion would take place.

"That was great," Yann said as he patted Thierry's back.

"Was I good? Did you like it?"

"It was great," Yann repeated. He lowered his voice and said, "Claude and Garrigue aren't even giving papers today. We were right to submit ours."

Thierry took off his wool sweater—he had sweated throughout his entire talk. He then said to Yann, "Your talk on Cluny's contribution to wine making was fantastic."

Yann smiled. "You really think so? That stuff about the monks giving France the concept of *terroir* wasn't too much?"

Thierry shook his head back and forth. "No, no! I had no idea that a wine that comes from one section of a vineyard can taste dramatically different from wine made from grapes grown on another parcel of that same vineyard. So it was the monks who taught us that? Cool. Dr. Leonetti and that beautiful law professor were nodding up and down in agreement."

"Marine Bonnet?"

"Yeah, her. Come on, let's get some food. I'm starving."

The students had just helped themselves to the remaining Petit Lu cookies when Claude Ossart strode past them and said, "Ah, who better to extol the frivolities of Cluny than you two."

Yann rolled his eyes. "Get a life, Ossart."

They walked back into the lecture hall and Dr. Leonetti was at the microphone, smiling her acre-wide smile. "She's so at ease up there," Thierry whispered to Yann.

"I know. I was so nervous, but she doesn't even flinch. She'd make a great politician."

Thierry laughed. "Yeah, in Corsica."

"Before we open up the discussion, I'd like to thank you all for coming today, and thank especially our participants: Dr. Rodier for his fine paper on Saint Bernard's contribution to the spiritual work of the Templar monks, Dr. Kahn from Toulouse for his study of Cluny's revitalization of the Norman church, and our graduate students, who bravely delivered their first papers in the presence of kind, but very knowledgeable, peers and colleagues."

Applause filled the room and Yann poked Thierry in the ribs.

"I'd now like us to pause for a minute's silence in remembrance of Dr. Georges Moutte, our beloved doyen, and his secretary, Mlle Zacharie," Leonetti said. Heads were bowed and silence filled the room, but only a few of the conference attendees were thinking of the recently departed. Thierry was concentrating on keeping his stomach from rumbling; Yann was going over, word for word, his interview with the judge and commissioner, worried that he and Thierry still might be expelled from school; Annie Leonetti forced herself to think of Georges and Audrey because she was at the podium, as if the audience could read her thoughts; Claude Ossart was still fuming over the excesses of Cluny and Yann Falquerho's conceit; Bernard Rodier had begun making a mental list of tonight's Picard shopping, then, ashamed of himself, he began silently reciting the Hail Mary; and Garrigue Druon was musing on the generous offer that had just come her way.

Questions began, with the elderly Dr. Florence Bonnet asking Dr. Kahn to what degree he thought Cluny had inspired Saint Dunstan in England. Drs. Bonnet and Kahn spoke back and forth and Thierry, try as he might, could not keep his eyes open. He had stayed up most of the previous night reworking his paper and now was feeling the effects. He drifted off for a few minutes to be woken up by loud voices and Yann poking him again in the ribs.

"What is it?" Thierry whispered, sitting up straighter.

"You're missing the fireworks," Yann replied. "Everyone is fighting. It's the drunken, debauched Cluniacs versus the pickle-up-your-butt Cistercians."

"Forty farms were needed to produce enough food for the monks at Cluny alone," Claude Ossart said, his voice cracking. "The black-robed monks ate roast chicken and drank fine wines"—here he threw Yann a look across the room—"while monks from other orders ate porridge and drank broth." Yann looked at Claude and shrugged, smiling.

Thierry's mouth watered at the thought of roast chicken, but he quickly remembered a fact he had read late the previous night and so he spoke up. "But the serfs who were transferred to monasteries under Cluny's reign were regarded as fortunate . . ." He paused, wishing he hadn't fallen asleep. He was feeling too drowsy to speak.

"Go on, Thierry," Annie Leonetti said, motioning with her hand to help him finish his sentence.

"These serfs, under the protection of Cluny, were less subject to transfers, or even being sold like slaves."

Annie Leonetti smiled. "Quite right, Thierry. Thank you."

"The Cluniac order's opulence knew no precedent, as Dr. Rodier so aptly proved, and should be condemned!" Claude now shouted. "The order was even too opulent for nunneries to exist, as they were not seen as cost-effective." With "cost-effective," Claude had bent his index and middle fingers to make quotation marks. "The monks at Cluny performed no manual labor," he continued, not drawing a breath, "and when their priests, wealthy themselves, died, they left everything to the order. It was like the Mafia!"

Marine Bonnet raised her hand and stood up from her seat in the back of the room. "With the Council of Altheim in 916, bequests of the clergy were honored, their holdings permitted to go to family or whomever they wished and not automatically to the church."

"There was strict discipline at Cluny under Abbot Peter the Venerable, as Dr. Rodier pointed out," Claude continued, trying a different tack. "But after Peter's death"—he paused and smiled— "in 1156 . . . the order began to fall to pieces, making room for a less corrupt, more disciplined order of monks, that of the honorable men in white, the Cistercians."

Annie Leonetti secretly moaned to herself: all this talk of men. Where were the women in the Middle Ages? Beside her, Dr. Bernard Rodier smiled weakly, embarrassed by his protégé's outburst and constant and unnecessary references to his mentor.

"Let us not forget," Marine said, once again standing, "that it was the rise of English and French nationalisms, as much as anything, that created a climate unfavorable to the existence of all-powerful, centralized monasteries such as what we had at Cluny."

Claude Ossart's face turned red. Thierry Marchive smiled and looked over at Garrigue Druon, who was staring at him, and although he couldn't be sure, he thought he saw her smile, raise her eyebrows, and then quickly look away.

Chapter Twenty-seven

❧

Dragonflies

*R*adia Habib picked up a shard of broken glass with a set of long tweezers and held it up to the light. "I've never seen one of these," she said, squinting.

"I beg your pardon?" Verlaque asked, not sure what she meant. She had certainly seen Gallé vases—they had passed a half a dozen on the way downstairs to her office in the basement of the Petit Palais.

"Sorry. Such a good fake. The dragonfly is exquisite, isn't it?" She held up one of the bigger shards that Paulik had brought along from Georges Moutte's apartment—about two inches square—so that both Verlaque and Paulik could see. The insect, with its black elongated body, was in flight, its translucent pale blue wings all the more dazzling against the vase's olive-green background.

"It is beautiful," Verlaque agreed. "So if it's so exquisite, how do you know it's a fake?" He looked at Mlle Habib, a dark-haired beauty with a long, aquiline nose and almost black eyes that she had accentuated with black eyeliner. She was a darker, thinner version of Annie Leonetti, he thought, a North African beauty, just further across the Mediterranean than Corsica.

The curator set down the dragonfly shard and picked up a smaller shard, this one dark brown, almost black. "This rim," she said. "The color is too shocking . . . it never would have been used by Gallé. But more important is the rim's cut itself . . . do you see it?" She held the shard up to her light for her visitors to see.

"It looks perfect," Paulik said, leaning in.

"Exactly. It was cut by a machine. Gallés were hand cut." She set the shard down and turned to Verlaque and Paulik. "Such a shame when the dragonfly was so well executed." She picked up another shard and examined it in silence. "Ah. Here's another giveaway. Look at this background color. Would you say it's matte or semigloss?"

Verlaque turned to Paulik in an exaggerated panic. "Semigloss," Paulik answered, smiling. He and Hélène had painted their restored village house in Pertuis room by room, and he never wanted to see a can of paint again.

"Right. But it should be matte. Gallé was so good at matte." Habib looked at Verlaque and smiled.

"How much would one of these be worth?" Verlaque asked.

"A vase like this one, a real Gallé, anywhere from five thousand to eight thousand U.S. dollars."

"Dollars? The buyers are American?"

"Yes, or Japanese, but the Japanese like only certain Gallés . . . flowers . . . and then only violets, roses, or poppies."

"Eight thousand dollars doesn't seem worth the effort to forge," Paulik said.

"Ah, but that's for this style of vase, and if you're a forger, you want to cover all the styles, the whole range, from this type to the more sought-after soufflé vases," Habib replied. Seeing her guests' raised eyebrows, she continued. "The soufflé vases are also called 'blown-out vases' . . . production began after World War I and continued after Gallé's death. The vases are built up with layers of colored glass, then cut back with hydrofluoric acid. The design is protected with a waxy resist, resulting in a raised design, like a slight relief. We have two examples upstairs I can show you. Gallé's atelier produced about fifty molds for blown-out vases, from large to small. The forms stay the same with each mold, naturally, but the colors change. The rarer vases and more expensive ones are done using rarer colors . . . some of those, especially the coveted white elephant, can get over one hundred thousand dollars at an auction house." Mlle Habib sat back, content with her lecture.

"One hundred thousand dollars?" Paulik repeated.

"Yes. But some people pay just as much for a car, or even a watch," Radia Habib replied, looking quickly at Paulik but then moving, and resting, her eyes on Verlaque.

Verlaque leaned back and folded his arms, hoping to hide what the curator had obviously already seen . . . his grandfather's watch, a Patek Philippe. "Would someone who collects Gallé know that this particular vase is a fake?" he asked.

"Oh yes, despite the good workmanship of the dragonfly. The machine-cut rim gives it away."

"Thank you," Verlaque said. "We won't take any more of your time."

"It's been no trouble. I rarely get visitors," Mlle Habib replied, picking up the shards of glass on the table and putting them back in the plastic container Paulik had brought with him. "Call me if you have any more questions," she continued, and she handed a business card to Verlaque.

After they had left, Radia Habib sat down and smiled, thinking to herself that not only did she rarely have visitors in the basement of the Petit Palais but seldom were they as oddly attractive as Antoine Verlaque. Physically he was, in her opinion, a knockout: thick black disheveled hair that was turning gray at the temples, a broad chest and shoulders, and lovely big hands with thick fingers that lacked a wedding ring. The broken nose only added to his charm. She imagined that he was a good cook or that he ate out a lot: his stomach gave that away. She too was a *gourmande*, she was just never able to put on weight, much to the chagrin of her four plump sisters. But what she liked most of all was his humor, the little bit of it she had seen. When she had made the reference to expensive cars and watches he had awkwardly tried to hide his own Swiss watch, and she had caught him smile and wink at her, as if to say, "Well, I tried to hide it!"

She allowed herself a few seconds to fantasize a scene in which she made the judge her famous lamb tagine, and as she cut the apricots in half she set one in the lovely wide mouth of the judge, who then licked her fingers. She jumped as the office phone rang; it was her boss, calling her upstairs for a staff meeting—no doubt to discuss more budget cuts.

Verlaque and Paulik made it onto the train with about two minutes to spare, dodging grandmothers with suitcases, students with enormous duffel bags, and the pigeons that fly about the Gare de Lyon. Verlaque was already asleep when the train was still on the outskirts of Paris, and Paulik stole a few minutes to listen to opera on his iPod, a gift from Hélène and Léa for his fortieth birthday. In Burgundy Verlaque awoke and Paulik suggested they stretch their legs and get a coffee in the bar car. They each ordered a double espresso and stood with their elbows on the counter, watching the vineyards of what Bruno Paulik considered the world's best wine fly past them. "So Georges Moutte knew that the dragonfly vase was a fake," Paulik said when they had both stirred one pack of sugar into their coffees and had a first sip.

"Apparently. Which explains why he set the vase on that dresser: he didn't care about it. But why display the vase at all, if it's an obvious fake?" Verlaque asked, tearing himself away from the view.

Paulik sipped his coffee. "Because he thought it was such a good fake? Was he dealing in fake Gallés . . . selling them to unsuspecting foreign buyers?"

"That's a thought. He'd have the best counterfeit on display, in his bedroom, where only he would see it."

"That could be a motive for murder," Paulik suggested.

"A pissed-off buyer?" Verlaque asked.

"I was thinking more along the lines of his partner, or associates, in the fake-glass business. A double cross? Or did Moutte want out and threaten to reveal their identities?"

Verlaque nodded. "That would explain his visits to Italy that Maître Fabre told us about. This all points to Rocchia," he said. "The fellow glass lover."

They watched in silence as the hills of Burgundy and Beaujolais gradually became flatter as they approached Lyon, and the vineyards disappeared and were replaced by fields of soy and grains.

Chapter Twenty-eight

✻

La Pata Negra

*I*t was just before 8:00 p.m. when Verlaque walked onto Aix's place des Trois Ormeaux. Despite the cold November evening, there were already a few occupied tables on the cobbled terrace that was named for the three elm trees that grew in each corner of the triangular square. Paul and Emilie, the owners of L'Epicerie, a food and wine emporium also on the square, had set out portable heaters, and on each chair placed a small woolen throw. Although Paul offered a good selection of reds and whites, this cool evening called for red, which most of the patrons that evening had ordered. In summer, Paul and Emilie put bottles of white and rosé in the square's fountain to keep cool. Verlaque had once seen a map of Aix that dated from the thirteenth century, and in the place of the fountain and well-dressed Aixois sipping wines were two gallows.

Verlaque flew into the shop and ordered an entire *pata negra* leg of ham and a case each of champagne and red wine. He phoned Arnaud to come pick up the wine, which Paul stacked on a cart, and Verlaque took the ham, wrapped in tea towels, under his arm. Paul opened the door for the judge and said, "Swing by Monoprix and buy a couple of heads of lettuce for a green salad . . . that's all you'll need for the *pata negra*."

The pig was heavier than Verlaque had predicted—he guessed it weighed twenty pounds—and by the time he got to the cours Mirabeau his arms were aching.

"Well, well," he heard a voice say behind him. "Looks like you have a hoofed friend with you."

He turned around and saw Annie Leonetti, smiling. She took ahold of the pig's hoof, which was sticking out of the towel, and shook it. She looked closer and peeked under a section of the tea towel. "Is this a *pata negra*?"

"Yes," Verlaque answered, embarrassed to be carrying a pig's leg.

"Don't ever tell any of my relatives this, but that is the best ham in the world, even better than we can get in Corsica." Annie Leonetti made the sign of the cross for slurring her island. "Imagine a black pig that has eaten only wild herbs, grasses, and roots, and then just before it's slaughtered, is fed solely acorns." She smiled at the thought of it, but Verlaque remembered that the last words Dr. Leonetti had spoken to him had also been about death.

"And then is cured for four years," Verlaque added, unable to stop himself.

Annie Leonetti threw up her hands in mock amazement. "*Ah, oui!* Well, it looks like you're in a rush. Can I help you with anything? Were you just about to go into Monoprix with your friend?"

Verlaque laughed despite himself. "You couldn't run downstairs and buy three heads of *salade frisée* for me, could you?"

"I'd be delighted!"

Verlaque braced the ham leg on his stomach and reached into his pants pocket and pulled out a handful of coins, handing them to Dr. Leonetti. She walked quickly into Monoprix and he waited on the sidewalk under a plane tree, trying to look inconspicuous. He thought of what they knew so far . . . that Moutte's big Gallé vase was indeed a fake; that Rocchia and Moutte had, no doubt, dined together in Perugia; and that Audrey Zacharie had recently come into money and she had expected the haul to continue. Could the killer have broken into Moutte's apartment only to break the vase as a warning to Audrey Zacharie? Is that why Audrey had run out of the apartment and why she'd screamed when she saw the broken vase?

"Voilà!"

Verlaque looked up as Annie Leonetti handed him a familiar red bag. "Have fun wherever you're going!"

"*Mille merci!*" Verlaque said as he took the bag and began walking away. He turned right onto the rue Clémenceau and saw Carole standing in her *tabac*'s doorway. "*Bonsoir, le Juge,*" she said, winking.

He felt doubly foolish, having had a murder suspect buy him three heads of lettuce and now having the lovely Carole see him carrying a leg of ham. "*Bonsoir* Carole!" he answered. He looked ahead and saw Arnaud coming toward him. "I've never been happier to see someone!" Verlaque said to him, laughing.

"I dropped off the wine, put a couple bottles of champagne in your freezer, and thought I'd run back down here and help you."

"Great . . . thanks," Verlaque answered, handing Arnaud the *pata negra*. "Carry this for me, if you don't mind."

"Some of your friends have arrived already," Arnaud said, taking the ham. "I let them into your apartment, as instructed. They've invited me to stay, providing I try a cigar."

Verlaque laughed and remembered his first cigar—with his grandfather Charles at their home in Normandy. He had been around the same age that Arnaud was now. It had been an instant love for Verlaque, but he knew that this was rarely the case. His brother Sébastien hated cigars, as did his father.

"You'd be more than welcome." They walked up the rue Gaston de Saporta and turned right onto the place des Martyrs de la Résistance and then down Verlaque's small street. He reached into his pocket and got out his own set of keys to open the outer green door to his building. "The guys must be starving," he said as he and Arnaud ran up the stairs.

"Oh no, don't worry. One of them bought two big pizzas after he parked his car . . . you know, that pizza truck across from the Parking Bellegarde that does the wood-fired pizzas. He was in your kitchen, cutting up the pizzas into little pieces, when I left."

A chorus of "Ooh la la"s was heard as Verlaque and Arnaud entered the apartment, the air already thick with cigar smoke. "*Pata negra!*" a few people called out. Fabrice, the club's president, yelled, "Bring that animal here, Arnaud! We've got the stand all ready and the knives sharpened. They were dull, by the way, Antoine!" Someone handed Verlaque a glass of champagne, and muttering thanks, he downed it.

"Give a glass of champagne to Arnaud, will you?" Verlaque said to no one in particular, yelling over his shoulder as he walked down to his bedroom. "I'm going to change."

Verlaque smiled as he pulled on his blue jeans. It was a treat to have his apartment full of people—friends—and it reminded him of being at his grandparents' house in the seventeenth, the frequent party guests a strange mix of artists whom Emmeline had known at art school, business acquaintances of his grandfather Charles's, and the odd neighbor who had, like Emmeline and

Charles, fallen in love with that treelined street in the most unlikely of Parisian neighborhoods.

"Arnaud is going to Cuba," José, one of the club's members, hollered as Verlaque walked back into his living room.

"I know," Verlaque answered, taking another glass of champagne from his friend Jean-Marc and smiling. "Arnaud saved me this evening, and he's agreed to clean up this mess, so after our cigars we'll raise a little tip collection for his trip, okay?"

The group vocalized its approval of this idea and Verlaque walked over to the bar that separated his kitchen from the dining room, where Julien was cutting thin pieces of ham and setting every second piece on a large oval plate and every first piece into his mouth.

"Julien, here, take a break and let me take over," Virginie, the club's sole female, said, winking at Verlaque and Jean-Marc. She took the knife from Julien before he could protest and began to quickly and deftly slice the ham. Jacob, an Egyptian Jew who commuted between his finance job in London and Aix, took the platter from Virginie and said, "I may as well pass this around since I can't eat it. Why don't you keep slicing and put some more on another plate."

"There's salmon, Jacob," Verlaque said.

"I know, Arnaud already showed it to me when I told him I couldn't eat this lovely *pata negra*," Jacob replied, smiling.

"You're a good worker, Arnaud. I always hire young people who have shown a drive to work," Jacob said to Arnaud, who was now standing beside Fabrice, who had his arm around the teen.

"I do too!" Fabrice echoed, pulling Arnaud in closer. "I have three daughters and each one worked in my shops after school and during the summer holidays. They never complained." Fabrice owned a franchise of plumbing stores that had started in Marseille but now went as far as Menton, just before the Italian border. Arnaud smiled at the two men and nodded, not sure what to say.

"Arnaud is going to try a wide Churchill from Romeo y Julieta now," Fabrice told the group. "It was one of Che's favorites," he told the teen, leaning in and squeezing him again.

At the mention of his hero, the teen lit up. "I'm ready!"

"You snip the end off with these cutters," Fabrice instructed. Arnaud took the cigar and cutters from the club president and his hands shook.

"Do it for him, Fabrice," Jacob said.

"Fabrice regrets not having a son, I think," Jean-Marc whispered to Verlaque. Verlaque smiled and nodded in agreement.

In no time the cigar was snipped, lit, and in Arnaud's mouth.

"Don't inhale!" Virginie yelled.

Arnaud coughed and his eyes watered. "I'm not sure about this . . ." He brought the cigar to his mouth and tried it again, coughing and blowing the smoke out of his mouth as fast as he could.

Fabrice looked over his large belly down at the floor, saddened that his new apprentice was obviously going to take longer than usual to learn how to smoke a cigar. "Good try, Arnaud!" José said, and the other members, except Fabrice, cheered.

Verlaque looked to his side to say something to Jean-Marc, but he was gone. He found Jean-Marc in the kitchen, washing the lettuce. "You'd make someone a good wife," Verlaque joked.

Jean-Marc smiled and then said, "I've been mediating divorces all this week, so please don't talk of marriage. That institution doesn't look that great to me right now." He placed the lettuce in Verlaque's salad spinner and turned the handle, watching the top spin. "How's Marine? I haven't seen her in a few days."

"I'm going to call her tonight. We got in a fight last time we saw each other. I insulted Sylvie, and for no good reason, if truth be known. I highly doubt marriage is in our future, so don't worry."

Jean-Marc drained the water out of the salad spinner and looked at Verlaque. "Apologies are always gracefully accepted by Marine."

"You're right. I was frustrated by this case, I think, and took it out on Sylvie." He silently made a note to slip into his bedroom before the dessert course and call Marine.

"How was Paris?" Jean-Marc asked.

"Somewhat fruitful. We spoke to the lawyer who has Georges Moutte's will and discovered that he had a pile of money, at least in one Paris account. And we had a mini-lesson in what constitutes a fake Gallé from a lovely curator at the Petit Palais. She confirmed that one of the Gallé vases the doyen had in his apartment *was* an obvious forgery, and that he probably knew it."

"Ah, Antoine. Always an eye for the ladies."

Verlaque looked at Jean-Marc, one of Aix's most competent lawyers and a reliable and sure friend to both himself and to Marine. He thought it strange that his friend, slim, tall, and broad shouldered, never commented on the women he was dating. Jean-Marc surely must get flirted with all the time, Verlaque thought, given his gentle manner, clear blue eyes, and short-cropped, always perfectly groomed blond hair.

Jean-Marc began ripping the salad and letting the pieces fall into a large glass salad bowl.

"That *is* strange, though," Jean-Marc said. "Why display a forgery among your treasures unless to say, 'I know this one is a fake'?"

"Moutte could have displayed that vase to remind himself what a forged Gallé looked like . . ."

"If he was in the business of forging antiques, yes," Jean-Marc answered. "Or, Moutte, even knowing it was a fake, couldn't bring himself to get rid of it. It could have been a gift, you know, like those gifts your mother gives you that you don't like but you hold on to anyway. Best find out, if you can, who gave him that vase."

Verlaque raised an eyebrow and said, "Hold that thought." He grabbed his cell phone off of the kitchen counter and texted Paulik and copied Officer Flamant on it. He set the cell phone down and was about to ask Jean-Marc about his love life when another club member entered the room. "Hello, men," said Pierre, a small-boned bookseller every bit as neat and tidy as Jean-Marc, only dark-haired and about six inches shorter.

"Hey," Jean-Marc said, smiling. "I was waiting for you . . . here, try my salad dressing."

Pierre dipped his finger into the thick, dark yellow sauce that Jean-Marc had just made. "Perfect, as usual."

Verlaque looked at Pierre and then at Jean-Marc. "You've cooked for Pierre before?"

Jean-Marc laughed and gently put a hand on Verlaque's shoulder. "You sound like a jealous husband!"

"I'm lucky, aren't I?" Pierre asked, laughing. The judge continued to look back and forth between the two men, whom, he now noticed, were both wearing neatly pressed jeans, expensive leather moccasins, and Lacoste polo shirts. It suddenly became clear to him: their similar looks and interests and the fact that they had both spent a weekend in Barcelona in September and nervously avoided Verlaque's eyes when he had asked them if they had bumped into each other that weekend.

Verlaque smiled and got a bottle of champagne out of the fridge. "I feel like we should make a toast. How long have you been a couple? And when were you going to tell me?"

"We're telling you now," Pierre replied. "We've been seeing each other for over a year." Laughter, José singing a ballad in Spanish, and the sound of Arnaud coughing could be heard coming from the living room.

"We need to rescue that kid," Verlaque said as he ripped off the aluminum around the bottle's neck and uncorked the champagne. He grabbed three glasses out of a cupboard and poured out the champagne and toasted his friends. "I'm thrilled for you both. Cheers."

"It's an amazing thing when it happens, Antoine," Jean-Marc said.

Verlaque sipped his champagne and frowned. "When what happens?"

"When you finally meet the love of your life." Jean-Marc winked at Pierre and the three men raised their glasses and drank.

Chapter Twenty-nine

❧

A Confession over Grappa

*I*t was after midnight when Verlaque walked into Marine's apartment. He hung up his coat on her coatrack and saw Marine standing in the doorway, her arms drawn around her chest, dressed in one of his extra-large cotton striped pajama tops and enormous fuzzy pink slippers. He walked across the entryway and hugged her, and when she kissed his cheek he drew her closer to him and held her tighter. She ran her fingers through his thick black hair and he finally leaned back a bit and looked at her. "I'm so sorry," he said.

Marine pulled away. "You have to learn to be kinder to my friends, especially Sylvie . . ."

"I will try to handle my temper with Sylvie. It's none of my business if she sleeps around. I'm sorry."

"Even Vincent," Marine continued, her face getting flushed. "Whom I know you think outrageous."

Verlaque sighed. "As for Vincent, it's not his being gay that I mind, it's the over-the-top outrageous bit that bothers me."

Marine stepped back and looked at her lover. "Are you sure Vincent's being gay doesn't bother you?"

Verlaque shook his head. "Rugby players aren't at all homophobic."

Marine nodded. "You're right. Now soccer players, on the other hand . . ."

"Marine, have you ever wondered about Jean-Marc?"

Marine laughed. "You've only just realized? Okay, I'm being unfair, as I didn't see the signs either until very recently." She laughed and pulled Verlaque close to her, kissing him on the lips.

"Stop trying to seduce me!" Verlaque said, laughing. "I only just realized this evening . . . and how long have I known Jean-Marc? I'm stunned!"

"Why are you stunned?" Marine asked. "Does it change Jean-Marc? No. Does it change the way you feel about your friend? No. Why does who he sleeps with interest or surprise you?"

"All right, all right. I guess I was surprised because he never talked about it."

"Why should he have? I sometimes think that that's all you think about."

"Sex? No, you're wrong." Verlaque pulled Marine in closer. "I think about wine and cigars too."

Marine gave him a friendly slap, but the look on her face wasn't a happy one.

"I'm crazy about you, Marine. You should know that by now."

Marine still couldn't bring herself to smile. Verlaque looked closely at the freckles that covered her face, neck, and chest. "If you're waiting for me to propose," he said, "it's . . ."

"A waste of time," Marine cut in. "No, I'm not waiting for a proposal. Those kinds of decisions are made by two people these days, Antoine. Even in the late 1950s my parents made that decision together, there was no kneeling down, no hidden engagement ring . . ."

"Okay, okay. I'm sorry . . . for all the times I've angered you, for all the times I've been so unclear, so indecisive. You are the most amazing woman I've ever met. That I'm sure of, I realized it today, in Paris. I was speaking to an old man, and he's just lost his wife, and . . ."

Marine broke in. "Antoine, would you like a grappa? Because I sure would."

Verlaque threw his head back and let out a roar of laughter. "Is the pope Polish?"

"I take that as a yes." Marine walked into the kitchen and opened the freezer compartment in her refrigerator, taking out a long, thin, icy bottle.

"Isn't that the grappa we bought last year in Liguria? You still have some left?"

Marine smiled. "I've been saving it for when my lover comes over to my apartment in the middle of the night and trips over his words, trying to tell me that he loves me." Marine looked at Verlaque, finally relieved to have said the words that she had kept inside for so long. Well, this is it, she thought. He'll either fess up right now, or run out of the door.

Verlaque stood with his back resting against the kitchen door for what seemed like an eternity staring at Marine, she would later tell Sylvie. He quickly moved toward her, pushing her against the refrigerator, wrapping his arms around her slender waist and putting his face in her hair. "My love, my love," he whispered over and over. He kissed her lips, his mouth moist and soft, and then kissed her cheeks and forehead and neck. "I love you, Marine." He took her head in his hands and looked at her, and kissed her on the mouth once again, running his hands up from her waist and over her small breasts, then up to her cheeks. "I love you," he repeated once more and then stepped back, looking at her.

"You just knocked over all my fridge magnets and Charlotte's drawing," Marine said. She leaned down to pick up the drawing, hiding her smile.

"Marine?"

She stood up, smiling, and grabbed Verlaque by the collar of his sweater, bringing him near her and kissing him. "I love you too, Antoine. Let's not talk about this anymore for now, okay?"

She took the grappa bottle into her living room. Verlaque followed her, sat down on her sofa, and watched the freckled beauty as she opened an antique corner buffet and took out two small crystal shot glasses that were etched with dragonflies.

"I had forgotten about these glasses," Verlaque said, leaning toward the coffee table to look at them, grateful for her elegance, grateful that she had not needed to hear, or say, more on the subject of love that evening. "See, you were everywhere with me today in Paris. That vase that broke in Moutte's apartment was also engraved with dragonflies."

"These were my grandmother's," Marine said, pouring the clear white alcohol into the glasses.

Marine sipped some grappa and winced. "I've forgotten that the first sip always burns, and then after that . . . smooth as silk." She took another sip to test out her theory, and nodded.

Verlaque told her about their discoveries in Paris, that Moutte has displayed a vase that he knew was counterfeit, and how the doyen had definitely been to Umbria, even a glassblowing factory near Perugia.

"Let's have a look," Marine said. She walked over to her bookshelves and pulled out a shoe box full of maps. She spread out a map of central Italy on her coffee table and rested her elbows on her thighs, looking down. "The lawyer told you that the town starts with an 'F'? Let's look as closely to Perugia as we can, since Rocchia grew up there. That's where he would have all of his contacts, right?"

"He grew up in Perugia?"

"Yes, my mother is full of information these days." She leaned over Verlaque and took a pencil off of the side table next to him. "By the way, she gave me a file for you, and I meant to give it to you that night I stormed off with Sylvie."

"I'm sorry about what I said," Verlaque said.

"I know; I'll tell Sylvie. Let's look at my mother's file. Basically, it contains the Dumas's bank statements."

Marine opened the file and put the bank statements on the coffee table. "None of the professors, my mother included, have ever wanted to take responsibility for the fellowship, and so only recently did they discover that bit by bit someone has been taking out money."

"Pardon?"

"In cash withdrawals, from the savings account."

"Who?"

"Well, in the Law Department it's only our head accountant who has this kind of authority," Marine said. "But my mother told me that the Theology Department's accountant retired two months ago, and they haven't yet agreed on a replacement."

Verlaque laughed. "And with all the unemployment in France!"

Marine bit her lip. "Well, tell me, who has banking privileges in *your* department?"

"Me, Roussel, and Mme Girard. So, someone was embezzling? Moutte? That could explain where he got the money for all that stuff and why he left all of his assets to the school, in particular for the fellowship."

"I should think so! My mother also told me that Audrey Zacharie was flirting with the doyen during that party on Friday night. What do you think about that?"

Verlaque sipped some grappa and then said, "Mlle Zacharie was fiercely protective of that department, from all reports. Perhaps flirting with Moutte was just another way to have more control over her little empire on the fourth floor. What do you think? You're a woman."

"Mmm. What if . . . there really was counterfeiting going on, which was confirmed today, yesterday now, by that curator you visited. Audrey, since she did try to control what went on in the department, might have found out about it. Would she then try to blackmail Moutte? She'd have one on him, right? So the flirting at the party was just reminding him of that, of her new power over him."

"Not bad. Wait a minute!" he said, pouring a tiny bit of grappa into Marine's glass. "Audrey Zacharie did have a mysterious windfall recently, her boyfriend told me about it and I saw some of her shopping splurges in their apartment."

"And if she was blackmailing Moutte and Rocchia, that would make Rocchia a suspect for her murder. Does he have an alibi for Monday night?" Marine asked.

"He was en route from San Remo the evening Mlle Zacharie was hit. And on the night of Moutte's murder, he was at home in Perugia with his wife."

"He could be lying. His marriage was one of convenience, my mother told me. And have you checked out the hotel in San Remo?"

Verlaque sipped some grappa and leaned back. "One of our officers was making phone calls today while we were in Paris. I'll know first thing tomorrow morning. I think that Mlle Zacharie came into the apartment to look for what the thief was looking for; and she then found us there," Verlaque said. "She left in a hurry too, when Bruno and I were in another room."

"What did she say she was doing there?"

"Looking for a grant application for one of the grad students."

"That would be easy to check, wouldn't it? Just ask the student. Speaking of students, I went to the symposium on Cluny today and heard some of the students give papers. Two of the boys, Yann and Thierry I think their names are, did very well. The female grad student just seemed to be tripping over her own feet the entire afternoon, and the fourth one . . ."

"Claude?"

"Yes, that's him. Well, he was enraged! Anything anyone tried to say in favor of the Cluniac order just sent him into a tizzy! Really a weird kid. I guess he was just defending his mentor, but really . . ."

Verlaque finished his grappa. "Yeah, grad students always get too enthusiastic about what they're studying, as if it's the only way to look at a certain subject. He'll calm down once he gets out into the real world."

"That's exactly what my mother said after the lecture."

Verlaque feigned outrage at being compared to Florence Bonnet, and Marine laughed. She took Verlaque's empty glass from his hands and stood up. "You look tired."

Verlaque looked up at her. "I'm so tired I could fall asleep on this sofa, fully dressed."

Marine reached out her arm and pulled Verlaque up. "Let's go to bed then. Tomorrow's another day."

Chapter Thirty

❧

The Persian Letters

*M*onique had come to Verlaque again in a dream. He bolted up and said, "You're dead, Monique." He was sweating and fell back onto the pillow, trying to slow down his breathing. He looked over at Marine, who was very still, both arms at her sides and her head tilted away from him, toward the window.

"Are you all right?" she whispered.

Verlaque sat up again and threw off the covers. "Bad dream, sorry if I woke you. Would you like some coffee?" There was no way that he could now explain his past to Marine. He was determined that Monique was not going to jeopardize his relationship with Marine. Or was he just afraid? Taking the easy way out?

Marine turned her face toward his and rested her head on her right arm. "When have I ever refused coffee?"

"Right! Give me five seconds." Verlaque walked into Marine's bathroom and splashed cold water on his face. He picked up his watch, which was sitting on the counter, and looked at the time. "*Merde!*" he hollered.

"What? Did we sleep in?" Marine called from the bedroom.

"Yes! It's almost 9:00 a.m.!"

"*Merde!*"

"What time is your first class?"

"10:00!"

A cell phone began to ring and Verlaque ran back into the bedroom and picked his phone up from the bedside table. "*Oui.*"

"Sorry, sir. Paulik here. I just wanted to warn you before you come in this morning."

"I'll be there in a few minutes. What's going on, Bruno?"

"It's Roussel. He's on the warpath. Just brace yourself."

"*Merde, merci.*" He hung up the phone and walked back into the bathroom and began brushing his teeth.

"Is my Montesquieu book in the bathroom?" Marine called from the living room. "I need it for today's class."

Verlaque looked at her bathroom counter, covered in a half dozen small jars of face creams; four lipsticks, each one with its cap off; a Chanel no. 19 perfume; a small volume of Rimbaud's poetry; and finally, under a battered and wet *Elle* magazine, Montesquieu's *Persian Letters*. "Found it!" he called out.

Verlaque looked at Marine as she walked into the bathroom and smiled. "Funny choice for a law class. But then your lectures are famous for that." He tapped her head lightly with the book. "I'll go make coffee. By the way, I put the lids back on your lipsticks for you."

As Verlaque was pouring the coffee into two cups Marine walked into the kitchen. She was wearing wide-legged tweed pants with high-heeled boots and a crisp, tight-fitting white blouse with a long narrow green tie. "Good morning, Annie Hall," he said as he handed her her morning drug. "It was one of my grandfather's favorite books," he continued, not able to take his eyes off of Marine.

"The *Persian Letters*? It was one of my grandfather's favorites as well," Marine answered, sipping her coffee. "'I may have lived in servitude, but I have always been free.' Poor Roxane. My grandfather loved that line in the book. I'm going to write it on the blackboard this morning and have the students write for twenty minutes or so a response to it . . . they could approach it from a number of different angles . . . the contrast between European and non-European societies, or the advantages and disadvantages of different systems of government . . ."

Verlaque broke in. "Or the nature of political authority, or even religious tolerance . . . didn't Montesquieu marry a Protestant?"

"Heaven forbid," Marine answered, smiling. The Verlaque ancestors had been Huguenots, and Emmeline, a devote Anglican.

"You're right, it will make for a great discussion." Verlaque smiled and put his hand through her thick auburn hair. "I wish you had been teaching in Bordeaux when I was a law student there."

"Ah, then we wouldn't be sleeping together."

Verlaque smiled. "Montesquieu may have been bleak, but I always found those two Turks—what were their names? . . ."

"Usbek and Rica."

"Thanks. I always thought they were quite funny, the way they misinterpret what they see."

Marine held the book to her chest and said, "But still Roxane is enslaved, and commits suicide because of it. So I guess it's bleak and funny at the same time." She brushed his cheek with the back of her hand and added, "Sort of like your English poet, *non*?"

Verlaque and Marine parted on the rue d'Italie and Verlaque carried on up the rue Thiers, hoping he wouldn't run into anyone he knew. As the road curved he saw ahead of him a roadblock, and for a few seconds thought perhaps the Palais de Justice was being roped off, but then remembered that it was Thursday, market day. Although he found the stands with their artfully displayed mountains of vegetables beautiful, zigzagging through the crowd was tiresome. Not today . . . all he could think of was Marine. He walked by one of his favorite sellers—a man who only sold what was local and in season—and today he had four piles of wild mushrooms sitting on his long wooden table: delicate little orange girolles; black trumpet mushrooms; pointy, pockmarked morels; and big fatty cèpes. Verlaque stopped at the stand and asked for two hundred grams of each of the mushrooms, which the vendor weighed and put into separate small paper bags. "Fry them with parsley and lemon, right?" Verlaque asked.

"And garlic," the vendor replied, smiling. He threw a bunch of flat-leaf parsley into one of the bags.

"Thanks." Verlaque paid, took the four bags, and crossed the street, already imagining the dinner he would make for Marine that night. On his way into the Palais de Justice, Verlaque ran into Alain Flamant. "*Salut*," the young officer said, shaking Verlaque's hand. "I made about a dozen phone calls yesterday, sir, including the hotel that Professor Rocchia gave us in San Remo . . . no Giuseppe, or Dottore, or Signore Rocchia stayed there on Monday."

Verlaque stopped on the stairs and looked at Flamant. "You're kidding? Thanks, Alain." He ran up the rest of the stairs two at a time, anxious to find Bruno Paulik. "Good morning, Mme Girard," he said as he walked past his secretary's desk.

"Hello, Judge," Mme Girard answered, and then held up her pen as if in warning. Verlaque nodded as he could hear Yves Roussel's voice around the corner.

"Sorry I'm late," Verlaque said as he saw Yves Roussel standing outside Verlaque's office door. "Come on in," Verlaque said, opening the door. "Giuseppe Rocchia didn't stay at the Hôtel des Anglais in San Remo on Monday night."

Roussel stayed silent and Verlaque looked at the prosecutor, surprised.

Verlaque continued, "He has no alibi for Mlle Zacharie's murder, has lied about his whereabouts that night, and lied to us about never seeing Georges Moutte in Perugia. Yves, I don't know if Bruno filled you in yet, but we have reason to believe that Rocchia is involved in making fake antique glass, and that Moutte knew about it. That could be why he was killed . . . he could have threatened to blow the whistle on Rocchia, or perhaps he had been involved all along, and suddenly got a bad conscience about the whole thing."

Yves Roussel smiled and walked across the room, pretending to be interested in Verlaque's leather-bound law books. Roussel, just under five-three, rocked back and forth on the toes and heels of his blue cowboy boots. "Fascinating, Antoine," he finally said, turning around. "Wrong, but completely fascinating."

Verlaque looked at Roussel and rolled his eyes. "Tell me, Yves, why it's wrong."

"Don't mind if I do. I've been waiting half the morning to tell you. I'm on my way to make my first arrest of the day, in fact. I could have done it without you, but wanted to be polite . . . fill you in on it."

"The bank machines? You found those idiots?" Verlaque asked, sitting down and placing the mushrooms on his desk. Roussel was such a moron, he thought, making a big display about arresting some small-time hoodlums who went around the countryside stealing from cash machines.

"No, my friend, that case remains unsolved for the moment." Roussel walked up to Verlaque's desk and put his hands on its glass top. "I'm off to arrest someone for the murder of Mlle Audrey Zacharie."

Verlaque shot up out of his seat. "What? Who?"

"Yann Falquerho."

"Are you crazy, Yves? On what proof?" Verlaque asked.

Bruno Paulik opened the door and came into the office. "Sorry I'm late."

"That's fine, Bruno," Verlaque said, looking at Roussel. Bruno Paulik's arrival was very welcome, even if late.

"I just met with Mme da Silva, Moutte's housekeeper," Paulik said. "I was following up on the text message you sent last night. She can't remember the name of the person who gave the doyen that vase, but she does remember it was an Italian."

"Rocchia," Verlaque said.

"He's not the only Italian on the planet," Roussel said. "As I was saying, I did some calling around while you two were up in Paris yesterday," Roussel continued. "My first call was to the precinct in the seventh arrondissement, where M. Falquerho spent an evening behind bars for breaking and entering."

"We know about that, Yves."

"Wait for it," Roussel replied, holding up his right hand, the palm facing Verlaque. "So I spoke to one of the officers, who looked up that evening's records, and the officer who arrested Yann Falquerho that evening, and who scared the pants off him, has now been promoted to Europol in Brussels. So, I called up Officer, now Sergeant, Addaoud, and spoke to him about that evening. After all, we've had a suspect with a crime record all along . . . so I thought it warranted some digging." Roussel looked at Paulik as if to blame the commissioner for overlooking that point.

"Come off it, Roussel," Verlaque said, his voice raised. "That kid broke into his father's club as a prank! A rich, bored kid in Paris looking for something naughty to do on a Saturday night!"

"Well, this rich kid has also had a run-in with the police in Brittany, in some little town where he spends his summers."

"Carnac," Paulik said, sighing. It infuriated him that Roussel couldn't remember the name of the town that held one of the greatest alignments of prehistoric standing stones in France.

Roussel ignored Paulik and continued. "Sergeant Addaoud told me that he had wanted to frighten some sense into the kid, because Paris wasn't his first offense. The summer previous to that, Yann Falquerho was detained for guess what?"

Verlaque threw up his hands. "You got me."

"Car theft. Seems the kid knows how to hot-wire a car, only this car belonged to a friend of his father's who didn't press charges. The kid has a thing for BMWs, apparently."

Verlaque sat down and put his head in his hands. "The poor kid. I almost wish you hadn't told me that, Yves."

"Alas," Roussel said, raising his hands in the air.

"Let's get Yann in here, and his friend Thierry too," Verlaque said. "They were together the night of both murders."

"Falquerho's lying and he's got his poor little friend to cover for him!" Roussel screeched. "I'm going straight there, to their apartment!"

"Like hell you are," Verlaque answered. "We'll bring both the boys here, since they're each other's alibis for both murders."

"Falquerho ran a car . . . a BMW . . . over an innocent woman, and he, with the help of his chubby friend, probably killed Professor Moutte! Let's go now and surprise him!"

"No, Yves!" Verlaque looked at Paulik and said, "Call them, Bruno, and get them in here right away."

"You're making a big mistake!" Roussel hollered, so loudly that Mme Girard had to put her hand over the mouthpiece of her phone. She had been giving her niece a recipe for an easy-to-make mushroom pâté, having seen mushrooms in the market on her way to work.

"Maybe, Yves, but we're going to do this in a civilized way and get some honest answers from these two kids. They're scared, and obviously lied to us about Yann's past, but they aren't murderers." As soon as he said it, Verlaque realized that he sounded every bit as naive, and possibly misled, as Usbek and Rica.

Verlaque's office phone rang and he spoke with his voice lowered to Mme Girard and then hung up. "You'll both want to stay for this," he said to Paulik and Roussel. "The maid who found Georges Moutte's body is in the waiting room." The commissioner and prosecutor exchanged surprised looks and turned to face the door, ready to greet the woman. Mme Girard knocked on the door and Verlaque answered it.

"Thank you for coming," Verlaque said as he reached over and took Mlle Winnie Mukiga by the arm and helped her to sit down. She folded her hands on her lap and looked down at them.

"Are you feeling better?" he asked, looking at the tall woman who sat so still. She raised her eyes to meet his, and he saw that in another life, born in another country and in another time, Mlle Mukiga could have been a famously rich fashion model. Her dark black skin shone, her face free of blemishes or wrinkles, and her cheekbones prominent. But she needed a haircut, and her eyes looked tired and sad. "Yes, I'm sorry I couldn't come sooner," she finally answered.

"It's not a problem. We have the report you gave the first policeman to arrive on the scene, and Commissioner Paulik has briefed me on the statement you gave him on Saturday afternoon.

Could you please tell me what exactly happened that morning?" Verlaque asked.

Mukiga swallowed and spoke. "I began my cleaning at the end of the hall as I always do. There's Dr. Rodier's office, which is spotless, so I dusted where I thought it needed it, and vacuumed, and then locked his office door. I have a master key."

"Go on," Verlaque said gently.

"I then cleaned the two small public restrooms . . . there's a women's and a men's . . . and the fourth door down that hallway is the doyen's office. I'm always a little nervous before I clean his office."

Verlaque looked at her. "Why is that?"

"Because of the artwork, all those glass vases. He was very particular about them."

Verlaque nodded and silently noted that although the doyen was particular about his Gallé collection, he had let one in his apartment sit on a dresser that was unsteady—the fake.

Mlle Mukiga took a tissue out of her purse and dabbed her forehead. "But that morning, as I reached into my apron pocket for the master key, I saw that his door was partly open. I opened it all the way and called his name, but no one answered. I went in to begin cleaning the room and saw a file on the floor, next to his desk. I crossed the room and picked it up, and when I looked over the side of the desk, I saw him lying there."

"And then?"

"I walked around the desk and knelt down beside him. I knew he was dead. I thought he had had a heart attack, and it was only when I leaned in closer, to close his eyes, that I saw the blood on the carpet, and blood on the side of his head." She closed her eyes but continued speaking. "And then I screamed. I didn't mean to, but it brought back too many memories for me. My family, in

Rwanda, they were killed, and when I came home one afternoon from my auntie's house, that was the way I found them. Heads bashed in, blood on the floor . . ." She closed her eyes and wrapped her arms around her thin waist.

Verlaque watched her, and when she had begun to breathe evenly and slowly, he continued his questioning. "You called the ambulance then?"

"No, I didn't have to, because Odette, one of the other cleaners, heard me and came running up from the floor below. She called the ambulance and then helped me get up and took me into the adjoining office to sit down. When I had finally calmed down it became chaotic again, with the ambulance attendants arriving, Dr. Leonetti in and out, and then finally the police . . ."

Verlaque sat forward. "Dr. Leonetti was there?"

"Yes, she too heard my screams. She must have been working in her office. I can't even remember if we spoke, I just remember her there, in the secretary's office with us."

"That wasn't in the police report taken Saturday morning at the school," Verlaque gently said.

The maid shook her head. "I'm sorry, that's possible, because it seems like I've only just remembered Dr. Leonetti's face in the office now, just this instant."

Verlaque became restless. "Thank you so much for coming in, Mlle Mukiga," he said, getting up and walking over to where she was seated. She too got up and he offered her his arm. "I'll walk you down to the front door," he said.

She smiled. "Thank you." Winnie Mukiga draped her long slender arm through his and leaned slightly into him, but Verlaque could tell that despite her exhaustion, this was a woman who was strong, and proud.

In a few minutes Verlaque was back in his office.

"Who gets to call that Ivy League show-off?" Roussel asked as he jumped up out of his seat.

"I will," Verlaque said. "I'll ask her to come in as soon as possible."

Roussel walked toward the door but turned to Verlaque and said, "He probably used a different name."

"I beg your pardon?" Verlaque asked.

"For the hotel. Rocchia's a celebrity, especially in Italy. He probably used a phony name at the hotel." With that Roussel walked out of the office, slamming the door.

Bruno Paulik got to his feet. "I'll call the boys, and have Flamant call Rocchia."

Verlaque nodded. "I'll call Rocchia. Have you ever read the *Persian Letters?*" he asked.

"No, I never have. Molière? Marivaux?"

"Close. Montesquieu. There are these two Turks, Usbek and Rica, who go on a grand tour of Western Europe, hilariously misinterpreting the people and customs they see along the way."

"Are you referring to Roussel?" Paulik asked. "Or Yann and Thierry?"

"No, us."

Chapter Thirty-one

≈

Frankly, My Dear . . .

"N ext time ask to speak with the manager and not some bellhop," Giuseppe Rocchia said into the telephone. "I stay in so many luxury hotels that I can't remember if I used my real name or not. Try under Signore Bianco . . . that's the name I usually use when traveling with . . . um, a companion. And ask for the manager . . . he recognized me, no doubt."

"You would have saved us a lot of time had you just told us outright," Verlaque answered.

"Like I say, I forget." Dottore Rocchia's Italian accent was suddenly thicker, and his French worse, as if he were blaming his imprecision on the language barrier. "The manager at the Hôtel des Anglais knows me, so don't you worry."

"I'm not worried, Dottore. And are you sure you were in Perugia with your wife, and not your, um, companion, last Friday night?"

Rocchia laughed. "Yes, Judge, I was at home that night. Let

me give you our home phone number . . . I've told my wife to expect your call."

Verlaque took down the number, remembering what Florence Bonnet had told her daughter—that the Rocchia marriage was one of convenience. He would call anyway and get the answer he knew he would get. "Thank you, Dottore," he said before hanging up.

"My pleasure."

Verlaque was about to dial the Perugia number when his phone rang in his hand. "*Oui*," he answered.

"Judge Verlaque?" a quiet but hoarse voice asked.

"Yes. Is this Maître Fabre?"

"Yes, Judge. As I was falling asleep last night, I remembered something that Georges told me about that town in Umbria. I'm not sure it will help, but . . . I don't have much else to do these days."

Verlaque got up and began walking around his office. "Go on, Maître."

"Georges told me that the town had a wonderful medieval museum, housed in a palace right on the main square. He was most impressed with their collection, given the town isn't well-known, so you can rule out Assisi, Todi, and Orvieto." The old man held the phone away as he coughed.

"That's a great help, Maître Fabre. Thank you."

"You're welcome."

Verlaque hung up and dialed Marine's number, hoping that she was between classes.

"*Oui*," Marine answered on the third ring.

"Can you talk? It's me."

"Yes, I'm having a coffee between classes. What's going on?"

"Could you ask your mother about towns in Umbria? We're

now looking for a town that has a quite good medieval museum—
that was her specialty, no?—in an old palace on the town square.
And it's not a touristy town at all. You've been to Umbria too, with
Sylvie, hunting down Annunciation paintings, haven't you?"

"Yes," Marine answered, chewing a piece of croissant. "But we
didn't have much time, so we only went to Assisi. And we bought
those cappuccino cups that you love, in Deruta. I'll call my mom
straightaway. And we still think the town begins with an 'F,'
right?"

"Yes, let's go with the maître's hunch. Thanks!"

Verlaque hung up and sat back down at his desk and dialed the
Rocchia residence. After speaking in very bad Italian to someone
he assumed was a young maid, he was put on the phone with an
older woman. He introduced himself and apologized for his
Italian, and Signora Rocchia laughed. "It's charming, Judge. My
English is better than my French, so I'd prefer to speak in English
if that's all right with you."

"English was my grandmother's language, so that's fine with
me," Verlaque answered in English. "I don't get much of a chance
to use it in Aix, except to give directions to lost tourists."

"Ah! Same with me in Perugia! I studied at the London School
of Economics many years ago. My student days are long over, but
my English, thankfully, has stayed with me." Signora Rocchia
then paused before asking, "You're calling to confirm my husband's alibi, yes?"

"Yes, Signora. We need to confirm everyone's whereabouts
on Friday evening." Judging by the conversation so far, Signora
Rocchia was obviously more refined than her husband. If she was
the same age as Giuseppe, that meant she would have attended
LSE sometime in the 1960s, when few Italian women went to
university, let alone a world-renowned one.

Signora Rocchia hesitated for the briefest of seconds before answering. "He was here, Judge."

Verlaque closed his eyes in disappointment. He had hoped that Signora Rocchia would have had a sudden change of heart, that her husband's well-known philandering would finally be acknowledged and challenged by her.

"He was here," she repeated. "But I was not."

Verlaque jumped up out of his chair just as Mme Girard knocked and came into his office. He shooed her away with his hand and pointed to the phone.

"I beg your pardon, Signora? Where were you?"

"I was at my family home on the Ligurian coast, near Lerici, closing it up for the winter. Last winter we had mudslides and the village road was closed for weeks." Verlaque thought of Lerici's orange and red buildings and its swaying palm trees. He had spent many vacations near Lerici, in a village just a few kilometers east.

"You realize you are going against your husband's word, Signora."

"Yes, I do," she answered, and then laughed. "And as Clark Gable once said, 'Frankly, I don't give a damn.'"

Verlaque threw a clenched fist into the air. "And how do you know that your husband was at home, Signora?"

"Our maid . . . she was the one who answered the phone . . . told me."

"Has your maid been with you a long time?" he asked.

"Do you mean to ask if I trust her?"

"Yes, Signora."

"I'm not sure if I trust her, she hasn't been working for us that long. My husband hired her, probably because of her breast size." Signora Rocchia laughed but Verlaque could hear that it was forced. He looked out of the window at a rare gray Aix sky and imagined a young Italian woman in 1960s London, with books under her arm, laughing.

"Thank you for your honesty, Signora."

Signora Rocchia stifled what he thought sounded like a sob, but continued talking. "Telling you the truth was easier than I imagined it would be," she said, sniffing. "Speaking in English helps, somehow."

"I may have to call you again, or the prosecutor here in Aix will. You understand that, don't you, Signora?"

She breathed so deeply that Verlaque could hear it on the other end of the phone. "Yes, of course, but . . . I may not . . . be here. Let me give you my sister's phone number in Rome . . . I may be there, or she'll at least be able to tell you where I am. I've just realized that my future plans are somewhat . . . up in the air, as they say in English. Do you have a pen?"

Verlaque took down the number and thanked her once more. "I'll keep you abreast of any developments or decisions we'll be making in the case."

"I'd appreciate that, Judge."

"Signora? Good luck with everything."

Verlaque walked out of his office, hungry for lunch but more desperate for a coffee. "I'm sorry about that, Mme Girard. I was on the phone with Dottore Rocchia's wife."

"My apologies, Judge, I walked in a bit too quickly. I just wanted to remind you that tomorrow is a holiday."

"Ah! The eleventh of November. Thank you, Madame, I had forgotten. Would you care for an espresso? I'm about to make one for myself."

Mme Girard stood up, straightening her tight skirt. "No thank you, Judge. I'm on my way to meet my husband for lunch."

Verlaque smiled, thinking of himself and Marine, and now

Jean-Marc and Pierre, and the Girards, who after thirty-plus years of marriage and three children still enjoyed regularly scheduled lunches together. "Pass my greetings on to M. Girard," he said. There was hope in the world. Perhaps Signora Rocchia would discover love in Rome, or on Lerici's Bay of Poets, under the bright pink and red bougainvillea flowers and near Byron and Shelley's beloved green-blue sea. Perhaps she already had.

Chapter Thirty-two

The Bay of Poets

"The hotel manager in San Remo recognized Rocchia," Paulik told Verlaque as they were eating their sandwiches.

"He could have been paid off," Verlaque suggested.

"I thought that too, so I made a few more inquiries—well, Officer Cazal did, since she speaks a bit of Italian. The hotel's barman recognized Rocchia from television too, as did the parking valet, who has all of Rocchia's books."

"*Merde.*" Verlaque looked over the counter at Fanny, the owner of one of his favorite restaurants in Aix, a small sandwich shop that served the best lunches in town and was a two-minute walk from his office. "Fanny, where do you buy your *pan-bagnats*?" he asked.

"Professional secret, but I've tried every baker in town and finally settled on this one."

Verlaque was eating the New Yorker sandwich, made with diced hamburger and onions and drizzled with olive oil on a thick bun. "I love this kind of place," he said to Paulik. "It's small, clean, and she uses such great products. I could just do without the students and the ladies from the passport office up the street."

"Hey, they need to eat too," Paulik answered, looking around. He recognized a woman who had been particularly rude to Hélène when she had needed to renew her passport in a hurry to attend a wine conference in California. It was one of the only times he had ever used his commissioner badge when not working. "Okay, the students can stay, but you're right about the passport ladies."

They finished up, paid for their lunch, and walked back to the Palais de Justice. Mme Girard was already at her desk, and she motioned with a tilt of her head at Thierry Marchive, Yann Falquerho, and Annie Leonetti, who were sitting in the small waiting area between her office and Verlaque's.

"Dr. Leonetti is waiting to see you, sir," Mme Girard said. Verlaque nodded and waved Dr. Leonetti to come into the office with him. He held out his hand and thanked her for coming.

"What's this all about?" she asked, more curious than aggressive. "I had to cancel a class to come here, and the students are already worried and shaken up over the two deaths at their faculty."

"I'll get right to the point then, Dr. Leonetti. I'd like to know what you were doing at the crime scene on Saturday morning. The maid told us during our interviews that she saw you go into Dr. Moutte's office before the ambulance arrived."

"I didn't know then that it was a crime scene, Judge. I was at school to get some work done. My husband was at home with the kids, and my youngest was in bed with a cold, so he couldn't take them to the park as he usually does. I can't read or write when they're in the apartment. So I went to school."

Verlaque and Paulik stayed silent, and so Dr. Leonetti flushed and sat down. "I heard the commotion . . . . the maid screaming . . .

from the hallway and went on in. You need to understand that I didn't know at that point that Georges had been murdered. I thought he had had a heart attack or something."

Verlaque stared at Dr. Leonetti. "Why did you go into his office?"

"To see if he really was . . . dead."

"Why didn't you tell us this during the interviews? Did you take something from the office?"

Annie Leonetti rubbed her hands together. "I've never been a good liar, so I thought if I said nothing it would be better. I needed to get something before anyone else got it, or it would be lost in that chaos of the ambulance guys coming in."

"I'll need more of an explanation, Dr. Leonetti."

"All right," she answered, sighing. "Just the day before, Georges had been showing off the Dumas folder to me, waving it around in my face but not showing me the contents. He said that it contained the name of the fellowship's recipient, and after we talked for a few minutes I saw him put it on his desk. That Saturday morning, with Georges dead and the maid hysterical, I thought I could slip in and fetch the folder before the ambulance attendants showed up."

"And did you find what you were looking for?"

Dr. Leonetti looked down. "Yes, on the floor of his office. I have the file in my briefcase, right here." She opened her briefcase, a battered satchel of worn light brown leather, and pulled out a manila folder. She handed it to Verlaque. "I didn't want Bernard to get ahold of it. He was fiercely competitive, and I don't trust his assistant, Claude. I was worried he, or Bernard, would change the recipient's name." Verlaque made a mental note of Annie Leonetti's mistrust of Bernard and Claude. It was easy, in times like this, to try to pin the guilt on someone else.

"Would Dr. Moutte have typed this?" Paulik asked, looking at a page with Verlaque.

Annie Leonetti laughed. "Georges! He couldn't type to save his life." Dr. Leonetti realized her faux pas immediately. "Sorry . . . Mlle Zacharie typed everything for him."

"And winning the Dumas is really that important?" Verlaque asked. "The boys broke into a building to try to find this, and you were desperate to get it as well."

"I wouldn't say I was desperate, *cher Juge*. But winning this fellowship is, yes, a big deal. It's a rare thing at a French university. The recipient has their postdoctorate funded and they get a free apartment in the same building as Georges. Employment afterward is almost guaranteed, and with the unemployment rates in France, not to mention for theologians, you can imagine the importance of this in a young person's life." Her speech, and pride in the fellowship, was almost word for word the same as Florence Bonnet's.

"And you didn't change the name when you found the file?" Verlaque asked.

"No. You can see Georges's signature right there," she said, pointing to the doyen's shaky signature, done with a fountain pen. And then she smiled, wide and fullmouthed. "I didn't have to change the name, Judge Verlaque. The Dumas goes to my assistant, fair and square, the quiet and steady Garrigue."

Verlaque, although happy for Garrigue, thought of the two students who were sitting outside his office, unaware that neither of them would win the Dumas. How pointless all the trouble they were in had been. He thanked Annie Leonetti for coming, still angry at her dishonesty. She left without her large smile, but quickly and quietly.

"Come in," Verlaque said to the young men as he stood at the door to his office.

Paulik brought in another chair from the waiting room and motioned for the students to sit down.

"I'll stand, if that's okay with you," Yann Falquerho said. "I'm too nervous to sit, and this entire thing is all my fault."

"Go ahead then," Verlaque said. "I'll sit and digest my lunch while you explain yourself."

Yann looked at his friend and then the judge. "I should have told you about Brittany, I'm so sorry. It's just that since my dad's friend didn't press charges . . ."

"You thought we might not find out about it," Paulik finished his sentence.

"Yes, basically. But what that policeman didn't tell your prosecutor dude . . ."

Verlaque cut in. "Prosecutor Roussel."

"Yeah, him, was that that night, which was many years ago, I was with the toughies of the town, you know, the townies, the guys who live there all year round, and I was trying to be cool. They showed me how to hot-wire the car, but I was hardly paying attention, I was so scared, and I'm sure I couldn't do it now, even if desperate."

"Thierry?" Verlaque asked.

"We found Dr. Moutte together, as we said. He was already dead, and the night that Mlle Zacharie was hit by a car we were at home together, studying. It's only November, and we have a whole year ahead of us. Despite the fact that two people have been killed, we still have to study."

Verlaque nodded and thought to himself that this was the first time anyone was speaking some sense since the death of Dr. Moutte. Thierry and Signora Rocchia spoke sense, and he believed them.

"And I thought of something else," Thierry continued. "Another friend called us that night, really late, wanting to know if we would meet him at a pub. We didn't go, we were too tired, but he spoke to both of us, if that helps."

"Give us his name and number. What time was it, Thierry?"

Thierry looked at Yann, who shrugged. "I think it was around 1:00 a.m., because we both jumped when the phone rang and commented on how it was after midnight," Thierry answered. "Listen, Judge, I know how serious all this is, I've even spoken to a priest about it . . ."

"You did? Which one?" Yann asked.

"Père Jean-Luc."

"Boys? Could we stay on topic?" Paulik asked.

"Sorry. I spoke to Père Jean-Luc because I feel so terrible. I know what we did was wrong, breaking into the school, but that's all we did. I swear," Thierry said. Yann finally sat down, exhausted.

The office door opened and Yves Roussel walked in. "Well. Did you two confess yet? It would save us all a lot of time."

"We didn't kill anyone!" Yann said, and then fell back in his chair.

"You both can leave now," Verlaque said, looking at Thierry and Yann. "Leave your friend's name and number with Commissioner Paulik." His cell phone buzzed with a text message and he glanced down at it, seeing it was from Marine. "Foligno, Umbria." He looked at the time, 2:30.

Paulik left with the two students and Roussel sat down across from Verlaque. "What if they kill someone else? The little Marseillais was shaking in his boots."

"Yves, come off it." Verlaque stood up and grabbed his jacket off of the coatrack. "I saw no such thing. I'm going to Umbria. Now."

"What? On a Thursday night?" Roussel asked as Verlaque gently led him out of the office.

"Tomorrow's November the eleventh. It's a long weekend for us, but not for the Italians. I've done the drive before; it's nine hours, including quick stops. Here . . ." Before Roussel could argue, Verlaque had handed the prosecutor the bags of mushrooms and locked the door to his office. Yves Roussel walked down the hall, his footsteps getting quicker as he looked through each bag. It wasn't too late—he still had time to call his wife before she began making their Thursday night dinner. Later in the afternoon he could slip out to his butcher's shop on the place des Prêcheurs and buy two *poires*, his favorite cut of beef. He had a Saint-Émilion Grand Cru in the cellar he had been saving; but what was the occasion?

Marine sat at her dining room table with a stack of papers to grade in front of her, with those essays written by her more promising and dedicated students on top. She had made a pot of green tea, whose health benefits she had read about but whose taste she still hadn't come to love. Next time, she thought, better to make a pot of Earl Grey, which took her back to her student days in Paris, and she at least liked its taste. Every few months she went off coffee for a few days, swayed by reports of its dangers to one's health. She put her pen down and thought of her trips to Italy, and how the Italians, or the French for that matter, despite a large daily intake of espresso, didn't seem unhealthy. On the contrary. Tomorrow morning, she knew, she would go back to her old ways and sit in her armchair, hugging a cup of strong coffee and reading the front page of *Le Monde*.

She forced herself to grade one paper and then took a stroll around the living room, dusting off Sylvie's framed photographs with a tissue she had in her pocket. She could no longer afford to buy her friend's photos; they went off to wealthy collectors in London and Zurich. As she straightened one of the photographs—

an eerily gloomy black-and-white of a church in northern Spain—
she thought of Antoine. He had called out in his sleep that night,
and had very clearly said the words "You're dead, Monique." It was
not the first time he had done so, but last night's words were very
clear, not the usual nonsensical mumblings made by someone still
asleep. His bad dream was as gloomy as Sylvie's fuzzy church,
where dark clouds swept across the sky and the foreground was
barren, reminding the viewer that this country church, once the
most important building for miles around, was now abandoned,
no longer necessary, even unwanted.

"All these things left unsaid," Marine said aloud. She had
grown up with dark clouds, and as a child had been confused
those times when her mother wouldn't come out of her room and
her father escaped to the garden, sneaking cigarettes that Marine
knew he hid in the toolshed. The reasons why were explained to
her on her thirteenth birthday, as if this knowledge was a gift
for her newly acquired stature as an adolescent. Ten years before
Marine was born she had had a brother, Thomas, who died of
crib death when he was four months old. There had never been
any sign of him in the house, nor would there ever be. At four
months Charlotte had already been a full being, with hints of the
same funny personality that she now had at ten. Marine couldn't
imagine her parents' grief, and because of it she always felt like
she was walking on eggshells around them, never knowing when
the memories of Thomas would come back, sending her normally
stiff mother off moaning to her bedroom. Sylvie had suggested on
more than one occasion to Marine that perhaps her parents, and
maybe even Marine herself, should seek counseling, but Marine
knew that her parents would never agree to such a thing. Her
father, a doctor, prided himself on never actually having to go
to one; and her mother was keenly aware of and sensitive about

the price the French taxpayer paid for a doctor's visit, let alone what a visit to *le psy* would cost.

Marine walked back to the table, took a sip of tea, and looked out of the window at Saint-Jean-de-Malte's steeple. How bad could Antoine's secret be, she thought. She looked at the church and thought of the centuries of pain and happiness it had seen, thousands of weddings and funerals and baptisms. Surely she could speak to Antoine about his demons, if that was even what the bad dreams were. Once in Cannes, late at night, he had tried to talk to her about his past, and then the phone rang, and the moment was gone. He loved her, he had made his declaration, and she was now determined to ask him about it, what Charlotte called "those sad-bad things." She looked at her watch. It was 3:30 p.m.; she had lots of time to finish her grading and then as a reward walk over to Sylvie and Charlotte's for a glass of wine. Sylvie was still angry at Antoine, and although Marine had originally defended her best friend, she understood Antoine's masculine point of view too, as Sylvie had never given Charlotte's father a chance to be just that—her father. Gustav was a photographer from Berlin, married, with two children who now must be in their twenties. Sylvie had never returned his letters, and he had no knowledge of Charlotte's existence. Marine had suggested to Sylvie that this had been perhaps an unfair—even egotistical— move on Sylvie's part, and Sylvie had responded to Marine's suggestion that she write to Gustav with a weeklong silence. Since then Marine and Sylvie kept their conversations to nonconfrontational subjects: Charlotte, the changing face of Aix-en-Provence, French politics, art and music, general gossip, and books (Marine was currently reading a French translation of a laugh-out-loud novel by David Lodge, where the petty office politics of a university located in a small English city very much reflected those of her own school; Sylvie was rereading Simone de Beauvoir's *Les Mandarins*).

Marine had just finished correcting the second essay when the phone rang. She didn't recognize the caller's number and hesitated before answering; she sometimes had multiple calls a day telling her she had won a set of porcelain or crystal, all she had to do was to answer some questions . . .

"*Allô?*" she said, sounding as angry as she could.

"Marine? It's Annie Leonetti. I hope I didn't disturb you."

"Oh! Annie, hello. I was afraid you were going to be someone trying to sell me something I don't need or want. Sorry."

Annie Leonetti laughed and revealed that she too averaged two sales calls a day. "But I *am* trying to sell you something," she said, "in a way, at least. I really enjoyed your comments during our lectures. I'm in the middle of a book on Sainte Dévote, as you may know, and need some of your legal history advice. Could I tempt you to dinner some night next week?"

"I'd be delighted," Marine answered just as a knock was heard at her apartment door. "Next week then! Someone's at my front door!" she said as she hung up, suddenly wondering if there were other intentions behind Annie Leonetti's invite. She walked into the front hall and opened her door to see her mother. "Some kid downstairs let me in the building. They ought to be more careful," Florence Bonnet said, kissing her daughter.

"Come in. You hardly look like a thief, Maman."

"What's that supposed to mean? Are you being racist?"

Marine was shocked. "No, Maman! What I meant was female senior citizens wearing raincoats from the seventies usually don't fit the profile." Marine immediately regretted what she had said about her mother's lack of fashion sense, but Florence Bonnet was so unaware of fashion that the comment went unnoticed.

"Well, I suppose you're right. Listen, I don't have much time as I'm late for a meeting at Saint-Jean-de-Malte—we're finally buying a new organ and are having a brainstorming session on how to raise money. Someone actually suggested that we sell wine, red *and* rosé, with a drawing of the church on the bottle! Can you believe it?"

Marine cut in. "It sounds like a great idea. I'd buy the wine, as would all my friends!"

"Well, I'm not here to discuss the church," her mother said, looking at her daughter, who was in turn thinking, But you're the one who started the conversation about Saint–Jean-de-Malte. "I still haven't heard from Judge Verlaque about that dossier I gave you."

Marine frowned. "I'm so sorry, Maman! I only showed it to Antoine last night." Marine wished that she could confide in her mother the way Sylvie did with hers. She wanted to tell her that Antoine—yes, he had a Christian name, although her mother never used it—loved her; he had finally declared his love. "I'll ask Antoine about it this evening, I promise," Marine said.

"If you would," her mother said, turning to go. "As I told you the other day, someone has embezzled all the funds. Now I ask you, whom? I don't trust anyone anymore."

Marine's cell phone began to ring and she kissed her mother and tried not to push her out of the door. "When it rains it pours," Marine muttered and picked up the phone.

"It's a long weekend and I miss Italy," Verlaque said as Marine answered. "I owe you a long weekend. There's work involved, but it is Italy . . ."

"Sounds great!" Marine screeched. "My mother was just here, asking about the file. We'll talk in the car. I'll go and pack my bag, and yes, I have to bring along grading. Are we going to Umbria by any chance?"

"Affirmative. I'll pick you up in the car in a half hour? Can you be ready?"

"I'm packing as we speak."

After six hours of highway driving and dozens of tunnels, they were finally close to their overnight stop. They had left Aix just before 4:00 p.m. and had been driving continuously, stopping only to switch drivers and drink a quick espresso. "Talking to Signora Rocchia on the phone reminded me of this little village at the end of a dead-end road on the sea," Verlaque said as he directed Marine off of the highway and through a valley that led to Lerici and the coast. "I think her family house may be in the same village."

"Do you want to see her?" Marine asked.

"Oh no, she closed up the house for the winter. But there's this great small hotel, with a fabulous restaurant, that my grandparents loved. They started going in the early sixties, and then in the seventies took me and Sébastien. It was a real family affair, with mama up front in the hotel and papa in the kitchen. The decor was really classy 1960s Capri-style: lots of bright color, handmade ceramics, lots of Murano glass." It now occurred to Verlaque that perhaps the hotel had been sold, or at least the decor changed, the golds and bright greens, blues and purples thrown out in favor of beige.

When they reached the top of the hill, the town of Lerici spread out before them, with its medieval castle guarding the town at the eastern tip and the sailboats bobbing up and down in the water. "The Bay of Poets," Verlaque said. "The poet Shelley died here, just shy of his thirtieth birthday. He had gone out for an afternoon sail around the bay. The sea here is incredibly rough for such a peaceful place, Sébastien and I used to get freaked out by the waves." Verlaque pointed to the sign for the village, another four kilometers along the sea. "Just follow the signs. Actually, pull over and I'll drive from here . . . I want you to have the view."

Marine squealed in delight as they drove along the road,

sometimes from awe at the view of the sparkling sea, sometimes from fear of the road's sheer drop into the sea. At the entrance to the village, Verlaque pulled the car over in front of a small yellow hotel and turned off the ignition. "Here it is," he said. "Let's hope the same family still owns it."

They walked in arm and arm, and a young man in his midthirties with thick black curly hair greeted them. Verlaque asked in English if they had a room, and Marine wandered around, looking at the varied collection of paintings and prints and Italian ceramics that adorned the small lobby. The young man informed Verlaque that they did have a room, with a sea view, that included breakfast at 9:00 a.m. sharp. Verlaque looked at the man, who was dressed in what looked like California surfer attire, and finally said, "Alessandro?"

"Sì."

"It's me, Antoine. Emmeline and Charles Verlaque's grandson. We used to come here, with my brother, in the seventies. You were just a kid, about seven or so."

The man slapped his forehead and came around the desk, embracing Verlaque and calling to the kitchen. "Mamma! Papà! È Antoine Verlaque! Il nipote d'Emmeline e Charles!"

An elderly couple hurried out of the kitchen, the father, gray haired with a big handlebar mustache, wiping his hands on his white apron. "Salve!"

They embraced Verlaque. "Is this Mme Verlaque?" the signora asked, looking at Marine.

Marine laughed. "I'm his girlfriend," she answered in Italian. "And sometimes we work together."

The signora said something else in Italian and Verlaque looked to Marine for a translation. "The signora says that she misses your grandmother," Marine said.

Verlaque smiled and said, "Grazie."

"Are you a lawyer, Antoine? You always wanted to be one," Alessandro asked.

"Yes. A judge, actually."

Alessandro translated for his parents and his father whistled.

"And this is Dottore Bonnet, my girlfriend," Verlaque continued. "She's a law professor, who, as you noticed, speaks very good Italian."

"*Permesso,*" the father said as he took Marine by the arm and led her into the kitchen, which, from what Verlaque could see through the open door, hadn't changed since he was a boy. In the middle of the room stood a surface used for rolling pasta that was simply an old wooden table covered in Carrara white marble, and above it hung copper pots, and all along the sides green-painted wooden cabinets held dozens of mismatched earthenware.

"And Séb?" asked Alessandro, who had one eye on the kitchen and Marine. "What's he up to? He wanted to be a doctor when we were kids."

"Ah, he's a real estate mogul."

Alessandro winced. "Don't mention that in front of my parents," he answered. "They've been trying all their lives to protect this little bit of coast."

"They're right to do so," Verlaque said. "By the way, your English is fantastic."

"Thanks. I've learnt it entirely from our Anglo clients. And our elementary school teacher in the village, she was nuts for it." Alessandro stood back and reached out his arms. "'Nothing of him that doth fade / But doth suffer a sea-change / Into something rich and strange.'"

"Wonderful!" Verlaque exclaimed. "Shelley?"

"Good guess. It's Shakespeare, from *The Tempest*, but it was engraved on Shelley's grave."

"Well done!" Verlaque said. Taking Alessandro aside, he whispered, so that the diners couldn't hear, "Does Giuseppe Rocchia, the television theology guru, have a summer house here?"

Alessandro nodded. "His wife does, it's been in her family for years. It's at the bottom of the via D. H. Lawrence."

Verlaque laughed. "I had forgotten that the streets are named for the English writers who loved it here. Do you know Signora Rocchia well?"

"Sure I do. She eats here almost once a week when she's at the house, and she and Mamma share gardening tips. They're great friends."

"Is she a woman of her word?" Verlaque asked. "I mean, do you trust her?"

"On my life," Alessandro answered without hesitating.

"Thank you. I'll put our bags in our room, if I may, and have a quick shower before dinner. You can send Marine up when your parents are through with their tour."

"Sure thing. Papà adores French women, and one who speaks Italian, well . . ."

Verlaque took the bags and the room key, started up the stairs, and turned back when he was halfway up. He surveyed the entry, thankful that not a thing had been touched. There was color and warmth everywhere. "Hey Alessandro. Does your father still make those deep-fried cod fritters as a starter?"

"Yep. They're on tonight's menu."

"Heaven help me."

Chapter Thirty-three

❧

Flying Bits of Color

"*T*he bed and breakfast where I stayed with Sylvie and Charlotte was around here, I recognize this road," Marine said as she flattened the map on her knees and looked out the window at the green rolling hills just south of Assisi. "It was owned by this guy, Piero, whom Sylvie was convinced was Saint Francis of Assisi reincarnated."

Verlaque puffed on an 898, which he usually smoked when he was alone because although he loved its flavor he didn't like the look of a man of his thick build holding a long, thin, delicate-looking cigar. He stole a glance at Marine and smiled. "Why? Piero liked animals?"

"Oh yes, he loved animals, but it wasn't only that. Piero had given up his fast-paced life in Rome to move to the country, just as Saint Francis had given up his soldiering and lofty inheritance. Both their mothers were French, from Provence . . ."

"Really?"

"Yes, weird coincidence, eh? And there were animals, dozens of them. Piero had this huge walk-in birdcage that Charlotte loved, but it freaked Sylvie and me out. He called the birds 'flying bits of color.' He had this otherworldliness to him." She looked at the landscape that was still very green but had suddenly turned flat. "According to the map we should be in Foligno any minute."

Once in Foligno they parked their car in the small downtown, beside a short, squat, red-stoned Romanesque church. "Just a quick peek!" Marine said as she hopped out of the car and ran into the church. Verlaque went up to the parking meter and by the time he had figured out how to use it and fumbled in his pockets, and then in the car, for change, Marine was back.

"Did you find an Annunciation?" he asked.

"Yes! And Mary was beaming! Really, really happy!" Marine put her arm through Verlaque's and they walked toward the imposing duomo, built from a pale pink stone.

"If we find this art museum on the main square we can ask to speak to a curator or the director about a glassworks around here," Verlaque said.

"You'll have to buy me lunch first. Mamma's fresh-squeezed orange juice and chocolate-filled croissant was a long time ago."

"I don't know how you could have eaten that croissant," Verlaque said, squeezing Marine's arm and bringing her close to him so that a cyclist could pass. "Leave it to the Italians to take something that's perfectly fine and then stuff it full of gooey chocolate."

"And then sprinkle sugar on top! You missed out, darling."

Verlaque laughed and looked at his watch. "It's 1:15, so everyone at the museum will be at lunch. Best we do the same, but let's just order one dish, not the full menu."

They walked onto the main square and looked up at the cathedral in wonder. To the left was a museum, the building marked as the Palazzo Trinci. It was indeed closed for lunch and would reopen at 3:00 p.m. "Okay, let's do a tour of the restaurants," Verlaque said.

Marine turned to grab Verlaque's hand, but he was already walking toward the other side of the square. He stopped to look at a menu that a restaurant had posted next to their front door. "A restaurant on the main square? Aren't you breaking Antoine's rule number one?" she asked as she got to his side.

Verlaque took her hand and led her away. "You're right. Let's get off the square."

Marine rubbed her stomach. "I'm going to sit down on that bench over there, beside the old lady, while you find us a restaurant. I know you'll be fussy about music and plastic chairs, and I'm too hungry to care about those things right now."

"Give me five minutes," Verlaque said.

They left the restaurant at 3:30 p.m. "I'm so full I can hardly walk," Marine complained halfheartedly, laughing. Indeed, they had ordered the five-dish tasting menu, which ended up being seven dishes, the restaurant's owner thrilled by their enthusiasm and Marine's beauty. Once sitting down at a table that was located beside the bar—lined with local wines and a collection of restaurant guidebooks—Marine had reasoned that it was financially wiser to order the tasting menu than à la carte, while Verlaque claimed that he wanted everything on that day's menu anyway, so ordering the set menu made things easier.

The palazzo was a fabulous medieval palace that had been restored with the help, by the looks of it, of a contemporary architect from Milan or Rome: large glass doors filled in the archways, and the lighting was sleek and discrete. Marine spoke to a bored-looking woman at the front desk and, announcing that she was with a French judge, asked to see the museum's director.

"She's really angry that we didn't phone first," Marine said as she joined Verlaque on a leather bench.

Verlaque looked around at the long hallway in front of them

and the exhibition room at the end of it, both empty of people. "Yeah, this place is really busy. She might have to get up off her ass and do something."

Marine sighed, not wanting one of his anti–civil servant rampages. What she really wanted to do was to lie flat on the bench and close her eyes. She leaned her head against Verlaque's shoulder and was just falling asleep when she heard voices and felt a nudge. A tall, thin man with gray hair that was a tad too long stood before them with his hand outstretched. "Good afternoon," he said in perfect French. "I am Dottore Camorro. Sorry to have kept you waiting. Please come with me." Verlaque glanced at Marine and wondered if she was thinking the same thing: that considering they had come to the Dottore unannounced, he was more than polite. He led them into his upstairs office, every bit as minimalist as the downstairs had been. He gestured to two black leather chairs. "Please, sit down."

"Thank you for meeting with us, Dottore," Verlaque said. "I am the examining magistrate of Aix-en-Provence, and this is Dr. Marine Bonnet of the University of Aix. We are here, on very short notice I'm afraid, to investigate some potential leads we have concerning the murder of one of Dr. Bonnet's colleagues, a Dr. Moutte."

The museum director frowned and nodded up and down. "You'll have to go on, Judge. I'm afraid I've never heard of this man."

"We're here, essentially, because Dr. Moutte collected art glass, and we know that he visited Foligno, possibly more than once."

"Ah, I see," replied Camorro, rubbing his long hands together, which Marine noticed were trembling slightly.

"We found in the deceased's apartment, among some rare and expensive French blown glass, some obvious fakes that were perhaps made here. Do you know of such a place in or near Foligno?"

Dottore Camorro shrugged. "No, not in Foligno. Surely Venice would be the place for glass studios, Judge."

"That's what we thought, but we know that Dr. Moutte was here, in Foligno."

Camorro looked from Verlaque to Marine and again shrugged. "I'm sorry I cannot help you. And now, you'll have to excuse me. I have a meeting in ten minutes that I must prepare for." The director stood up and shook hands with Marine and Verlaque.

"Thank you," Marine said as she shook his hand. "This is a beautiful building," she added. "Have you been the director here for very long?"

"Ah, for ten years, Dr. Bonnet. I'm glad you like the renovations. They took four long years to complete."

"It's lovely."

Verlaque held the door open for Marine as they left the museum and walked out onto the square, which was slowly getting dark. "I don't understand," Verlaque said. "You'd think that he would know of the glass studio. Maître Fabre's information must have been wrong, poor old guy."

"Oh, there's a glass studio here, all right," Marine answered, stopping in the middle of the square. "And I also think that if we were to slowly turn around we would see Dottore Camorro watching us from the plate glass windows of his sleek office. Who has better eyesight?"

"You do. I'll sweep you in my arms and kiss you, and you look over my shoulder at his office." Verlaque took Marine in his arms and kissed the side of her head. She whispered into his ear. "Bingo. He was there, clear as day. He's gone now."

Verlaque took her arm and they walked away. "How did you know all this?" he asked.

"That old woman on the bench."

"What?"

"I asked her if there was a glass studio in Foligno, and said that I was tired of majolica pottery and that I wanted to buy glass. She said that there's a glass studio outside of town on the way to Bevagna, and that her great-nephew even worked there for a short time, but he left because it was *sporco*."

Verlaque looked at her with his eyebrows raised.

"Dirty," Marine answered. "In the sense of dishonest, judging from her expression."

"Why didn't you tell me this before we met Camorro?"

"Because I didn't want it to influence your questions."

Verlaque put his arm around her shoulder. "Well done, Dr. Bonnet! Is that why you asked him how long he's been the museum's director?"

"Yes. Ten years is a long time and this is a small town. Surely he'd know of a glass factory just outside of town. Let's get to the car and drive by the place."

Verlaque stopped. "They'll see our French license plates. He's probably called them to warn them that we'll be driving around Foligno snooping. What a great guy to have on your side, right? A museum director would be able to instruct them on how to design perfect-looking antique glass."

It was Marine's turn to pull Verlaque toward her as another cyclist, an old man with his front basket full of cabbages, whizzed past them. "I've never seen so many cyclists in an Italian town," she said. "It must be because it's so flat." She then ruffled Verlaque's hair and added, "And I know just how we're going to get around. Come on!"

Chapter Thirty-four

❧

Hot Chocolate

*B*runo Paulik walked up the cours Mirabeau to meet his wife and daughter for a coffee. It was already getting dark, and it was still a half-hour drive before they would be home in Pertuis. Each winter they questioned their decision to have enrolled Léa in a school in Aix. But in Pertuis there wasn't a music conservatory that had a public school next door, where gifted students could float between their academic subjects and music classes, all paid for by the state. It was rare that the three of them could meet in Aix—even though it was a holiday, Hélène had attended a local winemakers' meeting downtown and Léa had had a voice lesson—and he quickened his step, happy to be with his girls. Tomorrow was Saturday and they had no commute and could sleep in.

The double rows of plane trees that lined the *cours* had lost their leaves, leaving white knobby-kneed skeletons, and the street-lights had come on, illuminating the golden-stoned mansions. As

Paulik crossed the rue 4 du Septembre, he looked down toward Georges Moutte's apartment and thought about the break and enter. Of his suspects, he thought Rocchia and Leonetti unable to swing themselves into the apartment from the roof; but each one of the students could have, including Garrigue . . . and what did they know of her, anyway? Who were her parents? And the other students, for that matter? And Bernard Rodier, who was in good shape . . . he had told them during questioning that he played squash regularly. Paulik resolved to check into their backgrounds more thoroughly tomorrow.

"Papa!" Léa squealed when she saw Paulik come across Le Mazarin's heated terrace. "I'm having an enormous hot chocolate!"

He kissed his daughter and wife and ordered a coffee.

"Mama's in a bad mood!" Léa added, blowing on her hot chocolate.

Paulik looked toward his wife. "It's true," Hélène answered, sighing. "The meeting was a total waste of time, everyone arguing and talking in circles, and now this!" she said, motioning with her hand at a double-parked souped-up VW Golf.

Léa rolled her eyes and began spooning off the whipped cream and putting it into her mouth. "What's so unusual about that?" Paulik asked, looking toward the car. "Those guys always double-park in front of the cafés. They see it as their right."

"It's so rude! Do they think that they're the only people on the planet? They sit here and sip their Coca-Colas and survey their hot cars. I took twenty minutes trying to find a parking spot!"

"You really hate Coca-Cola, don't you?" Paulik said, teasing his wife.

Hélène Paulik laughed out loud. "You know it!"

"You once gave it to me when I had an upset tummy," Léa said.

"Yes, *once*, dear!" Hélène answered, hugging Léa.

"But I don't feel so well," Léa said, staring at her unfinished hot chocolate.

"I think you started drinking that too quickly," Hélène said. She turned to ask Bruno about his day but he was walking toward the VW. She watched him as he leaned down and looked in the window of the car. A young man wearing a gold jogging suit with a Louis Vuitton shoulder bag jumped up from a table at the edge of the terrace and ran to the car. Hélène watched, amazed, as her husband flashed the young man his police badge. The owner of the poorly parked car ran back to his table, threw down some coins, and went back to his car and drove away.

Léa clapped for her father when he got back to the table. "I can't believe you did that!" Hélène whispered. "Just like you did in the passport office."

"I was just thinking of that yesterday. But your indignation over that double-parked car gave me an idea about the case we're working on." Paulik put a ten-euro bill on the table and hugged Léa. "I'll be home late; eat dinner without me." Before they could protest, he was gone, up the rue Clémenceau toward the Palais de Justice. He stopped in front of a lingerie store and, looking at the lacy pink matching bras and underwear, dialed Verlaque's cell phone number.

"*Oui*?" answered Verlaque, sounding out of breath.

"Sorry to bother you in Italy, sir, but I just had a revelation on the *cours*," said Paulik. He continued quickly, worried that he might be interrupting something between Marine and Verlaque. "You know how those punks always double-park on the *cours* at night, in front of the cafés?"

"Yes, it irritates me to no end," Verlaque said, puffing.

"Think about it for a second," Paulik said. "Where do they leave their keys when they do that?"

Verlaque replied immediately. "In the ignition."

"Right."

"So the punk who stole the BMW in Marseille could have driven it up to Aix and parked it in front of a café, leaving the keys in the ignition while he had a celebratory drink," Verlaque said, thinking out loud.

"Exactly. That's what they'd do, isn't it? Drive up to Aix to show off the car. And Mlle Zacharie's killer could have been in the right place at the right time, seen the car parked there with the keys in it, and driven off."

Verlaque huffed into the phone. "And even if the thief saw the guy . . . or woman . . . drive away, there was nothing he could do about it."

"Right. It was a stolen car. I'm on my way back to the Palais de Justice to try and calm down Roussel a bit. Sorry to have bothered you."

Verlaque coughed and told Paulik what he and Marine were doing.

"You're doing what?" Paulik exclaimed into the phone.

Verlaque repeated what he had said, annoyed. "That's why I'm out of breath," he explained.

"Well, I'll leave you to it, sir," Paulik said, smiling.

Paulik hung up and walked up into the small place Saint-Honoré, deserted at this time of night, the only noise the bubbling fountain. He zigzagged his way through a few more narrow streets until he came to the Palais de Justice and hurried in, hoping to catch Roussel before he went home, Paulik imagined, to watch television with his wife and their yappy little dog. November eleventh was an important date in French history, and he remembered that Roussel had planned to spend the day with the mayor visiting World War I monuments. With luck he would be in his office.

"Yves!" he said as he caught sight of the prosecutor making his way up the stairs.

Roussel turned around. "I'm on my way out, but I forgot something in my office. Have you heard from Judge Verlaque?"

"No," Paulik lied. "But do you have a second to talk about the Moutte case?"

"In my office then," Roussel answered, ushering Paulik into his office and closing the door. "What is it? I told you Rocchia would have an alibi."

"You were right," Paulik answered. He then went on to explain what he had just seen on the *cours*.

"Interesting theory, Bruno. I can see it happening like that. So who doesn't have an alibi for Monday night?" Roussel walked over to a whiteboard and began writing down names with a red Magic Marker. "Bernard Rodier, Claude Ossart, Garrigue Druon . . . and this is assuming that the two murders are related."

"Let's stick with that assumption. Annie Leonetti was at home with her husband; Thierry and Yann were together; and Rocchia was in San Remo," Paulik said. "Mlle Zacharie's boyfriend says he was at home, asleep in front of the television."

"Crimes of passion," Roussel added.

Paulik grabbed his coat and made for the door. "Have a good night, Yves. See you tomorrow." He walked quickly down the hallway and then down the stairs and out into the night. He mused to himself that the closest bar to the Palais de Justice was in fact the rough-and-tumble Bar Zola, and he was there in under two minutes. He pushed his way into the smoky bar—the patrons had long since forgotten the Somme and Ypres—and looked around for an empty table. There weren't any, so he squeezed himself into a spot at the bar next to a kid who looked like an art student—spiked hair and a nose ring, uncertain gender—and was relieved to see the same barman with the poet Rimbaud's verse tattooed on his forearm. The barman nodded when he saw Paulik, and Paulik ordered a pint of Guinness.

"This isn't my preferred genre of music," Paulik said as he waited for his beer to be poured, "but I like it. Good old seventies rock."

The barman looked at Paulik and asked, "So what *is* your preferred *genre* of music?"

Paulik took his beer, said "Cheers" in English, and had a sip. "Opera."

"Good town for it then," the barman answered. He looked again at Paulik and then leaned in closer, resting his forearms on the wooden bar. "That's where I've seen you before."

"You had that feeling too?" Paulik asked. "At the opera festival?"

"*Non, le conservatoire.*"

"Ah! That's it!" Paulik replied, shaking his pointer finger at the barman. "You're one of the other parents, aren't you?"

"I'm sure as hell not a student," the barman said, smiling. "My kid plays the piano."

"He's not Matthieu, is he?" Léa Paulik talked nonstop of a thirteen-year-old pianist who had not only raced through his music exams but was also an ace skateboarder.

"That's him." The barman reached out his hand. "I'm Patrick. Matthieu is the star of the family. My other two kids are total delinquents."

"Bruno, Léa Paulik's father. She sings." They shook hands and the barman asked, frowning, "You're here alone tonight?"

"He's okay once you get to know him," Paulik answered, defending Verlaque.

"If you say so."

"So, did you tell us everything that night?" Paulik asked.

"No. I don't really like cops. No offense. But I was also in shock at the news of Audrey's death, and that you were treating it as a homicide. I was actually going to call you tomorrow; my wife insisted. Should we go downstairs? It's too cold to stand outside."

Paulik took his Guinness with him as they walked to the end of the bar and Patrick opened a small door that led to a flight of stone stairs. "Don't worry," the barman said, smiling. "Nothing down here but cases of booze and perhaps a few odd ghosts." The cellar was damp, with a slight coating of water covering the floor.

"Is it true that all the cellars in Aix used to be connected?" Paulik asked.

"We've never found an opening, but it could have been blocked up decades ago." Patrick took out a cigarette and offered one to Paulik, who refused. "What I didn't tell you is that Audrey came in here a few times before she died with some kid I didn't know," Patrick said.

"Kid?" Paulik asked, trying to hide his concern. Perhaps they had all been snowed by Yann and Thierry.

"Yeah, early twenties, a real nerd. The weird thing was, she seemed freaked out by him—I mean, kind of scared."

Paulik nodded. "Can you describe him to me? Did she introduce you?"

"No, she didn't introduce us, she hid with him in a corner, which rang warning bells too. She always talked to me when she came in, but not when she was with him. Can I describe him, you ask? That's a good question, because I kind of figured you'd be back here, with the posh judge, and I've been racking my brain trying to think of what this kid looked like, but all I can remember is, *nerd*."

"If I bring in some photos, would that help?" Paulik asked.

"Yeah, it might. Come in tomorrow after 4:00 p.m."

"Is he the only person she came in with recently?"

Patrick stubbed out his cigarette on the wet stone floor. "Well, there was one other person, but I don't think you'd be interested in him."

"Why not?"

"He's harmless. He's in a wheelchair."

Chapter Thirty-five

≫

Ex-Votos

"*I*t's so green here, so peaceful. It's easy to imagine Saint Francis in this countryside," Marine said as she stopped at the side of the road to look at a meadow.

Verlaque's bicycle bumped into the back wheel of Marine's. "Warn me when you're going to stop," he complained.

Marine turned around and laughed. "Sorry! Are you all right?"

Verlaque took out a pressed handkerchief and mopped his brow. "I don't know why anyone would choose to go out on one of these things. I can't believe how uncomfortable the seat is."

"We look like tourists, which was the goal, right? Especially you, with that cigar."

They had rented bicycles at a garage that mostly rented out scooters and motorcycles; Marine had spotted it on the way into town. Examining their Michelin map, they had chosen to take the southern route into Bevagna, on a small departmental road instead of the busier S316 that led to Bevagna out of the northwest corner of Foligno. "That old woman on the bench definitely said 'south' of Foligno," Marine said, pointing on the map.

"We can always do a loop and come back on the S316," Verlaque suggested, looking at the map with his reading glasses. He sighed and added, "I can't believe we're doing this. How long would the circuit be, assuming we have to go to Bevagna and back?"

Marine bit her lips as she looked at the map. "About fourteen kilometers." She purposely rounded down the estimate a few kilometers.

"That's around eight or nine miles; doable, but it will be dark when we come back. Well, you lead, dear."

Marine thought it droll that Verlaque, despite being brought up in France, always thought in miles, like an Englishman, for distances. "Just holler if you need to stop," she said, beginning to pedal, and smiling to herself. She turned around when she smelled cigar smoke. "It would be easier if you didn't smoke!"

"It's hard either way, so I'd rather get a little enjoyment out of it."

Marine laughed. "At least we'll look more like tourists with you puffing away."

They rode on, Marine stopping to take photos with a small camera. "Look at the vineyards in the distance," she said at one break. "They're turning red." She pointed at a small steeple peeking up from a thicket of small trees. "A chapel! I know, I know, we don't have time to go in."

Verlaque stopped to catch his breath, thankful that Marine wanted to stop so frequently. His cell phone rang and he answered it, seeing Paulik's number. They spoke for less than a minute and he hung up and told Marine of Paulik's theory of the stolen car.

"It's so much greener than Tuscany, isn't it?" he said, looking around.

Marine took another photograph. "Yes, more like our bit of Provence." She put her camera back in her purse, which was sitting in the bicycle's front basket, and looked ahead, up the narrow road. "There's a lane up ahead on the left, with a little sign," she said. "I'll ride ahead and tell you what it says."

Verlaque nodded and puffed on his cigar, watching Marine ride off and then cross the deserted road. She got to the small wooden sign and then turned around to Verlaque and gave him a thumbs-up. He rode to meet her.

"Vetro Corvia?" he asked, looking down at the sign. "Is 'vetro' what I think it is? Glass?"

"Yes!" Marine exclaimed. "Let's go down the lane a bit."

Verlaque watched Marine in admiration as she led the way. They walked their bikes, hugging the left side of the laneway, and stopped in less than twenty meters. A small concrete-block building with a corrugated metal roof stood in front of them. There was a car parked in front of it, a beat-up older-edition Fiat 500, and a light was on in the building.

"Let's hide behind this toolshed," Verlaque whispered, putting out his cigar. "And hope he, she, or they haven't seen us."

"And I hope they don't smell the smoke!" Marine hissed.

They laid their bikes down in a thicket and crouched down, leaning their backs against the small brick toolshed. Marine looked at the photos she had just taken on her camera, and Verlaque watched the clouds race across the darkening sky. He checked his messages before turning off his cell phone, and there was one from Officer Flamant: "I just met with A. Zacharie's bank manager. Mlle Z made several deposits, each one 5,000 euros, beg in Sept and ending Nov 1. She also made a dep of 10,000 euros Monday afternoon. Tomorrow we're meeting with an accountant from another department who has been called in to help. Best, A. Flamant." Verlaque showed the message to Marine.

A door closed and they instinctively froze, listening. The car door opened and closed, and the car started, backed up, and drove down the lane, turning—Verlaque saw through the bushes— toward Foligno.

"Let's go look around," he whispered, getting up and then pulling Marine up with his hand.

The building's small, multipaned windows were dirty with layers of dust, making it difficult to see anything inside the studio. "The door is locked," Marine said, twisting the handle. "Let's walk around and see if we can open a window."

Verlaque looked at her in surprise but quickly decided that it was worth the risk. There were no windows on the east side of the building, but a window in the back, high up, was without the iron bars that the other windows had. Verlaque rolled an old, rusted iron barrel and set it upright against the wall. "Do you think you can stand up on this and then try to open the window and slip in? You're considerably thinner than I am."

Marine said nothing but put her hand on his shoulder and with his help got on top of the barrel. She reached up and pulled on the right side of the window. "Nothing," she said, looking down at Verlaque. She then pulled on the left, and the window budged slightly. She pulled harder and the entire left-hand side of the window almost fell into the building, Marine stopping it just in time from coming off its track.

"Well done," Verlaque whispered. "Can you see in?"

"Yes, although it's dark without the light on. If you boost me up, I can slip in and fall into the room." She heaved herself up more and stuck her head through the open window. "It looks like there's a beat-up sofa just below!"

Verlaque nodded, pushed Marine's buttocks, and she heaved

herself up by her trembling arms and then fell below. "Okay!" she said from within the building. Verlaque saw that she had turned on the lights and he quickly walked around to the front door.

"Are you okay?" he asked as she opened the door for him.

"I'm fine, I landed on that sofa, although it hardly has any springs left." She rubbed her right arm.

"Let's be careful not to leave any traces of our presence," Verlaque said, putting his arm around Marine, kissing her forehead, and closing the door behind him.

"What are we looking for?" she asked. "Links to Rocchia?"

"Yes, and/or Moutte. Let's hope they have left a paper trail . . . receipts, letters, that kind of thing."

They separated, each looking on opposite sides of the studio, which was surprisingly small. Glass objects covered every flat surface and existed in various forms, from small colorful animals to large, clear vases. Verlaque took out his handkerchief and tried to open a metal filing cabinet but it was locked. "Too bad Bruno isn't here," he whispered to Marine, who had come over to his side. "He could open this and close it again, not leaving a trace."

Marine wandered over to a desk and carefully sat down on its chair. She grabbed a Rolodex and flipped through the cards, one by one, but didn't find Rocchia's or Moutte's name anywhere. The desk was covered with a large paper calendar from a hardware store in Foligno. She leaned down, her chin resting on the palms of her hands, and looked at the doodles on the calendar's first page. There, in the top right-hand corner, under a drawing of a small dog with pointy ears, were the initials "GR" and a telephone number.

"Antoine, come here," she whispered. "Do you have Rocchia's phone number in your cell phone?"

Verlaque put on his reading glasses and saw the initials and phone number. "I have his cell phone number and home number in Perugia." He took out his phone from his jacket pocket and searched for Rocchia's name and then glanced down again at the scribbled number. "That's Rocchia's cell phone. Perfect."

"You'll need that piece of paper as evidence," Marine said.

Verlaque shrugged and tore off the November page, folded it, and put it in his pocket. "It's December now," he said, looking down at the new page. "With any luck, they'll think that someone else in the shop tore off the page to get to December. Better get cracking on those Christmas orders!"

They opened drawers in the desk and sifted through a small pile of papers but couldn't find anything else linking Rocchia to the Vetro Corvia. "It's not as if we're going to find a receipt that says 'three fake Gallés to the order of Giuseppe Rocchia,'" Marine said.

"I know," Verlaque answered. "Plus it's getting dark. Let's get back to Foligno while we still have a bit of light. We'll close the window and lock the front door when we leave. It won't be double-bolted, since we don't have a key, so they'll know someone was in here."

"Or they may think that they locked the door but forgot to double-lock it on the way out. I do that sometimes at home."

Verlaque jumped up on the sofa and pulled the window shut, and turning off the lights, they walked out of the building and collected their bicycles, riding off in the direction of Foligno. They hadn't gone far when Verlaque, who was riding behind, said, "Car behind us, Marine! Get far over to the right."

The car slowed down when it approached the cyclists, then moved over as if to pass, but instead of passing the car drove beside Verlaque and Marine. Two men were in the newer-model black Lancia, and they looked at the cyclists, then slowed down and stayed behind Verlaque. "What's their problem?" Verlaque called out to Marine. He motioned with his hand for them to pass. Again, the car drove up beside them and the passenger, who wore Ray-Ban sunglasses despite dusk setting in, looked at Verlaque, then turned and said something to the driver, and they finally passed.

"That gave me the willies," Marine called over her shoulder to Verlaque.

Verlaque didn't reply as they watched the car slow down, turn into a driveway, and begin to turn around. Marine continued riding and instinctively veered her bicycle to the right, forcing it through a narrow gap in the stone wall that surrounded the chapel they had seen earlier. Verlaque followed, and they jumped off their bikes and ran, holding on to the handlebars, toward the chapel. In silence they parked their bikes behind the chapel and ran to the front door, which was mercifully open.

The inside of the chapel was almost dark and smelled of wax. "Let's go to the front," Verlaque said, taking Marine's hand. "I'm not sure they could see the chapel from the road in a car, and there's that small side road they might go down looking for us." He didn't want to admit that they were sitting ducks in the chapel alone. Marine's heart raced and she was about to speak when they both heard a car door close. Verlaque held on to Marine. They could just barely see each other, and would not be seen from the front door. The sound of footsteps coming up the path was heard, the doorknob turned, and the front door opened. The visitor coughed, moved a few feet into the church, and then turned on the lights, coughed again, and then switched them off. The front door quickly closed, and both Marine and Verlaque heard very clearly the sound of a key turning in the lock.

"That wasn't the guys in the car, was it?" Marine whispered.

"*Merde*. I bet it was the caretaker." Verlaque looked at the lit-up time on his cell phone: 6:05 p.m. "He probably closes up at six."

They ran to the front door and pulled at the metal door latch, knowing it was locked but double-checking nonetheless. Marine called out and ran to the light switch and turned the lights on and off a half dozen times, hoping to get the caretaker's attention. They heard the car backing away down a gravel road. "There must be a way in here by another road," Marine said.

Verlaque gasped. "Look at this place."

Marine left the lights on and turned around to look at the chapel's white walls, every inch covered in small rectangular paintings. They moved closer to one and saw that they were not paintings but majolica earthenware plaques, each one painted in glorious colors—greens and bright yellows—similar to the dinnerware of the region.

"They're ex-votos," Marine whispered. "Giving thanks to God, or Jesus, or Mary, for being saved from some threat . . . illness, accidents, et cetera. I've only seen ex-voto paintings, never ceramics."

Verlaque slipped his reading glasses on. "Look. This guy is flying off his motorcycle. Look at that vintage bike!"

Marine moved along the wall. "This woman is sick," she said. "Her children are gathered around her, crying. The perspective is totally off. It's so charming."

"Wine barrels!" Verlaque almost shouted. "The winemaker is about to get crushed by wine barrels falling off his truck! These are amazing!"

Marine snapped a few photos. "I have to show Sylvie these. She loves folk art."

They stayed silent for a few minutes, moving along the walls, looking at each plaque. Marine then sat down on a wooden pew and Verlaque came and sat down beside her. "We're in a bit of a fix," he said, smiling.

Marine laughed. "You could say that. We need to call someone to get us out, or sleep here until the caretaker comes back tomorrow morning."

Verlaque pulled the Palazzo Trinci curator's business card out of his jacket.

"But I don't trust him!" Marine exclaimed.

"Marine, he's the only person we know around here." Verlaque slipped on his reading glasses and called Dottore Camorro's phone number.

"Pronto," Camorro answered on the third ring.

Marine took the phone and explained in Italian where they were. She did not mention the black car, or, naturally, the glassworks.

"Ah, the chapel with the ceramic ex-votos. Don't worry, I'll be right there. I know the caretaker and can get his phone number from one of the security guards here at the museum . . . they're cousins." Marine frowned, as she was sure that the Dottore spoke to someone else in his office. "Sit tight," he continued, "I just have to drop my son off at his karate lesson, get ahold of the caretaker, and then drive out with him to the chapel. I'll be as quick as I can."

"Grazie mille," Marine said, hanging up the phone.

Marine and Verlaque wandered around the chapel for another half hour until Verlaque went and sat down. "I'm on ex-voto overload," he said, taking off his shoes and putting his jacket on the pew to act as a pillow. He stretched out and closed his eyes while Marine continued to take photos.

Verlaque woke up to the sound of a car and then voices outside the chapel. He sat up and looked for Marine, who was fast asleep on a pew opposite his. He quickly put on his shoes and called, "Marine! They're here!" He walked toward the front door, putting his jacket on as he walked.

"We're here!" Dottore Camorro called. The noise of a key turning in the latch was heard and the door opened, Camorro the first to enter. Marine stood up and quickly walked toward the door, almost bumping into the men who followed the curator into the chapel. It was the driver of the black Lancia, and his passenger.

Chapter Thirty-six

❧

A Magnificent Ivory

Verlaque grabbed Marine's hand and pulled her close to him as Marine blurted out in Italian, "You're in this together! I knew it!"

Dottore Camorro smiled, but only slightly. "Yes, Dottore Bonnet, but not as you think."

The passenger of the Lancia reached into his jacket and pulled out an Italian state police identification badge. "I'm Dottore Sylvio Donadio, and this is my colleague Sergeant Tramenti. We work in the Guardia di Finanza's division for the Protection of Archaeological Patrimony in Rome, and have been following Giuseppe Rocchia's movements for some months. We've linked him to an extensive network of fraudulent art glass sales, as I believe you have as well. Dottore Camorro has been advising us in the investigation and called us as soon as you left his office this afternoon. I do hope, for the sake of our investigation"—Dottore Donadio paused and sighed heavily—"that you haven't trespassed onto the premises of Vetro Corvia."

Marine looked at Verlaque and stayed silent. Verlaque replied in English, "I'm afraid we did, Dottore, but we left no signs of our presence except the fact that we couldn't double-bolt the door, as we had no key." He still didn't know if he wanted to show them Rocchia's phone number from the calendar page.

Donadio nodded at Sergeant Tramenti, who quickly left the chapel. "We have a key," Donadio explained in accented English. "My colleague will go and lock the door properly. Now, what right did you have to go into that building? Do you realize that you may have jeopardized months of hard work and put yourselves at risk as well? And did you find anything in the studio that perhaps we Italian police overlooked?" Donadio sighed and raised his eyebrows to the curator, who folded his arms and looked angrily at Verlaque, waiting for an answer.

"First, I apologize that we broke into the studio; we had no idea that the glassworks was being investigated," Verlaque said.

"A few phone calls would have answered that question, Judge Verlaque," Donadio said.

"Secondly," Verlaque continued, "we found Rocchia's initials, and his cell phone number, written down on a piece of paper."

Donadio flashed a look of surprise. "Really? We just looked over everything in the studio yesterday. We found no such thing."

"It could have been written down today," Marine replied in Italian. "At first it looked like a . . ." She searched for the word in Italian. "A doodle."

Verlaque handed Donadio the folded calendar page and the policeman unfolded it and looked at it, smiling. "This is the number of one of Rocchia's cell phones," he said. "While we're waiting for my partner to return, perhaps we could sit down and you can tell me why you thought it necessary to come to Umbria, unannounced, and break and enter where you see fit."

"I'm working on a murder case," Verlaque said. He was beginning to get angry over the policeman's tone of voice. "Two murder cases, in fact," he added. "Rocchia is one of my chief suspects, and he's lied about his alibi for the night of the first murder. He said that he was at home with his wife in Perugia, but she has just told me that she was in fact not even there."

Dottore Donadio raised his eyebrows. "Signora Rocchia told you this?"

"Yes. She's willing to testify."

"I'm happy that she has, how do you say . . . 'seen the light'? But that doesn't mean that he is guilty of murder," Donadio replied. "When Sergeant Tramenti returns we'll check Rocchia's movements and whereabouts on our computer. What night was it?"

"Last Friday," Verlaque replied. "The murder happened in the middle of the night, the victim was a professor but also a specialist in the glass of Gallé."

"Ah, art nouveau glass from Nancy," Dottore Camorro said. "What was the victim's name? I've forgotten."

"Georges Moutte," Verlaque replied. "Does it mean anything to you, Dottore Donadio?"

Donadio looked as if someone had just punched him in the stomach. "Dottore Moutte? The theologian?"

Verlaque and Marine said yes in unison and Donadio began quickly whispering to Camorro in Italian. Verlaque nudged Marine forward so that she could listen and she brushed his hand aside, annoyed. Of course she was going to try and listen! What did he think? After a few seconds she gasped, looking at Dottore Donadio. "What?" she asked. "You knew him? You used the word 'informant.'"

"Yes, he was our informant," Donadio answered. "As one of Europe's glass experts, and as a colleague of Giuseppe Rocchia, he provided us with expert advice."

Verlaque was now the one to raise his voice. "If he was your informant, why didn't you even realize that he was murdered?!"

"We had phone interviews with Dr. Moutte set up only once a week, every Friday night. We were going to call him later. We had no reason to suspect anything since last week."

"It seems to me that you could have called us, as you suggested we should have done," Verlaque said. He remembered Paulik telling him that the call Moutte had received a week ago Friday came from Italy but couldn't be traced. Now he knew why—it was an unlisted number.

Donadio smiled weakly and then his shoulders relaxed. "You're right; we both should have called each other's local police. Please, let's sit down."

Sitting on opposite pews, with Marine and Verlaque turned around to face the Italians, Verlaque continued speaking. "Your investigation is very extensive for some forged early twentieth-century glass."

Donadio looked at Verlaque and answered, "It's more than glass, Judge Verlaque."

Verlaque leaned forward over the back of the pew and asked, "They deal in other antiquities as well?"

"Yes, they've begun stealing and selling, or forging and selling, precious religious objects from our churches and museums. This chapel itself was broken into several years ago. We lost many of the ex-votos, and thanks to our investigations, with the help of Dottore Camorro, almost half of the artworks have been re-covered, while some others have been expertly reproduced. Roc-chia's name keeps popping up, but we don't have enough evidence to charge him. We take these crimes against our heritage very seriously, Judge."

"As you should," Verlaque replied. "Dr. Moutte was killed, hit over the head, by an object that my pathologist tells me is wooden, and over seven hundred years old. Does this mean anything to you?"

"The Pisano," Sergeant Tramenti, who had just walked into the chapel and overheard Verlaque's question, said.

Donadio nodded. "Yes. A rare Andrea Pisano sculpture in ivory, but it has a large wooden base; it's a Madonna and child that stands about a foot high, stolen from a monastery in Sicily last year. It's priceless; Andrea Pisano sculpted the doors of Florence's cathedral. Marco, could you look up Rocchia's whereabouts a week ago, last Friday night?" Sergeant Tramenti went back to the car and brought with him a tiny computer and opened it and turned it on. While they were waiting for the computer to start up, Donadio told his sergeant of Moutte's death. Within a few minutes Tramenti had the information they needed. "He was at home, in Perugia," he said.

"How do you know? Are you watching the house?" Verlaque asked.

Tramenti answered, "We're watching the outside, yes, but the inside is being covered by someone working for us. She's the new maid. Rocchia was there all night, she reports."

Donadio turned to Verlaque and Bonnet. "That gets Rocchia off the hook."

There was silence, then Donadio continued, almost whispering. "We are certain that Rocchia was behind the theft. The statue belonged to an elderly priest in Ragusa, and Rocchia had visited him the same week that the statue went missing. Giuseppe Rocchia operated in this way, visiting the faithful elderly. Since the victims were old they often didn't notice the theft until days or weeks after, giving Rocchia plenty of time to sell the artwork. With that theft we do have a weak link to France, however." Donadio turned to Tremanti and asked, "Marco, could you look up that phone call we listened to just after Rocchia came back from Sicily?" Verlaque and Marine exchanged glances. Although as examining magistrate Verlaque was permitted to wiretap, he seldom did.

Tramenti pressed a few keys on his computer and waited. "Sorry," he said, shrugging. "This church has a lousy connection." The group, fatigued and stressed, all laughed. "Here we go," he continued, squinting at the screen. "The call was made to a number in Aix-en-Provence, belonging to Signor Bernard Rodier. In their conversation, which mainly involved Rocchia complaining about the food at the conference, Rocchia asks, quote, 'Is the item I gave you at the conference in Turin safe?' unquote. This Bernard Rodier answered, quote, 'Yes, it's in my office,' unquote."

There was now a touch of impatience in Verlaque's voice. "Why didn't you call us in Aix?"

It was Tramenti who spoke up. "The call was made on Rocchia's cell phone, and there was traffic in the background. We could hardly make out what either man was saying. The recording has only just been cleaned up by our guys in the tech lab in Rome. They were supposed to call your police headquarters in Aix, in fact, this afternoon. They may have, and you just haven't been told yet; or they may not have, given they're Roman . . ."

"Even so," Marine said. "As you said, it's a weak link, this telephone conversation linked to the stolen Pisano." She somehow felt an urge to protect Dr. Rodier, or any of her mother's other colleagues, although the pain in her stomach told her that one of them may be guilty.

Dottore Donadio raised an eyebrow. "I agree, but passing a stolen sculpture off on an unsuspecting colleague at a conference where he'll have to cross a border would have been highly convenient for Rocchia. Not that there are customs officials at the border between Italy and France anymore, but there could have been. Do you know this Rodier?"

"Yes," Verlaque answered, looking at Donadio and then Marine.

"I do too," Marine said. "He works with my mother in the Theology Department."

"Trustworthy?" Donadio asked.

Marine nodded. "Yes. If I had something to hide or get rid of quickly, I would give it to Bernard Rodier. He's dependable, quiet, and . . ."

Donadio leaned in and waited for Marine to finish her sentence.

"And just a tiny bit naive. He's also a devoted follower of the Cistercians, who as you know reject wealth, so a sculpture of value would be of no interest to him. Rocchia would have been leaving the Pisano in safe hands. But what Rocchia probably didn't know is that people are in and out of the Theology Department daily. The buildings are in dire condition, and the *facultés*, including my Department of Law, are understaffed. Anyone could have taken the statue from Bernard's office."

Verlaque thought to himself that what Marine said was very true. Thierry and Yann had easily broken into the humanities building. However, he wasn't quite ready to let Bernard Rodier off the hook. People change, especially when in possession of priceless art. Rodier could have since sold the statue; he'd call Paulik this evening and have him demand a search of Rodier's bank account. And was this the murder weapon? Why kill someone with a Pisano statue? He finally said, "We'll head back to Aix tomorrow morning and arrange to meet Dr. Rodier in his office at the end of the day. We'll call you as soon as we have any information on the statue's whereabouts."

The group exchanged business cards and Marine was wondering where they would get a warm shower and clean bed that evening. As if reading her thoughts, Dottore Camorro spoke up. "There is a very nice *enoteca* in Foligno that rents out a few rooms upstairs. Would you like me to call them and see if any rooms are available? We can leave the bicycles here and deal with them tomorrow."

Marine looked at Verlaque. "A wine bar that rents out rooms sounds perfect. And your wines are so hard for us to buy in France," Verlaque answered.

"Ah, the French protect their wines as the Italians do. It's hard for us to buy French wines as well, except for champagne," Camorro said, smiling.

"This statue," Verlaque said, turning back to the policemen, "how old is it? Will I know it when I see it?"

Tramenti turned his computer toward Marine and Verlaque. "Here's a poor-quality photograph of it that Father Rossellino had taken last year. You'll recognize it, yes."

"It's magnificent," Marine said, looking at the color photograph on Tramenti's screen.

"Did Georges Moutte know about this statue?" Verlaque asked.

"Yes," Donadio answered. "In fact, we told him about it late last Friday night, the night you now tell me he died. He said that he would look for it, but obviously didn't get the chance."

The group looked at the photograph and Tramenti spoke up. "There's a wonderful quiet elegance to this statue that we later see on the cathedral doors. And the amplitude of his forms points to the influence of his contemporary, the painter Giotto." Verlaque looked up at the young policeman, who was looking at his computer screen, now lost in thought. Verlaque was sorry he didn't have more time to spend in the company of these men. Tramenti briefly closed his eyes and Verlaque thought of the painter Paul

Gauguin's quote on the creation of art, one that Emmeline had painted on the south wall of her studio in Normandy: "I shut my eyes in order to see."

"Look at how she leans back," Marine said. "How she adores her baby."

"Yes," Tramenti said. "It's a proud mama's pose, not a queen's."

"We think that the statue was made in Florence before Pisano began the doors to the cathedral, so before 1330," Donadio said, breaking the silence. "That would make it roughly seven hundred years old."

Chapter Thirty-seven

❧

Empty Bookshelves

*B*runo Paulik wished he had been able to return to the Bar Zola with photographs of the students on Friday night, but Léa had started throwing up as soon as she and Hélène got back to Pertuis. When he and Hélène had changed Léa's sheets for a second time and he was getting undressed for bed, Verlaque, who sounded like he was in a restaurant, called his cell phone, explaining the connection Georges Moutte had with both Giuseppe Rocchia and the Guardia di Finanza. They agreed that fingers pointed at Rocchia, and Paulik told Verlaque that he would go into Aix on Saturday and go over the files again. Perhaps Rocchia was working with someone in Aix? They needed to find out whom, and quickly. "I have more to tell you," Verlaque had said. "But as it's late and you have a sick child, I'll call you back tomorrow."

Hélène needed to rush to the vineyard in the morning, so it was agreed that Bruno would stay and nurse Léa until Hélène got back. He kept his cell phone by his side as they watched *The*

Sound of Music, Léa complaining that she didn't like the songs and, despite her weakness, was alert enough to grab the remote control and fast forward every time a Von Trapp family member began singing. "Léa, this is a musical!" Bruno complained. "The songs are a big part of the movie; and besides, they're great songs!"

Léa shifted on the couch to get more comfortable. "I hate the songs. They're stupid. I only like the story part."

"But you're a singer!"

"Not like that I'm not."

Paulik sighed, worried that they had created an eight-year-old snob. Léa fell asleep just before the wedding scene, and Paulik was able to finish watching the movie, humming along, before Hélène walked in just around 1:00 p.m.

"I'm so sorry," she said, sitting down to take off her running shoes. "I thought I'd be back hours ago. It always takes longer to move soil around and spread manure. I left my rubber boots at the winery, don't worry."

Bruno Paulik smiled and watched his wife kiss the sleeping Léa on the forehead. He sometimes forgot how physically demanding Hélène's occupation was. She rarely complained about the corporeal strain of her job; only the cold. Compared to him she was tiny—just over five-three—and her wiry, muscular build looked great both in the overalls she wore when in the cellars or fields and in the glimmering evening dresses and high heels she wore for promotional events and dinners.

He sighed, sorry he had to go into Aix but anxious to go over the files again and to show Patrick the photos.

Verlaque and Marine were on the road back to Aix by 9:00 a.m. on Saturday, later than planned. They had spent an enjoyable evening dining with Donadio and Tramenti, who were staying in the wine bar's two other guest rooms. A fair amount of wine had been drunk, Donadio wanting to show off the whites of his native Friuli and Tramenti the rich dark reds of his sun-drenched Calabria. The conversation, a smattering of English, Italian, and French, had ranged from art to World Cup soccer to jazz and, of course, food. At the end of the meal the wine bar's owner, a fellow cigar aficionado, joined the group and brought out his uncle's rosolio, a digestive made from rose petals.

At their first rest stop, just south of Florence, they drank strong espressos and a glass of freshly squeezed orange juice. Verlaque stepped outside onto the terrace, littered with cigarette butts and abandoned coffee cups, to call Paulik. "*Salut*, Bruno," Verlaque said, watching Marine through the glass windows, who was buying an outrageously enormous glass jar of Nutella for Charlotte and a block of Parmesan for Sylvie. He filled Paulik in on their conversation with the Italian police in the chapel and asked him to visit Rodier in his office as soon as possible.

"I'll call him straightaway and arrange to meet him at the university," Paulik said. "I'm running late because of Léa."

Verlaque described that statue to his commissioner, who would, they agreed, discreetly look around Rodier's office for signs of the rare Pisano instead of asking him about it. Even if Verlaque and Marine had good traffic around Genoa, there was no way they could arrive in Aix before 5:00 p.m. "At 4:00 p.m. I have an appointment with the Zola's barman, Patrick," Paulik told Verlaque. "He told me that Audrey Zacharie went in a few times with someone he referred to as a nerd, but it was the barman's impression that he scared her. I'm taking photos of the theology students to see if Patrick recognizes anyone, but it's possible that the mystery nerd wasn't even a student. I would have tried to see

Patrick this morning, but he's in court; last month his oldest son was caught stealing a moped."

"How did you get all of this information out of the barman?" Verlaque asked. "I was under the impression that he didn't like us."

"His youngest son is in the *conservatoire* with Léa," Paulik answered with a partial truth. "I went back for a beer the other night and we recognized each other. There's something else too. Patrick told me that Audrey Zacharie went to the bar a few times with a man in a wheelchair."

Verlaque almost dropped his phone. "Lémoine?"

"I don't know. I'm taking a picture of him as well. I'll call you after I meet with Rodier and Patrick."

They drove on, Verlaque complaining about the other motorists. He signaled to pass an ancient Fiat 500 that was going along at about eighty kilometers per hour and as they passed, the elderly couple in the Fiat looked up at Marine and smiled, and she smiled and nodded in acknowledgment. It was one of the things Verlaque loved about her. She was unaffected by her beauty, and so very kind. "Marine," he began, and pulled back over into the slow lane as a Ferrari raced up behind them, flashing its lights. To Marine's surprise Verlaque didn't give the Ferrari driver a hand gesture but instead continued speaking, "you're wonderful."

Four hours later Marine and Verlaque were eating sandwiches of arugula and ham at a gas station rest stop just past Imperia. Verlaque was thrilled to find his favorite coffee, Illy, available for sale cold, in a can, as an iced coffee. He bought a bagful to put in his refrigerator back home, and Marine was taking a photograph of him with her cell phone, clutching his purchase, when Bruno Paulik called back. "I'm standing outside the humanities building right now," Paulik said. "Rodier met me, no questions asked, and I made him go over his whereabouts the night of Audrey Zacharie's murder while I looked around the office. The office is filled with bookshelves, two of the shelves have been cleared. There wasn't a sculpture in sight. He seemed more nervous than before, but that could have been because he was troubled by my visit. I had been there for about twenty minutes when guess who walked in?"

Verlaque ventured a guess. "Giuseppe Rocchia?"

"Yep. I stayed on when it was obvious to me that Rocchia didn't have any more of a reason to be there than I did. He made up some weak excuse about wanting to discuss the Cistercians with Rodier that even Rodier seemed confused about. It became a farce, with me sitting in a corner and Rocchia walking around the office glancing at the bookshelves and tables, both of us pretending to be listening to Dr. Rodier. Rocchia seemed panicked that I wouldn't leave and he finally left, mumbling something about being late for a meeting, and I left about three minutes after. I'm going to hang out at the snack shop across the street and have a coffee and see if Rocchia comes back to ask Bernard Rodier about the sculpture, but it's already 3:30 and my appointment at the Bar Zola is at 4:00 p.m."

Verlaque smiled at the thought of Bruno Paulik sitting in one of Dr. Rodier's armchairs, not budging, watching the panicked Italian take fleeting glances around the room. "Well done," he said. "Call me after your barman friend sees the photographs. We should be in Aix by 5:00 p.m."

Verlaque hung up and his cell phone rang again; this time it was Officer Flamant. "Sorry, Judge. Can you talk?"

"Yes, Alain. I have a driver," Verlaque replied, smiling at Marine. "Did you meet with the accountant?"

"Yes. Those first five-thousand-euro deposits all came from the university, sir."

"What?"

"Mlle Zacharie was embezzling; the funds came from a fellowship, the . . ."

"Dumas," Verlaque answered. Marine shot a look sideways at Verlaque, her mouth open.

"Affirmative, sir. This is a new accountant, and he's just caught up with all the books. The previous accountant has just retired, and didn't do much when on the job, apparently."

"And the bigger deposit, made on the day she died?"

"We don't know," Flamant answered. "But it wasn't from the Dumas, and it was cash."

Marine drove the rest of the way, nervous at first, but by the time they reached the French border she was passing cars and trucks in the tunnels as if she had driven this route hundreds of times. Verlaque had fallen asleep for about a half hour, and she envied his ability to sleep anywhere at any time. When he awoke he asked her about her family, which surprised her. He had never asked her about the Bonnets, and she thought that this may be a sign that he was ready to be asked about his own family, and the mysterious Monique of his dreams. Marine enjoyed the precision needed to drive on the coastal highway, and once they got past Nice and Cannes the highway evened out and became an easy drive past the rolling green vineyards of the Var, she relaxed, and during the last hour of the drive she told Verlaque all that she knew about baby Thomas. When she had finished Verlaque was silent, and she joked, "Do you have dark family secrets?"

"Yes," Verlaque answered. "I'll tell you about them sometime, maybe even tonight." They came to the last toll and slowed down. "Fifteen minutes and we'll be back in Aix," Verlaque said. The toll, Verlaque thought to himself, had mercifully cut off their conversation about families.

Chapter Thirty-eight

✕

Bruno Paulik Tries Bicycling Too

At the Palais de Justice, Bruno Paulik found the case file, immediately dropped it on the floor, then shoved the photographs back in and ran out of the office and out the front doors, heading to the Bar Zola. The streets were crowded with people of all ages, doing what Aixois do best on a Saturday—shop. He weaved his way in and out through the crowds, angered when more than one person stopped smack in the middle of the pedestrian streets to check a message on their cell phones.

The barman nodded when he saw the commissioner, said something to his coworker, and walked toward the cellar door, Paulik following. "Since when have we let cell phones rule our lives?" Paulik asked as they walked down the stone stairs.

Patrick shrugged. "I don't know. I still don't have one. Let's have a look at those photographs," he said.

They stood under the bare lightbulb, placing the file on top of a pile of wine cartons. Paulik intentionally showed the barman photographs of Thierry Marchive and Yann Falquerho, the barman carefully looking at each and then shaking his head back and forth. "No, sorry."

"There's one more," Paulik replied, handing the barman the photograph of Claude Ossart.

"That's him," the barman said, tapping the photograph. "No doubt about it."

"Thanks," Paulik said, trying to imagine how someone like Claude Ossart could possibly be mixed up in art fraud. He was a nut about the Cistercians, wasn't he? Weren't they anti-art? "How about this guy?" Paulik asked. "Is he the one in the wheelchair?"

Patrick took the photo, held it to the light, and nodded. "That's him."

"You've been a huge help. Do you mind if I use your cellar as an office for a few minutes?" Paulik asked.

"No problem. Would you like me to bring you a beer? It's on the house."

"No thanks, but I'll take a rain check, with pleasure," Paulik replied, shaking Patrick's hand. The commissioner sat down on a wooden chair and dialed Verlaque's number, which went straight to the message service. He hung up and went through the file until he saw the list of names and addresses. Ossart lived at 8 rue Constantin, not far from where Paulik was now. He got up and called the Palais de Justice, asking them to send another officer to meet him on the rue Constantin. Claude Ossart could have been friends with Mlle Zacharie—they were almost the same age—so the gnawing in his gut could be for nothing. But Patrick had said that Audrey Zacharie was uncharacteristically nervous around Ossart. What did he have on her? Or vice versa? And where did Lémoine fit in?

Paulik left the bar, saying "*salut*" on his way out, and walked north, turning right on the rue Chabier and then left on rue Matheron, a street with some fantastically run-down seventeenth-century mansions. He turned right on Constantin and saw Officer Cazal standing under a lamppost. "Does one of the students live on this street?" Cazal asked the commissioner. "I remember from when I took down their names."

"*Salut.* I'm glad it's you they sent. Yes, Claude Ossart lives at number 8. Let's see if he's at home and then I'll fill you in after. Sorry, but I'm eager to talk to him right now."

Officer Cazal nodded. "That's fine," she answered. "I'll follow your cues."

They rang Ossart's apartment buzzer but there was no answer. Impatient, Paulik leaned into it and rang again. A window opened from an upper-floor apartment and a young man, heavily studded, stuck his head out. "Ring any more and I'll come down and . . ."

Paulik cut him off. "Police. Do you know where Claude Ossart might be?"

"If I did I wouldn't tell you."

"Could you buzz us in, please?" Paulik yelled up. He made for the front door—he was suddenly desperate to look in Ossart's apartment but he wasn't sure why—and the pierced youth leaned further out the window and said, "I assume you have a warrant."

"I'm the commissioner of Aix and am working with the examining magistrate," Paulik hollered up.

"Oh, great. Congratulations. Now show me the warrant, because I know that while your boss doesn't need one, you still do."

Paulik turned around and looked at Officer Cazal, who had her hands on her hips and was sighing. "Does this kid read law procedure manuals for fun?" he asked.

"So it would seem. Let's go," she answered.

They had walked down the street and turned left toward the

Palais de Justice when Paulik asked, "Since when did everyone begin to hate us?"

Officer Cazal shrugged. "It's been slowly happening over the past few years. I used to dread pulling over cars. Drivers, even when they're at fault, have become more and more insulting and belligerent. And kids, like that one, aren't afraid of anyone. My sister teaches math at a junior high and says the same thing. They have no respect for anyone with authority."

"Bring back the cane," Paulik joked. "Let's phone Dr. Rodier and see if he knows where Claude hangs out on Saturdays." Cazal opened the file and read off the professor's phone number and Paulik dialed. This time his call was answered on the first ring.

"I was hoping you might be Claude," Rodier said as a greeting. "I've been sitting next to the phone, waiting."

Paulik stopped walking. "Go on, Professor. Have you heard from him recently?"

"Yes. He called here about two hours ago, ranting and raving against the other professors, the other students, the Cluniac order, almost everything under the sun. Claude even blasphemed that poor dead girl, Audrey Zacharie. His mother even called me, so he must have called them too. They've been estranged for years."

"*Ah bon?*" Paulik asked, the knot in his stomach tightening. "Why don't they speak? Do you know?"

"Their wealth, of course," Rodier replied. "Claude had forsaken his inheritance, calling it dirty money . . . the father is an industrialist in Paris, and they have a château in the Loire somewhere. Mme Ossart told me that Claude asked them for money recently, and he dipped into his inheritance, a rather large amount I'm told, which he has never done before."

Paulik asked, "Do you know where Claude could be?"

"You could try the library or the gym. He goes to the gym next to the parc Jourdan. I'll wait here in case he phones back."

Paulik thought of Lémoine . . . the parc Jourdan was one of Lémoine's favorite stalking grounds. He thanked the professor and hung up, then filled Officer Cazal in on his suspicions.

"The parc Jourdan overlooks the humanities building, at least part of it does, the hilly part, next to the swings," Cazal said. "I noticed that from Dr. Moutte's office you have a clear view of the park."

"And from the park you would have a view right into Moutte's office," Paulik added.

"Especially at night."

"Let's get an unmarked squad car and take it to the park," Paulik said.

"Bikes would be faster today," Cazal said. "That way we could ride right into the park and we'd be more inconspicuous." They ran to the Palais de Justice, signed two bikes out, putting the file folder into one of the saddlebags, and rode off down the rue Thiers toward the park.

Chapter Thirty-nine

❧

Sympathy for the Guilty

"You know," Marine said as she exited the highway and drove around Aix's first roundabout, "I think I could drink rosolio all the time. All day long, I mean, straight out of a flask that I could keep in my purse."

Verlaque laughed. "I know what you mean. I've never had any liquor quite like it. It was incredibly delicate, but at the same time, even with my cigar, I could taste roses."

"I don't envy that wine bar owner having to pack up everything to renovate this winter," Marine went on. "It's why I keep avoiding repainting my apartment . . . it would be like packing up in order to move, wouldn't it?"

"You could have offered to keep his rosolio for him," Verlaque said, glancing at Marine. He then slapped the dashboard and said, "Packing up. Someone packed up for Bernard Rodier, he told us during our first interview with him. Bruno told me that two of the shelves in Rodier's office were already empty."

"Why? He's moving offices?"

"No, but he was hoping to. Rodier told me that Moutte had promised him the doyen position, and on Friday afternoon, prematurely as it would happen, he had his assistant—now I remember—Claude begin filing and sorting through his office, getting ready for the big move down the hall."

"Claude? Do you think he could have taken the statue?" Marine asked as they stopped for a red light on the avenue Gambetta. "It's probably the murder weapon, right?"

"I think so. And you said that Claude was losing his temper at that conference you attended."

Verlaque grabbed his phone and called Paulik, getting no answer. He then called Flamant, who replied on the first ring. Verlaque ordered a search of Claude Ossart's apartment, describing the statue to Flamant.

"Yes, now that I think about it, Claude really was quite hysterical that day," Marine whispered to herself. The light finally changed and she put the car in first gear, going a little faster than she normally would on a city street.

They double-parked in front of Marine's apartment. Verlaque was helping unload Marine's suitcase and purchases into the building's front hall when his telephone rang. "Are you sure you don't need help with this?" he joked as he handed Marine the oversize jar of Nutella.

"No, I'll make two trips up the stairs . . . but thanks. See you tonight?"

Verlaque nodded in the affirmative and waved. He got back into the car and drove slowly down Marine's street and answered his phone on what must have been the tenth ring. Whoever it was, he or she was patient.

"Sir?" the caller asked.

"Bruno? I'm on my way to the Palais de Justice. Listen, I've ordered a search of Claude Ossart's apartment . . . that statue I told you about . . ."

"Great. I have to cut you off, sorry. Meet us in the parc Jourdan, near the swings. I'm on my way there by bike. I think that Ossart is there too, and he's somehow tied up with Lémoine."

"Lémoine?" Verlaque asked. "I'll be right there." He hung up the phone and turned left on the rue du 4 Septembre, glancing up at Georges Moutte's apartment as he passed by. He and Paulik had gone through the list of teachers and students capable of breaking in via the roof to Moutte's apartment but had overlooked Ossart—his physique had been hidden under the bulky clothing he had worn every time they had spoken to him. Ossart went to the gym, and Verlaque now heard the voice of either Thierry or Yann when they had said of their fellow student, "Claude was coming home from the gym when we were leaving the party . . ." and "that's all you ever get out of Claude, five seconds . . . ," which at the time had just sounded like nervous ramblings. He crossed over the ring road, turned right behind the Hotel Roi René, and stopped his car at the black gates of the park, putting his badge in the window. The gates were still open and Verlaque ran through, clutching his cell phone, he realized, as if it were a gun. He had no idea where the swings were, and so ran past the *boules* court on his left and ran up the wide steps to higher ground, where once at the top of them he stopped to get his bearings and catch his breath. Ahead he could see a bright red slide, and he took a step forward, about to run, and then stopped. To his right, coming from below, someone had moaned.

He ran to a set of stairs that led down to a small concrete utility building, from which a humming sound came. Halfway down was a landing where the steps changed direction, and lying on the landing was Lémoine, his wheelchair on top of him. Verlaque ran down the stairs and lifted the wheelchair up, pushing it down the rest of the stairs. He knelt down and saw that Lémoine was conscious but very weak. "Don't say anything, stay still," Verlaque said. "I'm calling for an ambulance." Lémoine hadn't fallen far but it looked like it had been a quick, brutal fall. Blood leaked from the side of his head and Verlaque took out a cotton handkerchief from his jacket and pressed as firmly but as gently as he could to stop the bleeding. Verlaque quickly called the ambulance with his left hand and then sat down, resting his back against the wall and looking at his watch. He dialed Paulik's number, but it was busy, and so he set his cell phone down on the concrete floor and looked up at a red anarchy sign that someone had spray-painted. He wondered how Lémoine got up the park's wide flight of stairs but then remembered that the east side entrances were on flat ground. Lémoine moaned once more, closing his eyes in pain, and Verlaque looked down at him. A rush of sentiment came over him for this man who was a convicted sex offender and was now perhaps battling for his life. Verlaque reached out and put his hand on Lémoine's upper arm and left it there, gently squeezing it now and again and whispering words of encouragement. It's what Marine would do, he thought to himself. "Marine, Marine," Verlaque said aloud, and Lémoine opened his eyes. Verlaque went on to tell the dying man about Marine Bonnet, how she didn't pay attention to what she was eating or drinking, but how she'd enthusiastically try anything new, infecting those around her with her joie de vivre and joyous laugh. He told Lémoine of Marine's law lectures, rumored to elicit applause, her modesty and kindness, the way she would close her eyes and sway to her favorite Brazilian jazz songs. Verlaque was just about to tell Lémoine of Marine's love of Italy when the ambulance attendants came. One of them saw Lémoine and whispered, "Not him," and Verlaque said, "Be careful, he's bleeding from the head and is in a lot of pain." Verlaque watched them lift Lémoine quickly and deftly onto the stretcher and take him up the stairs, then down the wide stairs to their ambulance, which they had managed to park next to the *boules* court.

Verlaque turned and ran toward the playground and soon saw a group of bystanders gathered in a semicircle around the building that faced the playground, a yellow-stoned, red-shuttered seventeenth-century bastide that belonged to the city and was the headquarters of the Provençal language association, the Oustau de Prouvènço. As he pushed his way through the crowd he looked up at the red-and-yellow striped flag waving and thought he saw someone on the roof, but he looked away as he heard his name whispered. Bruno Paulik grabbed Verlaque by the sleeve and said, "That's Claude up there, on the roof."

Verlaque turned to Paulik. "How did he get up there?"

"The building was open; it's the language association's Saturday night meeting. A police psychologist is on her way."

"Is that what we're waiting for?" Verlaque asked. "I just found Lémoine lying at the bottom of some stairs."

"Is he . . . ?"

"No, I hope he'll make it. How long has Ossart been up there?"

"Since I got here, thirty minutes or so. He's called out a couple of times, threatening to jump. We cleared away the mothers and children from the playground, but as you can see there's still a crowd," Paulik said, motioning with his shoulder behind them. "They're mostly members of the *oustau* who refuse to leave."

Verlaque half-turned his head to listen to an elderly couple whom he guessed were speaking in Provençal, a language he had never heard spoken.

"Mon Dieu!" the woman behind Verlaque yelled, forgetting her enthusiasm for the lost language of southern France. Verlaque and Paulik looked up and Claude was teetering over the edge of the bastide's red tile roof, swaying as if in a trance.

"Where's the bloody psychologist?" Verlaque whispered. "Claude," he called, stepping forward. "Enough, Claude! Enough deaths."

"Right. What's one more?" the youth asked, quietly but loud enough for Verlaque to hear.

Thoughts raced through Verlaque's head: what could he say? He thought of pointing out to Claude that a jump off a three-story building might not kill him, but paralyze him instead, like Lémoine. Instead he called up, "Claude, I'm coming up. I don't want these people to hear our conversation."

Without looking up Verlaque walked into the bastide and headed up the stone steps to the first floor and kept walking up the second flight until he got to an open window that looked out over the park. *"Merde,"* he whispered aloud. Claude had once again gotten himself up onto the roof by way of a window and his muscular arms. Verlaque then gasped and stepped back as Claude's upside-down head appeared in the window, reddened and wild looking. "It's harder getting up here than it looks," Claude said.

"Claude, can't you come inside and we can talk quietly here?"

"So you can convince me to turn myself in? Whatever for?" And he disappeared.

"Then I'll have to come out and join you on the roof," Verlaque said. He took off his shoes and socks to get a better grip, and took off his jacket and laid it on the floor. He thought very quickly that what he was doing, risking his life, and Claude's, was absolutely insane, but before the other half of his brain had a chance to argue back he was out on the stone ledge, standing up, with one hand on the roof tiles above him, the other on the red shutter. He looked at the shutter and saw its wrought-iron handle, about eight inches in length, and put his bare foot on it and with a groan lifted himself up and onto the roof.

"Impressive for a fat guy," Claude said. The student was sitting cross-legged, watching Verlaque.

"Thanks," Verlaque said once he had caught his breath. He had scraped his forearm and ripped his shirt getting up onto the roof, but otherwise felt fine. He sat down facing Claude and said, "This is a strange place for a conversation." Verlaque had almost used the word "interrogation."

"You called Moutte to meet you at his office last Friday night?" Verlaque asked.

"Yes, from a phone booth on the rue Mistral, on my way home from the gym. I saw those idiots Thierry and Yann and then turned around and called Moutte."

"And Lémoine saw you in Moutte's office from the park, didn't he? Was he blackmailing you?" Verlaque asked.

"Of course he was! He and that know-it-all Audrey Zacharie. I gave them one payment, and then got so angry I arranged to meet Audrey in this park. But then I saw what happened," he said, closing his eyes, "and she couldn't come . . . she was dead . . . but I didn't do it!"

"Claude, what happened Monday night?"

"I called her and told her to meet me here in the park. I lied and said I had the next installment of money for her and that creep Lémoine. I knew the route she would take, so I waited for her on the boulevard Roi René, but all I wanted to do was scare her, you know, not kill her, and as she crossed the street a car came screaming up from the back near the train station, and it hit her." He put his head in his hands. "They hardly even slowed down."

"So you left," Verlaque said.

Ossart nodded.

Verlaque didn't add how very un-Christian it was of Ossart to have left Mlle Zacharie lying there in the middle of the street, but he didn't have to. The remorse was written all over the young man's face. But did he have any remorse for killing the doyen?

"Why did you kill Dr. Moutte, Claude?"

"Because of everything he stood for—the wealth, the opulence, the lies," the youth answered, as if bored. "He told Dr. Rodier that the position was his, only to change his mind at the party."

"But you didn't know that on Friday night."

"Yes I did. I overheard Dr. Rodier call his slutty ex-wife from a phone booth just after he left the party."

"The same phone booth on the rue Mistral?" Verlaque could see it, the one he and Marine joked about as being one of the last in town.

"Yes. I was on my way to the gym, and I hid in a dark doorway. Dr. Rodier deserved that post, he walks the talk . . . he lives as the men he studies. He's pure." Claude went on, "The Dumas was promised to me by the dearly departed Moutte on Friday afternoon. And when I got to his office late Friday night he had changed his mind. My parents thought I couldn't do anything, unlike my business-school brothers. I needed that scholarship to show everyone. He had promised. And then he saw the ivory sculpture in my gym bag and he went crazy. He said that it was Italian, Pivano, or something, but it wasn't, Dr. Rodier told me that it was a reproduction. We fought over it, and I hit him. At first lightly, and then I gave him three hard bangs. It was quick; much kinder than the slow agonizing deaths that Henry VIII subjected priests to." And that Sir Thomas More subjected Protestant preachers to, Verlaque silently added.

Ossart started losing his concentration, and got up when he heard voices below.

"Claude, come back here," Verlaque said, slowly getting to his haunches in case he had to run to catch Claude.

The student looked over the edge of the roof and turned back toward Verlaque and laughed. "They've put one of those stupid white trampolines down. And if I were to jump off in another direction? Off the back of this glorious building that protects a language that no one speaks anymore?"

Verlaque smiled, pretending to be amused. "You're right, you could jump off from any direction; but suicide is a sin, Claude, and you're a believer."

Claude Ossart looked at Verlaque with a sad face, before changing his expression into a serious one. "Yes. 'I killed in order to save myself.' Saint Bernard said that."

"But your killing was different, Claude. Saint Bernard said that about the Crusades. He also wrote that the soul which sins shall die. Do you want your soul to die along with your body?" Verlaque silently thanked Florence Bonnet, who had once quoted Saint Bernard during an uncomfortable family dinner, for Claude seemed to be listening intently.

Claude sat down. "I'm so tired," he whispered, and he lay down on his side, putting his head down on the red roof tiles.

"Should we wait for the firemen to extend a ladder, Claude? I don't feel like crawling back in through the window, tubby guy that I am." Verlaque inched over toward Claude and saw that the youth had closed his eyes. Once again that day, Verlaque put his arm on a man's shoulder, and whispered, "The bad dream is over, Claude."

Chapter Forty

Still Hoping to Be Appointed the New Doyen

*I*t was close to nine o'clock when everyone had left the park and its gates were locked. Verlaque left his car where it was and called Marine as he walked around the hotel and crossed the busy ring road. "Any food in the house?" he asked when Marine answered the phone.

"There is, in fact. There's a chicken in the oven. I was hoping you might be free to join me. Where have you been?"

"I'll explain when I get there," he answered. He looked up at number 11 as he walked around the Quatres Dauphins fountain, wondering to himself which one of the professors would be living upstairs in a few months. His money was on Rodier. "Could you do me a favor and light a fire? I'm chilled."

"I've already lit one, with the help of those little white waxy cubes. I must have put four or five in the fireplace."

Verlaque smiled and was about to hang up when he said, "Marine, there are things I need to tell you, but not tonight . . . I'm just too wiped out. But I will, and soon, I promise."

"Don't worry about it," Marine answered, but she secretly worried that perhaps Antoine would never tell her about his bad dreams and Monique. She opened the oven and reached in to baste the chicken, and then she poked the potatoes and carrots with the tip of a knife . . . they were ready. She opened a bottle of red Burgundy that her *caviste* on the rue d'Italie had recommended. It was a good domaine, from Mercurey, that he assured her was almost as good as its more expensive Burgundian cousins while being a third of the price. She still couldn't bring herself to pay the prices that Antoine did for a bottle of wine. She sat down in her favorite armchair and waited for the doorbell, realizing that she was a domestic creature after all. She would be so happy to spend the rest of her days like this, waiting, with dinner in the oven, for Antoine to walk through the door; or, to have him be the one to greet her after a day of lecturing. He was the better cook, after all.

"I didn't even bother to pour myself a cup of policeman coffee after tasting yours," Bruno Paulik said as he walked into Verlaque's office on Monday morning.

"You did the right thing. Come, let's get ourselves some espresso from my machine, then we'll go and talk to Claude Ossart. I had his apartment searched yesterday, and they found the statue, bloodstained, still in his gym bag." Neither man admitted to the other that they had each slept almost twelve hours on Saturday night and had done nothing productive on Sunday except Paulik phoning his parents.

"How is Claude doing?" Verlaque asked. "Do you know?"

"Yeah, I went down to the holding rooms on my way in. He ate a big breakfast, apparently, and seems calm. His parents are arriving from Paris this afternoon, and Bernard Rodier is already down there, waiting his turn to speak to Claude."

"Let's go then. We can talk to Dr. Rodier before we see Claude."

Yves Roussel burst into the room, almost upsetting Paulik's coffee over his clean white shirt. "We found the BMW," he said, pacing around the office. "And the brats who did it."

"Is it the car that killed Mlle Zacharie?" Verlaque asked.

"Yes, no doubt about it. They left the car in a forest near Rians, a hunter found it early Sunday morning. I sent a crime team to Rians and they worked all day and were able to lift some fingerprints off of the car that match the prints of two repeat offenders from Marseille. And then, guess what, the punks laid low all last week and then late last night tried to blow up a bank machine in Gardanne and were caught by two patrolling policemen. It's the same guys. I'm going to Gardanne right now to bring them back here and then read them the riot act." Roussel paused, out of breath. "How's the kid downstairs?"

"We're going down to talk to him now," Verlaque answered.

"Good luck," Roussel said. "I'm off!"

Bernard Rodier was sitting stiffly, in a clean pressed beige suit, on a wooden bench against the stone wall of the Palais de Justice's cellar. He quickly got up when he saw the judge and commissioner. "I need to see Claude. When I got your message last night I couldn't sleep. I came here as soon as they would let me in."

"Come into this room with us," Verlaque said, holding the door open to a small office.

Paulik told Rodier what he had told Verlaque: that Claude seemed calm and had eaten.

"What bothers me most is that Claude killed for me," Rodier said, taking out a handkerchief and patting his forehead.

"Don't torture yourself," Verlaque said. "We had a long talk Saturday night, on the roof of the Provençal language institute. Claude killed for himself first, and then for you."

Bernard Rodier looked up in surprise, either from Verlaque's cold answer or the fact that the conversation had taken place on top of a roof. "Did he kill the girl too?" Rodier whispered, this time with less narcissism.

"No," Verlaque said. "He saw it happen, but it wasn't him. Claude called Mlle Zacharie to meet him at the gates of the parc Jourdan. He knew where she lived and the route she would take, and he was waiting for her on the boulevard Roi René when he saw her get hit. She, and a man named Hervé Lémoine, were blackmailing Claude."

"Poor Claude," Rodier mumbled.

"I beg your pardon?" Verlaque asked. "He did kill Georges Moutte, and he threw Lémoine, who's a paraplegic, down some stairs. Now, I'd like to ask you about an ivory sculpture, which was used as the murder weapon."

Bernard Rodier looked genuinely surprised. "Giuseppe's reproduction?"

"Is that what he told you? That it was a reproduction?"

Rodier nodded quickly. "Yes, a nineteenth-century reproduction. Is it no longer in my office? I hadn't noticed!"

"No. Claude removed it a week ago Friday when you had him clean up your room. He told me on the roof the other night that he packed up all of the books from two of your shelves and then ran out of boxes. He was late for a meeting with Dr. Moutte, and so threw the statue in his gym bag, thinking he'd ask Audrey Zacharie for a box, but then he forgot all about it. The statue isn't a reproduction; it was carved by Andrea Pisano in the mid-fourteenth century."

Genuine shock lit up the handsome face. "I had no idea!"

There was a touch of impatience in Verlaque's voice. "That's clear to me." He thought about just how apt Marine's description of Rodier as "naive" was.

Seeing the frustration set in on the judge, Paulik spoke. "I'm afraid it will be hours before you can talk to the boy. Why don't you go home, and I'll call you when you can come in."

Rodier stood up and smoothed out the creases on his pants. "Fine, fine. I'll do that."

They accompanied the professor to the stairs that led up and out into the November day. Without speaking they turned around and headed toward the interrogation room where Claude was now waiting for them. Opening the door, Verlaque saw that the half-crazed wisecracker from the rooftop was now a pale, quiet young man.

"Good morning, Claude," Verlaque said as both he and Paulik sat down. "I know that your father has arranged for you to have a lawyer, and he's on the train with your parents right now, so it's your legal right not to say anything to us until you see Maître Blanc."

"I think I told you too much already," Ossart answered. "I'll wait for my lawyer now."

"Your apartment was searched yesterday and we found the statue," Verlaque said. "In your gym bag, like you told me." Verlaque didn't tell Ossart that there was dried blood still on the statue. He then told Ossart that the BMW that killed Audrey Zacharie had been found, and the youth put his head in his hands. Verlaque glanced at Paulik, who remained motionless, staring at Ossart. They agreed later that neither were sure if Ossart had called the young woman Monday night "just to talk," as he had said, or to kill her.

"Would you mind just telling me why you broke into the doyen's apartment?" Verlaque asked. "That's the only bit I can't work out."

Ossart shrugged. "I wanted to throw you off of my trail; make it look like theft. I threw a big vase on the floor and was about to wreck the place when a noise in the hallway freaked me out. I quickly left by the window and then so did the cat who had followed me in."

"All right," Verlaque said, and he got up to leave. "I'll see you later."

"Do you think if that sculpture hadn't been in his gym bag that Georges Moutte may be alive today?" Paulik asked as they walked down the hall.

"Perhaps, and Audrey Zacharie too."

Paulik's cell phone rang and he answered it as they walked up the stairs together. "You're kidding?" he asked the caller, and then grimaced. Paulik hung up and then said to Verlaque, "Well, Hervé Lémoine is feeling fine and back to his old tricks."

"What?"

"He insulted one of the nurses. She's filed a complaint."

"What an ass!" Verlaque exclaimed. "I should have left him lying there!"

"But you wouldn't have," Bruno Paulik said. "Even if you knew what I just told you."

Epilogue

Thierry Marchive walked as quickly as he could without breaking out into a sweat. It was a difficult balance to achieve, and one he had been working on since hitting puberty, for he was often late, and he was a natural sweater. The last thing he wanted was to show up at the Bar Zola with perspiration marks under his arms. He got to the cours Mirabeau and looked at his watch . . . he should be at the bar now, and it was still another five minutes' walk. Just then a Diaboline, one of Aix's electric minibuses, pulled up behind him to let two elderly passengers out and two in. He jumped on behind them and put fifty centimes in the cashbox. He sat opposite the man and woman, both in their seventies, or even eighties, he wasn't sure, and smiled. Normally he would have been embarrassed to be taking the Diaboline, but this evening he didn't care. He couldn't be late. The bus made its way, painfully slowly, but at least he could stop sweating, up the rue Clémenceau, through the small place Saint-Honoré, and then continued up the rue Méjanes. Thierry pulled the cord to signal a stop and jumped out at the cross street of Méjanes and Fauchier, thanked the driver, and said good evening to the elderly couple, who returned greetings and waved.

The Bar Zola was packed. It was a Friday night and it was too cold for most people except the most hardy—usually students from northern France—and he slipped past the crowd that always seemed to be blocking the front door. He smiled to himself as Leonard Cohen was playing, and he thought of Yann and felt the tiniest bit of guilt that he hadn't told his friend of this evening's meeting. Yann would have teased him, and besides, he didn't really know himself why he had been summoned here. He would fill in Yann tomorrow, over breakfast.

Thierry looked around for the familiar wire-rimmed glasses and hunched-over shoulders, but couldn't see anyone like that. He walked slowly through the bar, looking at each table, trying not to look too much like someone who had been called here, perhaps on a hoax. There were three small tables at the back, and at the middle table he saw a girl, alone, with red glasses and red lipstick that matched the glasses. She smiled and quickly waved, and then put her hand down and held on to her beer glass as if it would race across the table. Thierry squeezed past two students who were standing at the bar arguing about Leonard Cohen and sat down across from her. "You got new glasses," Thierry said, immediately regretting his opening line. He should have said, "You look fantastic." That's what Yann would have said.

"Yes, Dr. Leonetti helped me pick them out," Garrigue said as she unconsciously lifted her hand up to the glasses and felt them, to make sure that they were indeed her new pair. "She helped me with my hair too, and the lipstick was a present from her."

Thierry ordered a beer from the waiter. He looked at Garrigue and smiled. "Super. It looks super. And congratulations on the Dumas. I'm really happy for you." He watched Garrigue as she sipped her beer and saw that the dark red glasses brought out her blue eyes, and that her hair, normally just pulled back in a ponytail, was now expertly piled on top of her head, like a crown, though slightly disheveled.

"That's what I wanted to talk to you about," she said, her hand grazing her beer glass and almost tipping it over. "The Dumas. I don't want it, and Dr. Leonetti told me that you were the runner-up."

Thierry looked at her in amazement. Tonight she really didn't seem like the same girl, physically or intellectually. But then he didn't really know her. "Are you nuts?" he finally asked. He was so caught up in looking at her beauty and he almost hadn't heard the word "Dumas."

Garrigue laughed and Thierry's beer arrived, but he didn't touch it.

"I've been offered a job instead," she answered. "In Paris."

Thierry stared at her and then shook his head back and forth. "Wait . . . Paris? I don't get it. Explain, please, now."

"I'm going to work in television."

"Television?" Thierry asked, shocked.

"It's not as bad as you think," Garrigue said. "It's for the station Arte. Dr. Leonetti has a cousin who works there, and she got me the interview. I'll be a research position on a new documentary series being filmed next fall. The salary is more than generous, it will keep me busy for two years."

Thierry whistled. "A lot of money, eh?"

"Yes, I'm embarrassed by how much. I'll be the consultant on both Saint Augustine and Saint Ambrose. It's the chance of a lifetime."

Thierry lifted his glass to hers and they clinked. "What can I say? I can't believe you're giving me the Dumas."

Garrigue smiled. "I'm not. You were runner-up. You deserve it."

"What can I give you in return?" Thierry innocently asked.

Garrigue leaned forward. "You can kiss me."

Thierry couldn't believe it. All this time, chasing after girls in every bar in Aix, and it was one of his fellow students who seemed to be in love with him. He leaned toward Garrigue and kissed her once, and liking the taste and feel of her lips, did it again.

Thierry and Garrigue's courting lasted seven years, never in the same city. Thierry finished his thesis, and thanks to the Dumas was offered an assistant professorship at a small university in Montana. The state was entirely different from his native Marseille, but he grew to love it, as did Garrigue. She finally left her high-paying job in London at the BBC and moved to join Thierry, they married, and she became the vice president of a local television station. Yann married Suzanne, they lived in Paris, he a banker and she a stay-at-home mother of their five children.

Every year Garrigue and Thierry sent Annie Leonetti a Christmas card to that coveted address on the place des Quatre Dauphins. Garrigue was always careful to include photos of their two children and Montana in every season. Annie put the Christmas card with the other ones on the black marble mantle in the apartment's elegant living room, watched over by the dancing figures on the ceiling's fresco, finally removing the cards sometime around Easter.